R.A.T.

R.A.T.

A Cadence Turing Mystery

ROBIN JEFFREY

Robin Jeffrey

To Sarah - Read & Enjoy!

To my mother, Terri Jeffrey.
You believed in me when I couldn't believe in myself.
Thank you.

Contents

I

Chapter 1

"Of course, you understand that Halcyon Enterprises can't be seen to take sides in a political debate," I said.

"But your company has taken a stand on political issues before, Mr. Hale," countered the aide to my left, a dark-skinned young man with piercing brown eyes.

I crossed my legs and leaned back in my plush office chair. "Yes, but that was when my father was running things."

The aide to my right, an older woman with curled white hair, fiddled with the campaign button fixed on her jacket. "You know that various representatives from the Archerusian political systems, including Representative Peyton, have already made statements condemning Charcornac and their allies for the systematic elimination of animanecrons. And that's to say nothing of their occupation of the animanecron moon itself–"

"Think of the weight your words would carry," her younger

counterpart jumped back in, squirming towards the edge of his seat. "Halcyon Enterprises could be a real force for good."

"We already are," I said, steepling my fingers in front of my face. "I understand Representative Peyton's position. It's not that I don't personally agree with him about the so-called 'Whiston Offensive', but it simply isn't the place of a private corporation – one which employs hundreds of thousands of workers across the system – to make a blanket statement on an issue like this."

The two aides shared a look. Sighing, the older woman shook her head. "We can respect that. But I don't suppose there's anything we can say or do to change your mind?"

"I'm afraid not." I stood, smoothing the front of my suit jacket with one hand.

"Perhaps if you met one-on-one with Representative Peyton," said the young man, standing as well. "He's hosting a fundraising gala tomorrow night; we'd love it if you could attend."

I flashed a smile. "Oh, I'm never one to say no to a party. Send the invite to my assistant, and I'll see if I can fit it in my schedule."

The young man beamed at my acquiescence, and we all parted ways amicably with a round of handshakes. I watched the door to my executive suite click shut, and then I collapsed behind my father's desk – my desk – the charming CEO smile fading as I drew my hands down my tired face.

Waking up my primary computer screen, I groaned at the fifty-seven new messages that had accrued during my hour-long meeting. Scrolling down the list, I had to remind myself that my father, Felix Hale, hadn't gotten himself murdered on purpose just to spite me. I had been the head of Halcyon Enterprises, the generations-old company my family had built, for almost eight months now. And, although working for a living was tiresome, I was showing a shocking aptitude for it, especially for someone with only an academic grasp of business. As expected, the public scrutiny of my life had increased, but I had found it easy to adjust to that as well; after all, charming the masses while retaining my privacy was a juggling act I had practiced for years. Even the responsibility of being the single largest employer across several planets in the system now hung on me well, like a competently crafted, off-the-rack suit.

I focused my attention on the screen, my smile folding into a grimace; several emails were from my assistant, Lily Taylor. I had handpicked Miss Taylor from a roster of other exceptionally talented candidates. Coming off a government post she had held for the previous ten years, our personalities blended beautifully – she enjoyed working hard, and I didn't. In fact, she did enough work for the both of us. I made a mental note to give her a raise, as I scanned the day's remaining appointments, meetings, and tasks to complete, shaded in all the colors of the rainbow.

One name in particular caught my eye. I sat bolt upright in my chair. My eyes glued to the appointment entry, I fumbled for the desk intercom, pressing down the red button. A hologram of Miss Taylor's face popped into existence. She turned towards the receiver, fingers still typing away on whatever work she had decided to conquer that morning.

"Yes, Mr. Hale?"

"Miss Taylor," I glanced at her and then back at my calendar, waving a hand towards it. "I see an entry here for a meeting with Ambassador Eamon Lech at two o'clock."

I thought I caught her rolling her eyes, but the holo-image was too grainy to be sure. "Yes, Mr. Hale?"

"I don't suppose it matters that I don't particularly wish to meet with Mr. Lech at two o'clock? Or at any other time, for that matter?"

Her typing ceased. Miss Taylor looked away from the receiver for a moment, blowing her curled bangs out of her eyes. After ascertaining that the room was clear of eavesdropping employees, she leaned back in towards the device and addressed me in a far less deferential manner. "Look, Chance – he's been calling every day for the past three weeks. I can only make up so many conflicting meetings and engagements before it starts to sound ridiculous."

"But–"

"But nothing," she cut me off with a growl, throwing one hand up, the other twirling a stylus beside her head. "Whether you like it or not, the Charcornacian Government is one of our biggest clients. They were none too pleased when we refused to sell them any more of our defensive smart tech–"

"You mean our weapons." I leaned back in my chair, my arms wrapped tight around my torso. I scowled, chewing the inside of my mouth. "I can't believe we even manufacture things like that, let alone that my father was selling them in bulk to a warmongering, short-sighted–"

"The point is–" Miss Taylor pressed on, hands coming down flat onto her desk. "–that the customer service division has been working to the point of exhaustion for three months to try and keep the Charcornacians from taking what is left of their business elsewhere." She sat back, shaking loose hair away from her face. "The least you can do is meet with one of their ambassadors for half an hour."

I threw up my hands, wheeling myself back under my desk with a powerful kick of my legs. "Fine! I'll meet with the bastard. But don't ever schedule something like this without telling me first, understand?"

I flicked off the hologram, cutting off her indignant snort. I chewed the inside of my mouth raw, before grabbing a stack of revenue reports and forcing my eyes down the page; correcting mathematical and grammatical errors helped release my anger.

It wasn't Miss Taylor's fault, I reflected after ten minutes of aggressive editorial therapy. I let out a long breath through my clenched teeth, leaning over the papers on my desk. I massaged my forehead with my free hand – I was going to have to apologize to her. I wrote myself a note in my task lists, before flicking the computer screens off to sleep and slouching back in my chair, mumbling to myself.

I couldn't exactly tell her the truth. My objections to Charcornac as a client of Halcyon Enterprises was more than philosophical in nature. Charcornac and their allies were directly responsible for the invasion of Whiston and the atrocities that were being committed against the animanecrons who lived there. Up until this point, I had worked extremely hard to keep any knowledge of my animanecron flat mate, Cadence Turing, away from the press and any other prying eyes. Henry and his family were the only ones who knew for certain what kind of company I was keeping, and that was the way I wanted it to stay.

A twinge of guilt squeezed my heart at the thought. I turned from my desk, staring out my office window. I couldn't deny it;

I didn't relish the idea of people finding out how deeply I had entangled myself with Cadence. I wanted her. I cared for her. On some level I accepted, even cherished, those truths. But what would people say if they knew I had feelings for an animanecron? What would I say if I knew it about someone else?

I pushed through the long, tedious hours of the morning, and spent the rest of the early afternoon watching the clock on my screen tick ever closer to two.

At exactly five after, the intercom on my desk rattled against the wood. I depressed the red button, bringing up the hologram of Miss Taylor.

"Is Mr. Lech here?"

"Yes, sir," she said, glaring eyes focused somewhere over my head. "Shall I show him in?"

"Please." I flicked the hologram off with a snap and braced myself.

While this was my first time seeing Eamon Lech in the flesh, it was not the first time I'd heard of him. With more planets lifting their ban on immigration from Whiston, the war there was gaining more attention, the actions of the Charcornacian government coming sharply into focus. Eamon Lech was the central ambassador for Charcornac, an advisor to the Prime Minister himself. The government had tapped him to be their interplanetary mouthpiece when it came to the war. He had traveled from planet to planet all summer, trying to calm the public's mind about events on Whiston, and lobbying for other governments to join the Charcornacian effort to, as he put it, "protect our borders, our livelihoods, and our very humanity."

When Miss Taylor showed him and his assistant into my

office, I rose to meet him. "Mr. Lech," I said, coming around my desk with an outstretched hand. "How do you do? I'm sorry we couldn't meet until today."

"No need to apologize, sir." Lech gripped my hand, displaying a wide smile of his own. "I'm sure a man like you is very busy."

It had taken some getting used to, men almost twice my age calling me 'sir'. Lech wasn't quite that old, but there was enough difference between our ages to make me smother a wince at the word. He had a strong grip and smooth hands. Everything about Lech suggested an innate sense of style and presentation. He stood a few inches taller than me, and he had the muscle mass I perhaps would if I ever stuck to a gym schedule long enough.

I turned my attention to the man behind him, inclining my head and offering my hand once more. "And is this your assistant?"

Thin and short, the man didn't look up from the datapad he had held in one hand, stylus flying over the screen with mechanical precision. His lips twitched up into a perfunctory smile, his head bobbing in my direction. He stepped neatly around both me and his employer, making for the interior of the office without a word. Lech seemed unperturbed by this antisocial behavior, answering for him smoothly: "My attaché, yes. Leo Trafford. Couldn't want better. He could whip your calendar into shape in no time. Need a man's mind for that."

"Oh, I'm sure," I laughed politely, and moved quickly to close the door to my office. I gestured to the chairs in front of my desk. "Please, sit. Mr. Trafford, you're welcome to as well, of course."

"Mr. Trafford prefers to stand, thank you." Lech settled into his seat with a wave back towards his companion, who had settled most unobtrusively behind him, his attention still fully absorbed by whatever work he had in front of him.

I could feel Lech's cornflower blue eyes follow me all the way back to my desk; his attentiveness put me on edge. I tried to fix him with an appraising stare of my own as I settled back into my chair, taking in his features as leisurely as I could. He was an attractive, if not a remarkable, looking man, with dark chestnut brown hair parted down the middle. His face was as statuesque as his bearing. But despite the pleasant nature of his appearance, there was something in his expression that radiated a barely concealed menace. He was like a predator in a zoo; I wished there were a pane of glass between us.

I pushed my misgivings to one side and asked, "What can I do for you, Mr. Lech?"

"I'm sure you're aware how far this whole animanecron issue has spun out of control over the last few months, Mr. Hale," he began, folding his hands in his lap. "We've done our best to keep the fraggers contained to Whiston and Charcornac, but it seems many have slipped through the cracks; spreading across the system like a virus." I did my best not to flinch at his use of the slur, but was hard-pressed not to smile when he continued, saying, "Planets like Römer lifting their immigration bans certainly haven't helped with the problem either."

That was one bit of good I'd done in my new position of power – spread some of our charity money around to the right organizations, anonymously of course, and help get the ludicrous ban my father had worked to get passed repealed. "I can only imagine how much that's...inconvenienced you, Mr. Lech."

"It's not about convenience, Mr. Hale," said Lech, lifting his hands, still clasped, out of his lap and pointing them at me. "It's about self-preservation."

"I'm afraid I don't quite follow you," I said, unbuttoning my suit jacket and leaning back in my chair.

Lech uncrossed his legs and moved to the edge of his seat, one hand clutching the armrest, the other gesticulating by his face as he spoke. "Humanity has existed for hundreds of thousands of years. We've brought light to the darkest corners of the universe, survived against insurmountable odds, and we have excelled at bettering worlds for our having existed in them. The animanecrons present a direct threat to this legacy, and to our future."

His hyperbole staggered me; not to laugh in his face was a heroic feat. I settled instead for staring at him with a bored expression, my own hands falling into my lap. "I wasn't aware the animanecrons had expressed a desire to harm humans in any way."

"It's only a matter of time. When you partner with machines, eventually everything becomes reduced to a factor." Lech straightened in his seat, his hand flattening against his chest. "For generations, we have been the ones setting the course of progress, with our mortal souls as guideposts to lead us towards brighter tomorrows. Can you imagine what would happen if machines got there first? If intelligent entities, devoid of our humanity, began to dictate the shape of the universe? Is there any question that our way of life, our very existence, wouldn't be in jeopardy?"

"You believe the animanecrons to be intelligent? Conscious?" I swallowed hard and met his cold eyes. "How curious."

"Oh, I've spent enough time with them to know, Mr. Hale." Lech rolled his shoulders back as he settled into his seat once more. "They are every bit our equals when it comes to the powers of the mind. Stronger, faster – all they lack is our empathy, our souls. And what a lack that is. What a poison." His finger pierced the air. "A poison for which we have a cure, Mr. Hale."

I ticked my head to one side. "Destroy them all. Of course."

Lech sighed, his shoulders falling, his jaw tightening. "Surely you realize that you have a responsibility, the highest responsibility, in this matter, Mr. Hale? After all, your company, your scientists are the fraggers' creators."

"I don't know if the animanecrons see it that way," I muttered, thinking of my friend who was, even now, somewhere in the Entertainment Market just trying to scrape by. We'd never discussed it, but I inferred from her apathy towards my company that she didn't hold Halcyon Enterprises in any high esteem.

"Animanecrons are not the creations of a god or nature, Mr. Hale," continued Lech, brows lifting over his eyes. "They are the creation of your family's legacy – of the scientists and staff behind Halcyon Enterprises, the company you represent to the world. You need to be seen to take a stand on this issue, and now is the time."

"Mr. Lech," I cleared my throat and stretched my arms across my desk, raising my voice a little. "Halcyon Enterprises' policy on this matter is as unchanged now as it was three hundred years ago, when the animanecrons were first banned. We can hardly be expected to take responsibility for a technology that evolved...shall we say, organically–" I lifted a brow, my hands tumbling over one another for emphasis, "–into its own state of consciousness. It was never our intent; we can hardly be held liable for an accident."

Lech nodded, his eyes never leaving my face, lips pressed tightly together. "Did you ever read *Frankenstein*, Mr. Hale?"

I clasped my hands together on top of my desk, wary of the man's sudden change in tact. "It rings a vague bell."

"It's an old earth text – pretty arcane, and hard to understand in the original common tongue. It tells the story of a scientist who seeks to create life out of death. He succeeds, and his creation runs amok throughout the civilized world – mostly because he fails to take any responsibility for the monster he's created."

I let out a breathy chuckle and shook my head. "I see what you're getting at, Mr. Lech. The animanecrons, as their name would suggest, were indeed originally created in an attempt to preserve some semblance of the mind after death. But not the actual soul, or life. The present situation is significantly more complicated than a mere science experiment gone awry."

"As the head of this company, you have the power to significantly influence the course of this debate on Arrhidaeus. And, frankly, in the entire system," pressed Lech, his tone earnest. "I understand your hesitation in making a firm statement, I do. But the time for such caution is past, Mr. Hale. You heard about the protest near the Entertainment Market today, I trust?"

My attention sharpened into alarm at the mention of the Entertainment Market, but I worked hard not to show it. "No, I hadn't. But there's been a lot of protests lately."

"The workers of the PT Dispatch Office for that District are on strike; picketing, for a week now, ever since Galaxy

Transportation announced its decision to hire fraggers as regular drivers at full pay." Lech huffed with disdain. "Ridiculous. They're machines; they don't need to eat or sleep. Living wage? They aren't alive! Of course, the pro-ani activists have come out to rabble rouse and make trouble for everyone else. Ergo Sum, they call themselves."

"And where they go, doesn't that other fringe group usually follow?" I grimaced, shaking my head. "The Anti-Fragger Organization?"

"The A.F.O. is a legitimate group of concerned citizens exercising their right to free speech and assembly." The line came out of his mouth with such speed I could tell it was well-rehearsed.

Leaning back in my chair, I fixed Lech with a cool stare. "They tend to turn protests into riots, I understand."

"Who is ultimately at fault for the violence that ensues at these demonstrations is still being investigated by the Enforcement Office," said Lech, shrugging. "But I would be very surprised if any charges were brought against the A.F.O."

So would I. Animanecrons found themselves in an undefined area of the law. They were still legal objects; possessions at best, walking and talking litter at worst. You couldn't exactly 'assault' a machine. Some forward-thinking public defenders were trying to get such cases seen under the heading of 'destruction of property,' but they were running into issues with compensation – the property in these cases belonged to no one but itself, so there was no one to pay damages to, except what was already defined, by law, as an inanimate object.

"My point is, Mr. Hale, that people are getting hurt and going to continue to get hurt. You're for peace and prosperity – so are we." Lech moved to the edge of his seat, resting his hand against the lip of my desk. "All the Charcornacian government is asking, is that you make a statement explaining to the public what the animanecrons are: machines, not people."

"What you want is for me to say it's okay to destroy them without prejudice," I smiled. "I won't do that. I'm sorry, Mr. Lech, but my answer is no."

Lech's blue eyes flicked over me once more. He shrugged. "I didn't expect you to be a man of such principle, Mr. Hale." He returned my smile with one of his own: a tight-lipped, toothless affair that left me feeling oily. "Trust me, in this business, you can't afford it."

"Thanks for the advice, Mr. Lech," I said, standing and re-buttoning my suit jacket. "But I'm managing so far with my ethics intact." Gesturing to the door, I plastered on a final charming grin. "If there's nothing else...?"

"I was very grateful for the opportunity to meet you, Mr. Hale," Lech stood, stretching out his hand to me. "You're something of an unknown quantity at the moment." We shook, and his grip was every bit as firm and commanding as before. "Coming into the spotlight so suddenly – what with your father's unfortunate death."

"I like to think I'm walking in his footsteps," I said, releasing his hand and slipping both of my own into my trouser pockets.

"Really?" His brows leapt up over his deep-set eyes. He turned to look at his assistant, who never glanced up from his pad, before returning his attention to me, one hand coming up to stroke his sharp chin. "Even when you use your own capital to get the immigration ban he fought for repealed?"

I bit into my cheek, tilting my head to one side. "Ah, I'm afraid you must be mistaken, Mr. Le–"

"I know all about your so-called 'anonymous' donations, Mr. Hale." He waved away my protestation like so much nix smoke. "I find it curious, if you really feel the way that you do, that you'd bother making them anonymous at all." He leaned forward and tapped my chest with his forefinger, smiling a much broader smile. "Perhaps you're not the man of principle you like to pretend to be."

Despite myself, I took a step back. Lech gave a happy hum and waved his hand again, gaze turning heavenward. "But it won't matter for much longer anyway. Once Kayin Oni is re-elected by the good people of Arrhidaeus, we're confident the ban will be reinstated."

"So," my hands curled into fists in my pockets, while my smile remained pasted onto my lips. "It's true what the pundits are saying: Chancellor Oni's campaign is being supported by other system politicians."

Lech shrugged. "Charcornac has no desire to see a pro-fragger gain a place on the IPC Council. And we're not the only ones."

"Well, everyone makes mistakes." I once more extended my arm towards my office door. "Have a good rest of your day, Mr. Lech."

With a slight nod, he and his assistant moved away. Lech was one of those people you were relieved to see the back of, and I'll admit, I allowed myself a shiver when I was sure he was no longer watching me.

2

Chapter 2

"Miss Taylor," I said as I stepped out of my office, pushing my arms through the sleeves of my raincoat. "Is there any way you can work your magic and clear my calendar for the rest of the day?"

Lily ceased typing. She stared at her main screen and took in a deep breath through her nose. With a quick jerk of her head, she turned to face me. "If I say 'no', will that stop you from doing whatever it is you're so clearly intent on doing?"

I froze partway through cinching my coat shut around my waist and considered her query. "No."

Lily nodded and returned to her work, rolling her shoulders back. "Then I suppose I better find a way." And then, because I knew she would move heaven and earth for me if I asked, despite our earlier tiff, she paused to look up at me as I crossed in front of her. "Is everything alright, Mr. Hale?"

"Just need to check on something," I replied. "I'll be back bright and early tomorrow morning." I began to move towards the lifts when I stopped, remembering myself with a wince. "Oh, and Miss Taylor?"

Lily folded her hands under her chin, watching me in expectation. I swallowed and avoided her gaze. "I'm sorry about earlier. Been a bit...on edge lately. Shouldn't have taken it out on you."

Her face softened into a smile. Shaking her head, she relaxed into her chair with a sigh. "My mum's birthday is coming up." She picked up a stylus and twirled it around in the air. "I was hoping to take her somewhere nice."

"Just tell me where and when, and I'll make the reservation myself."

Smile widening, she dipped her head in a nod. "Thanks, Chance. Have a good night."

With a final wave of my hand, I hopped on the lift, riding it down to the four hundredth floor, where the executive PTs waited to whisk weary workers from our building to their home sweet homes.

I stepped outside onto the PT dock, yanking up the collar of my coat with one hand to protect myself against the pouring rain. I jogged to one of the waiting PTs as quickly as I could, tumbling less than gracefully inside it through the open door. "The Entertainment Market, please," I said, rearranging myself in the backseat.

A nod from the driver and we were on our way, through the dark, heavy clouds and the steady, beating rain. Late summer meant the beginning of the rainy season on Arrhidaeus. The rains would fall until winter, saturating every part of the planet, except the poles, where it was always too cold, and it snowed almost year-round. Most of the drinking water for the planet was harvested from these yearly rains. Huge reservoirs and retaining pools were set up in every district of Römer, siphoning the rain off the streets and into treatment tanks that lurked beneath the city like laboring golems, pumping out the lifeblood of civilization daily.

Arrhidaeans had adapted to the months of dark clouds and constant wet. In fact, as I looked out the glass windows of the rapidly ascending PT, I was reminded of how much I loved the city at this time of year. Every building was a beacon of light, every room a cozy and dry haven. The people were friendlier, sharing bumbershoots and holding open doors. The sounds of the city became muted, almost melodious, under the thick blanket of grey mist.

When we arrived at the entrance to the Entertainment Market, the rain had eased from a pounding storm to a drizzle. As I exited the PT and entered the Market, I paused for a moment underneath the multicolored awning to shake off the wet from my coat, and to adjust to the sudden change in atmosphere.

The Entertainment Market was a chaotic hodgepodge of sounds and bodies, all flowing in and out and around each other, until one was indistinguishable from the other. Screens of every shape and size flashed out into the crowd. Discordant tunes fought for dominance above my head; one moment a sweet melody, the next a raging backbeat.

At the end of the dizzying maze of streets, story cubes glittered on stall shelves, sometimes placed out of reach, like precious jewels, other times jumbled together in multi-colored bins, begging to be nicked. Several of the cubes were plugged into modified audio devices, spewing their secreted words out into the atmosphere, filling the air with the sound of stories.

Half of the stalls sold everything, every genre, every era, every author. The rest, the less trafficked stalls, were the specialty sellers. These merchants didn't bother coming up with catchy names for their stalls, less interested in grabbing your attention than in giving you information. 'Existentialism' was written above one, 'Fantastical Romance' over another. Tucked in its own little corner was a stall with a simple, hand-printed sign that read: 'Mystery'.

As I headed for the stall which I knew belonged to Cadence, it occurred to me that lately the only time I came to this area of Römer was to see her. Five months ago, not long after we had solved the mystery surrounding my father's sudden death, I had also found myself in District 49 of Römer, wandering through the Market, looking for her.

I had watched her from behind the Political Satire booth for several minutes. Rearranging cubes at the front of her stall, Cadence pulled items from boxes at the back, and placed them with care on top of and beside each other. She had abandoned the simple white outfit in which I had first seen her, opting instead for a blue blouse, tight brown vest, and loose brown pants, her tattoo hidden entirely.

With faltering steps, I had made my way towards her, timing my strides so that when I arrived, she would be in the back, sorting through boxes. I picked up a cube and examined it, controlling the tremor in my voice. "Do you have any Agatha Christie?"

Her hand froze halfway out of a box. I wished then that I had done this with Cadence facing me, but I wouldn't have been able to read her expression anyway. I never could. She stood and, after a moment, turned to look over her shoulder, watching me with narrowed eyes. "I don't think you even know who that is."

"Course I do. I did a report about her at school." Cadence raised a brow. Placing the cube down with a huff, I shoved my hands into my pockets. "Alright; Henry did the actual report, but I presented it. Fascinating."

The edges of her mouth betrayed her, twitching and jumping as she tried to smother a smile. Stepping forward, she pulled a cube from a bin marked 'Conan Doyle' and tossed it at me. "Try this one."

Catching it one-handed, I plugged it in to the reader she had on display, the words dancing above it. I skimmed the text but was too busy noticing the way Cadence's hair danced around her cheeks, the way she picked at the threadbare cloth laid out over her stand, and the way she looked at me.

"I didn't think I'd ever see you again," she said.

I lifted my head, blinking in surprise. "Really?"

"Maybe." Cadence started tapping against the table but stopped, holding one hand in the other as she shrugged. "I thought you might be glad that I left." She frowned at her hands. "A little."

"I think I was."

Looking back up at me, the bridge of her nose wrinkled.

I unplugged the cube from its station, handing it back to her with a grin. "For about five seconds."

Taking it from me with her summer smile, she tossed it from

hand to hand, catching it each time without looking. "How have you been?"

"Good. Bored, actually. Being responsible is everything I ever thought it would be. I was right to avoid it for as long as possible." I ran my hand through my hair, chewing the inside of my mouth. "I'm selling Hale Manor."

Like lightning, Cadence's shoulders tensed. "What?" She placed both hands flat against the counter. "No. Why?"

"It's too big for me. And there's so much... sadness in that house. Now that I know– I just can't stay there anymore." Clearing my throat, I began to straighten my collar. "I'm thinking of getting a place here in town, actually."

Cadence nodded. "That will be nice."

"Closer to the office."

"Yes. Much more convenient."

"Yes." I fiddled with a box of cubes marked two-for-fifteen-credits. "Where are you living?"

"District 30, up on 29th and Pine."

I groaned. Cadence tilted her head to one side. "Is that bad?"

"Well, it's not the best part of Römer, is it?" I leaned against her stall, folding my arms over my chest. "How much are you paying?"

"Five hundred credits a month."

"Shameful!"

I waited for Cadence to look away, but she didn't move.

"Hold on." Closing my eyes, I put a finger to my lips. "Here's a thought: all the places I've looked at in the business district are two-bedroom apartments; they expect businesspeople and their families, you know? Well, they run about a thousand credits a month, and I'd only use one room..."

Opening my eyes again, I found Cadence had remained just as she was. Dropping my hands to my sides, I attempted a laugh. "Well, of course I can afford that, but maybe it would be better – for you, I mean – if you and I – if we..."

Cadence blinked at me several times but said nothing. Fisting my hands into my pockets, I finished with a mumble, "...it'd still be five hundred credits a month..."

Stepping closer, Cadence rested against the other side of the stall. "Why?"

Scowling, I leaned forward until my face was inches from hers. "Because I miss you, damn it. I miss you so much that I can't stand the thought of being even a block away from you."

Still blinking at me, her breathing stilled, and she stood, bringing her hand up to her chin and stroking it with an earnest air of contemplation. "I wouldn't mind having my own kitchen."

Then she smiled. Her smile outshined the multicolored lights which she had strung along the front of the shop, outshined the sun itself, and warmed my shivering soul with its sweet sincerity. Dazzled, I smiled back, hoping to bask in her brilliance forever.

Now, I came upon her shop, and it was dark and unlit. No cubes sat out for browsing, but were hidden inside tall, locked cases that were themselves covered in thick, tan sheets. The front register's screen was turned out, facing the public, and flashed a simple one-word message: CLOSED.

I tried peering into the dim depths of the stall but saw no signs of movement. My mind raced, my unease growing more intense by the moment. Surely, she wouldn't be foolish enough to go to an Ani-Rights protest... She must know how dangerous that could be for her... She wasn't reckless by nature...

A clatter from behind me broke my concentration, and I looked over my shoulder. Across the way from Cadence's stall was a hexagonal shop with a sign above it that read, 'Myths and Legends'. A rotund, bald man was standing behind the shop's front counter, grumbling to himself as he picked up a box of story cubes that he had fumbled to the ground.

Making my way through the crowd, I approached the cube seller, and cleared my throat. "Excuse me." I gestured to the deserted stall behind me. "The woman who usually runs this shop–?"

The man blinked at me, shifting the box under one arm. "You mean, Miss Turing?"

"Yes. Any idea if she'll be back today?"

The round gentleman puffed out his cheeks and shook his head. "Oh, to be honest, I'm not sure. Saw a young man stop by her booth, and then she closed up shop and they headed towards the Galaxy Transpo Offices."

I gritted my teeth. A young man. No points for guessing who that was; we'd been trying to connect with each other for weeks, and I had encouraged Henry to look up Cadence at the Market – but taking her to an Ani-Rights protest was not what I had had in mind. I nodded to the shopkeep in front of me and turned towards the other end of the Market with a sharp, "Thank you," more intent than ever on tracking down my friends.

The man called after me, his own concern obvious in his strident tone. "Say, sir, I wouldn't go down there if I were you!"

I waved behind me and shouted back, "I'll be fine, thank you!"

I fought my way through the crowds until I reached the opposite end of the Market, which opened back onto the public walkways. I was surprised to find the walkways choked with bodies, but soon realized that this was the protest for which I was looking. The flashing pink and purple neon sign of the Galaxy Transportation offices glowed bright in the rain. Closest to the building was a line of picketers with crude, handmade signs on dowels. "Living wage? Not alive!", "Not Here, Not Ever!", "Arrhidaeus for Arrhidaeans!" were some of the most popular slogans featured, although some simply were emblazoned with images of blocky robots strangling humans.

These picketers, drenched to the bone, hurled expletives and insults at the large group on the other side of the walkway, a more prepared looking bunch with umbrellas, ponchos, and waterproof pre-printed plastic signs that read "Right to Work, Right to Live", "Stand Against Hate", and "Think, Feel, Fight!".

I recognized the slogans of Ergo Sum, the pro-animanecron organization, and surmised that if Cadence and Henry were anywhere, it was somewhere within that crowd. I pushed my way into the group, making my apologies when I trod on feet, or bumped errant elbows, all the while hunting for my missing companions.

"Shouldn't you be at work?"

I spun around to find the object of my search standing behind me, her mouth crooked in a confused scowl, her arms crossed low over her belly. I don't know how I could have missed her – even in a crowd, Cadence Turing stood out. Standing as tall as any man, her wavy black hair pulled back from her sharp face, her dark blue eyes flashed out from under dark brows.

"Cay!" Without a moment's hesitation or thought, I embraced her. "Thank God, you're alright!"

"Why wouldn't I be?" She rubbed my back with her hands, but I felt her pull away to look at me. "Chance, why are you here in the middle of the day? Won't the office be missing you?"

Shaking my head, I gave her one last tight squeeze before releasing her, stepping back as far as the crowd would allow. "I heard about the protest on the news, and since it was so close to the market, I wanted to make sure you were okay."

"Better than okay." The happiness in her voice, so long absent, stayed my upset momentarily. She was smiling her wide summer smile, blue eyes sparkling under her raised brows. "Gav, it's wonderful, Chance! Look at all these people! I never thought I would see so many humans supporting us. And I haven't seen so many animanecrons in one place since I left Whiston. It's incredible!"

Glancing at the sea of bodies around us, I drew her in close to me. "I think you mean it's incredibly dangerous; especially for you," I said, my voice low. "How did you even find out this was going on, Cay?"

Her inky blue eyes narrowed before she rolled them at me, shaking my hand off her arm. "Sarc, I listen to the news too, Chance. I'm not an idiot, you know." One hand on her hip, she gestured to the assembly surrounding us. "I know what's been happening out here since the ban was lifted. I just wanted to see what it was like."

I scoffed aloud, crossing my arms over my chest. "Oh, well: is your curiosity satisfied?"

She mimicked my stance and stared at me, grimacing. "I don't know why you're acting like this, Chance. I may not look it, but I am very much older than you. And I may not know what a nix is, or how to hail a PT, or a lot of other things, but that doesn't mean I'm naïve."

I sighed, rubbing at my forehead as I tried in vain to let go of some of my distress. "I know that."

Cadence clicked her tongue off the roof of her mouth. I took another step back from her, my hands falling to my sides. "I do, I really do!" I tilted my head to one side, my gaze focused on the top of her shoes. "Listen: you're right," I said. "I'm sorry. I just worry about you out here, with things the way they are right now. I don't want something to happen to you when you're alone."

"She's not alone." A thin, elegant hand fell onto her shoulder. "I'm here with her."

I glared up at my oldest friend, Henry Davers, from under my brow. "I'll get to you in a minute, chum."

Henry crooked a brow up over his chocolate brown eyes. "Well, hello to you too, Chance." He removed his hand from Cadence and pushed it into the pocket of his open raincoat. "Yes, it has been a long time. Yes, it certainly is good to see you."

It really had been a long time since we'd last seen each other; too long a time, as Henry was a bit leaner than I remembered, and his usually trimmed and coiffed hair was verging on shaggy and disheveled. But his eyes were as bright and lively as ever, and I didn't care for the hint of judgment I saw brewing inside of them.

"You know that device in your pocket? A phone?" He rocked

back on his heels. "Amazing thing. Can make calls as well as receive them. You should try it some time."

I looked away, not trusting myself to hold on to my displeasure with my oldest friend if I kept eye contact with him. "I know we've been trying to catch each other for weeks but colluding with Cadence to go to an Ani-Rights Rally seems an extreme way to get my attention."

Shrugging, Henry rolled his eyes at my purposeful hyperbole. "Whatever works." A small smile snuck onto his lips, and he reached forward to grip my shoulder. "I am glad to see you here, though; the more the merrier."

"As nice as it is to see you, chum, I'm not here," I said with an emphatic swipe of my hand. "It'd be a PR nightmare if it got out that I was here, so I'm going to be leaving as soon as possible. And so should both of you." I leaned in so only they could hear. "The A.F.O. are on their way, if they aren't here already, and we all know that spells trouble."

"Those bastards?" Henry's thin face reddened, and he released me, scanning the crowd. "I've got to let Elea and Simone know before they speak."

"Who?"

But Henry was not there to hear my confused query. Striding with purpose, he made his way towards the front of the crowd, where I could now see a small stage erected in the center of the public walkway.

"Henry!" I shouted after him, but it was no use. All my call did was attract the attention of the protestors nearest to us, a couple of whom looked at me once, and then again with something that was too close to recognition for my liking. I turned around and pulled my coat collar up around my chin in an ineffectual attempt to hide myself. "Blast," I exclaimed under my breath. I reached for Cadence's arm and started walking back in the direction of the Entertainment Market. "Come on, let's get out of here."

But Cadence stayed where she was and moved not an inch in the direction I indicated. She looked from the hand I had placed on her to my face, her brow furrowing. "I'm not leaving without Henry."

I shook my head, gaze going heavenward. "He's a grown man, he can take care of himself."

"And I can't take care of myself?" countered Cadence, flicking my hand off her appendage as if it were a piece of lint.

"That's not what I meant," I said, lips firming into a stern line.

"But that's clearly what you think."

"Cay–"

"Goddamn fragger lovers!" The shout, louder and lustier than the others being exchanged between the two groups of protestors, drowned out my words to Cadence, and forced me to turn around. A bottle flew through the air from the direction of the Galaxy Transpo offices, the liquid and powder inside of it sloshing and mixing together. It exploded above the heads of the Ergo Sum protestors at the front of the crowd, sending a shower of glass shrapnel hailing down, alongside a sickly green smoke that descended slowly onto the screaming crowd of bodies.

Chaos erupted. Three more bottles soared into the air, exploding one after the other. One hovered directly over Cadence and me. I stepped in front of her, intent on shielding her with my body, but she was, as usual, far more practical than I.

Before I knew what was happening, I was on the ground, the wind knocked out of me. Cadence crouched over and around me, covering me as best as she could, her head hanging down over mine.

I heard the bottle explode. Heard Cadence cry out in pain as the shards of glass slashed into her flesh. But she didn't flinch. She didn't move a muscle. Instead, she merely shouted in my ear, "Try not to breathe!"

I squirmed against the ground, attempting to free enough of my coat from under my body to hold it to my nose and mouth. The ground of the public walkway shook as protestors ran in every direction around us. The green smoke, thick and heavy, filtered down to our level, unaffected by the rain. I screwed my eyes shut and tried to keep my breathing shallow.

Without warning, the warmth of Cadence's body left me. At the same instant, I felt a spongy piece of plastic being pressed against my nose and mouth. I started and opened my eyes to see Cadence crouching to one side of me, watching me with concern, blood from a gash on her neck dripping down her collarbone. Henry knelt on the other side of me, pressing the air filtration node tight against my face, holding an identical node to his own.

Scrambling up into a sitting position, I held the node to my face and nodded at Henry. Returning my nod, he stood, reaching his hand down to me and pulling me up with him. Communication was impossible with the nodes fitted tightly over our faces, but we all understood that we needed to get clear of the area as quickly as possible. Cadence led the way, cutting through the heaving crowd like a scalpel through rotten flesh. Henry and I followed behind. The filtration nodes were doing their jobs, but all around me I saw protestors who weren't so lucky succumb to the effects of the noxious fumes, doubled over in pain and retching, hallucinating and jibbering. I tried to keep my eyes forward, keep my eyes on Cadence, but when I did so, I could not avoid seeing the shredded mess of her clothes, the gashes in her back from the glass, and a singularly nasty slice on the back of her calf, which was causing her to limp.

3

Chapter 3

We fought our way into the Entertainment Market, which had been thrown into pandemonium by the riot just beyond its borders. I dropped my filtration node from my face and slid it into my pocket, hurrying to catch up to Cadence.

"Cay–"

But Cadence cut me off with a shake of her head, smearing blood across her forehead as she swiped her hand across it. "We need to get out of here before–"

The shrill sounds of EO sirens became louder and louder with every passing second. Cadence skittered to a halt a few feet from the main entrance of the Market, her eyes widening as she took in the sight of three EO PTs blocking the way.

"This way," said Henry, darting to the right, giving Cadence and I little choice but to follow him.

Leading us on a winding path through the side streets that

made up the Market, Henry ducked into a small, dingy cyber-cafe at the dead end of an alleyway. By the time Cadence and I followed him inside, he was already in deep conversation with the gentleman behind the cafe counter.

"It'll just be for an hour or two, Sal," Henry was saying, his tone strident and pleading.

Sal looked up as we entered and sighed, pushing a hand back through his shoulder length black hair. He leaned away from the counter, his hands held up in the air. "Fine. Fine! An hour, Henry. No more, okay? I don't want any trouble."

"Okay." Henry nodded and smiled. "Thank you."

Shaking his head, Sal just said, "You know the way," before returning to the opposite end of the counter, where a screen junkie waited for a fix of caffeine.

Henry turned to face us and jerked his thumb towards a set of metal stairs in the back corner of the space. "Sal has a spare room you can lie low in for a while until the EO clears out."

"'You'?" I blinked at him in confusion. "You're not staying?"

Henry shook his head, already moving past me for the door. "I have to get back out there; see what I can do to help." He waved at us. "I'll call you later, Chance, I promise!"

There wasn't even time to call out to him, let alone argue. I watched him disappear out the door, my mouth opening and closing uselessly.

"Are you coming?"

Cadence's voice snapped me back to the moment at hand, and I turned to see her standing across the room on the bottom stair. I nodded and followed her, trudging up the stairs.

The door on the landing opened into a modest, pre-furnished

studio apartment that appeared to have been unoccupied for some time. I flicked the light switch on the wall, and a pair of weak, yellow bulbs buzzed into life, hidden under a dusty, faded lampshade in the corner. There was a single bed shoved against the right wall, its bare mattress blue, worn, and exposed. A small kitchen area sat directly to the left, with a closet of a bathroom in the back corner. A loveseat sat across from the bed, collapsed in the middle and altogether untrustworthy looking.

I lifted my brows and smacked my lips. "Charming."

"It's not so bad," answered Cadence, moving stiffly towards the bed.

Now that we were no longer running, I could take clearer stock of her injuries. There must be a cut somewhere under her hair, a steady stream of blood trickling down her forehead and across her cheek. The cut on the side of her neck didn't look deep, nor did the many nicks and slices across her back and shoulders. But the gash in her leg was a nasty piece of work, bloody and jagged, and I blanched at the sight of it.

"You sit down," I said, moving back towards the staircase, "I'm going to–"

"Hey."

Sal stood on the landing, shifting from foot to foot, his eyes downcast. He was a younger man, with a rough voice that did not match his kind eyes and soft face. Held in his outstretched hands was a standard issue emergency medkit.

"Thought you guys might need this," he said, jutting the medkit out to me.

I took it from him, heaving a sigh of relief. "Thank you. We'll be out of your way as soon as we can."

"It's no problem," Sal scratched the back of his neck, his dark face blushing. "You stay as long as you need. It's no problem. Any friend of Henry's is a friend of mine."

I made a mental note to ask Henry about Sal later, but settled in the moment for shaking his hand, and thanking him once again. He closed the door behind him as he left.

Opening the medkit, I looked over the supplies and began to form a treatment plan for Cadence's injuries. The skin patch would be for her leg, the anticoagulant foam for her head, the antiseptic swabs and butterfly bandages for the cuts on her back and neck...

By the time I glanced up at my patient, I had crossed the small room and was standing beside the bed. Cadence was splayed out face down on the mattress, her legs and arms spread wide to either side.

"I'm in pain," she said, the words muffled by the springs and stuffing.

"I can fix that. A little, at least." I tugged at the hem of her long-sleeved pink shirt. "Could you take this off for me? I need to get at those cuts."

A tired sigh, but then Cadence complied, sitting up and gingerly pulling the shirt up and over her head. She tossed it to the floor, and was about to lie back down, when my hand on her bare shoulder stopped her movement.

"Let me see to the cut on your head and the one on your neck first."

She obeyed without a word, growing still, her hands falling to her lap. I shook the pressurized canister of anticoagulant foam twice before parting her hair, my fingers probing hesitantly for the cut.

"It's a little to the left."

I moved my hand to the left and felt blood. Sweeping her hair out of the way, I revealed a jagged slash in her scalp, about two centimeters long. With the end of the nozzle hovering over the wound, I pressed the plunger down. The foam covered the cut with a hiss, expanding as it met blood. I felt Cadence shiver under my hands.

"Oh!" She exclaimed. "It's cold!"

"Yes, sorry." My brows knitted together in concern. "I should've warned you."

"It's okay. It feels nice." Cadence started to roll her shoulders back but seemed to think better of it. "I get so overheated in this humid weather. I wish I could sweat like you..."

"It's overrated." I activated the antiseptic swab and cleaned up her neck wound as best as I could. The butterfly bandage closed it nicely. She would need skin patches for everything, eventually. Given her unique biological make-up, her skin didn't exactly regenerate the same way a humans did – it needed a little help.

"Now you can lie down," I said, taking a step back from her. "It'll be easier for me to get at your back and leg that way."

"Right." Cadence pivoted and lay stomach down against the mattress, trusting as always.

I sat next to her hip, trying hard not to think of anything, just robotically performing the task in front of me, but failing miserably. Every mark on her, every cut, was a reminder of how useless I had proven. I had come down here to protect her – and in the end it was me who needed protecting.

"Cadence," I said, drawing my hands away from her and closing my eyes. "I'm sorry."

When there was no immediate response to my apology, I opened my eyes again. Cadence had twisted onto her side and was looking at me, one brow quirked upward in confusion.

"For earlier. I was acting like an ass." I lifted my hand and let it drop into my lap, tongue clicking off the back of my teeth. "I was worried about you, that's all. But you're right. You can take care of yourself."

A small, weak smile struggled onto her pale lips. She reached down and took my hand, squeezing it. "Not all the time."

Now it was my turn to look confused. She answered my grimace with a laugh and shook our joined hands. "I couldn't very well patch myself, could I?"

Some of the tension left my shoulders at the sound of her laughter. I lifted her hand to my lips and brushed them against her knuckles. "No. No, I suppose not."

With a last smile in my direction, she turned back onto her stomach, asking, "So... how was work today?"

I smothered a disbelieving smile, my gaze going heavenward. Affixing another butterfly bandage, I smoothed the taupe-colored fabric against her skin, swallowing hard. "Are we really going to talk about that now?"

"What else would you like to talk about?"

I shook my head, averting my eyes from hers. "It was dull. Dull, like it is every day."

"You could always quit." Cadence looked at me from over her shoulder, and I immediately busied myself with picking another swab and bandage from the medkit.

"My father would turn in his grave." I broke the bulb on the antiseptic swab and watched as the tip became soaked in the germ-killing liquid.

Cadence wriggled against the mattress with a huff, pulling her arms under her chin. "I doubt that very much."

My lips twisted into a humorless smirk as I traced the tip of the swab over the cuts. "There must always be a Hale at the head of Halcyon Enterprises, remember?" I tossed the used swab into the medkit, shuddering a little. "Anyway. How was your day?"

She moved her hand back through her hair, forcing the locks out of her face, but careful to avoid her fresh hurt. "Slow. I don't know what it is about modern humans, but you don't have any taste in classic literature."

I allowed myself a weak chuckle, unwrapping several butterfly bandages in preparation. "I'll try not to take that personally."

Cadence pushed herself up onto her forearms, one fist coming down against the mattress with a thud. "I sell wonderful stories! They have danger, romance, intrigue, death; everything you could want!" She rested her chin in her hand, her words coming out in a barely intelligible grumble. "But if it doesn't have a half-naked person in the visual appendix, no one will touch it these days."

I stared at the back of her head, my movements slowing. "Is it really that bad?"

Her head bobbed up and down. "It really is. I can barely afford to pay my bills."

I placed the last butterfly bandage on her back, my mind whirring, and cleared my throat. "What bills?"

Her entire back tensed, a shot of heat going through her

that caused me to instinctively jerk my hand away. Cadence swung her feet down to the floor, shaking her head as she stood. "Chance, no." There was a firmness in her words that brooked no argument. She reached down and out for her discarded top. "We've talked about this."

Collapsing back against the wall, I scowled. "We've talked about it; I've never agreed with you." I gave an aggravated grunt as I leaned forward to stand, nudging the medkit out of my way as I did so. "I don't see what's so wrong with me occasionally helping you pay off some of your bills."

Cadence gave the bottom of her recovered shirt a firm tug, head shaking back and forth. At last, she turned around, her arms akimbo, face creased with lines of worry. "You've done so much for me already. I couldn't ask you to do any more."

I sighed, my head lolling to one side as I reached forward to lightly grab her elbows, pulling her closer to me. "You're not asking," I said, my thumbs rubbing at her soft skin. "I'm offering."

She slid out of my hands, knees bending in a mocking curtsy. "Then I shall continue not to take advantage of such offers."

"Hey." I reached for her once again, the seriousness in my voice surprising even me.

She stopped and looked back at me, gaze bouncing between my eyes and my outstretched hand.

I almost told her then. How I felt. How I really felt about her. That I hadn't come to the Entertainment Market that day five months ago on a whim – I'd come because I was scared. Scared to lose her. I'd come because she was special to me; different from any other person I'd ever known. She was inside me. I felt her there with every beat of my heart, and I had needed her back in my life not because I was lonely or bored, but because not having her was like missing a piece of myself.

"I…" I closed my outstretched hand into a fist. "I haven't finished yet." My hand fell to my side. "Your leg. I still need to patch your leg."

Cadence looked down at her shredded pant leg and sighed. "Sometimes having a corporeal form is very tiresome."

"I like to think the benefits outweigh the frustrations." I forced a smile onto my face. "Come on: back on the bed."

Cadence returned to the mattress, and I swallowed down the words that had almost escaped from me. They were the truth, but the truth was also that I didn't want to damage what we had: a friendship the depth of which I'd known only one other time in my life. And, when I was being completely honest with myself in the cold, lonely depths of the night, the thought that Cadence – inorganic, immortal, inhuman Cadence – might be the one I would want forever? The terror of it nearly overwhelmed me.

When our hour was up, we exited the cybercafe, thanking Sal once more for his impromptu hospitality, and imposing on him just a little further to direct us to the nearest PT. Turns out we were on the outer edge of the Entertainment Market, and a PT station was only two blocks away.

It was late, dark, and still raining, by the time our PT pulled in front of our apartment building. *The Feathers* derived its name from its design; shaped like an archaic writing quill, the wide base of the complex tapered upward into an elegant, silver-capped point that pierced the skyline. Personally, I had always thought it looked more like a flame than a feather, but I never had any taste in modern architecture.

The wind howled outside the cab as we hurried out onto the platform. A door attendant met us halfway across the tiled patio, a blue-gloved hand holding his cap in place, as he struggled to keep a large purple umbrella over our heads. We scurried inside the lobby without a word, although I made sure to tip him a few extra credits for his trouble, once we were all indoors.

Neither Cadence nor I spoke as we rode the lift to the fifty-first floor and stepped out directly in front of our apartment door. It was one of the larger flats in the complex, taking up a whole floor all to itself. We were near the tip of the feather; the privacy and the view were well worth the extra cost of the space.

We entered the luxury flat soaked, wounded – exhausted. I was too tired to even think about food, and Cadence didn't technically need to eat, so we instead said our goodnights and headed to our separate rooms.

When I awoke the next morning, the rain had temporarily abated. I undimmed the privacy screen on my windows, a scowl forming at the sight of the city blanketed in a thick layer of grey fog. Even up here, the sun was hidden between a high, thin layer of haze.

I showered and shaved, slipping on the grey suit and red vest that I felt somehow matched my mood. I wandered out into the kitchen, stared morosely into the refrigerator and cabinets, and wandered back down the hall again. I couldn't force myself to eat this early in the morning, no matter what Cadence said about breakfast being "the meal most necessary to consume, if you wish to operate at peak efficiency."

Cadence. She had come to Arrhidaeus because she had no other choice; the war that consumed her home had forced her to flee or risk a horrible end. Escape was her only option. But she had found friends here. She had found a place to start over. A place to feel safe again.

Now, thanks to people like Eamon Lech, and thanks to groups like the A.F.O., that tenuous sanctuary had started to crumble. More than that, Cadence herself was in trouble. Her business was failing. I had peeked at the earning reports for the past few months – a breach of confidence about which I felt sincerely guilty – but what else could I do? It's not as if she shared such things with me. In many ways, Cadence was as closed off from me as ever. As the days and months wore on, she was getting worse; more secretive, withdrawing into herself a little more every time we spoke. I was losing her.

I sat in the back of one of Halcyon Enterprises' many corporate PTs, my thoughts consumed with Cadence, when I was interrupted by a sudden and persistent buzzing from my suit jacket pocket. I dug out my phone, watched the call indicator flash blue a few times, and then popped the bud into my ear. "Hello?"

There was silence.

"Hello?"

"My God, I actually got through to you." Henry's low tones echoed down the earpiece like distant bells. "I don't know what to do now; I hadn't prepared for such an eventuality."

"Henry, love of my life," I leaned back in my seat, stretching out my legs in front of me. "Good to hear your voice. Half expected you to have gotten yourself arrested."

"Well... not this time," said Henry. "Listen, Chance, I wanted to say: I really am very sorry."

I sighed. "Oh?"

"I didn't mean to worry you by taking Cadence to the protest."

"You have nothing to apologize for, Henry." I crossed my feet at the ankles and rubbed at my forehead. "Cadence is right. She's not a child; she can make her own decisions. If she wanted to go, I'm glad she had someone like you there to look out for her." I furrowed my brow, chewing at the inside of my mouth. "Why were you there, anyway? What's your interest?"

"I'm working for Ergo Sum."

I sat up straighter in my seat. "Well. I know that the political events of the last several hundred years have always been your area of interest–" I shook my head. "–but I confess, I always thought it was a strictly armchair interest; strictly academic."

"Even I can't stay on the sidelines this time, Chance." Henry's tone grew serious, almost stern. "Whiston and the animanecrons need help. I'd like to do what I can." Some of his previous joviality returned as he exclaimed, "Say, I have an idea! There's a fundraiser tonight for Representative Peyton at the Sanctorious Hotel. Are you going?"

I frowned, my eyes remaining closed. "I wasn't planning on it. Why?"

"Come along tonight," Henry suggested. "I'll be there, and it's the first chance in ages we've had to speak properly."

"A political fundraiser? You?" My hand fell to my chest. "Henry, you're a historian for goodness' sake!"

"And history is happening right in front of our eyes, in case you haven't noticed." Henry drawled, his tone falling from matter of fact to judgmental. "I never thought I'd have to beg you to come to a party."

He was right. Still, I felt compelled to put up one last feeble attempt at protest, groaning. "I was planning on cooking for Cadence tonight..."

"Bring her along!" Henry rejoined. "It'll be a great cultural experience for her, and I'd love to spend more time with her too."

"Oh, alright, alright." I wasn't sure how Cadence would feel about going out, but I was confident I could convince her it was a promising idea. "Sounds dull as dishwater, but you know I can't say no to you."

"Great. How about we meet up at your place, and then head over together. Six?"

"Six it is." I looked out the window to see that the PT was pulling up to the Halcyon Enterprises transportation platform. "Now I'm sorry to rush off but–"

"You've got work to do, I'm sure." Henry chuckled. "The system's biggest company doesn't just run itself. See you soon, Chance."

"Goodbye."

4

Chapter 4

The atrium of the primary office building of Halcyon Enterprises' campus was abuzz with bodies, bustling their way towards a new workday. Campus Security hated the fact that I used this main hub, insisting that doing so was putting myself at "unnecessary risk". My response was that my employees were not viruses to be avoided, and I had no intention of treating them as such. I would enter and exit through the same doors as they for as long as I ran Halcyon, security be damned.

Shaking the rain off my coat, I cut across the lobby towards the bay of elevators, waving hellos at a few familiar and unfamiliar faces. I stood patiently, waiting in line for the lifts, checking the thin gold band on my wrist for any messages from Miss Taylor that couldn't wait until I got upstairs, when a voice from behind made me jump.

"The rains just aren't letting up this year, are they, Mr. Hale?"

My stomach clenching, I turned to face Eamon Lech, who stood beside me, a smile lighting up his blue eyes. His assistant, Trafford, lingered a few feet behind him, scanning the crowd around us. "What's that old Earth saying?" continued Lech, hands sliding into his trouser pockets. "It never rains, but it pours?"

"Mr. Lech," I frowned and did not offer him my hand. "I didn't expect to see you again so soon. I don't believe we have a meeting–?"

"We don't," he said, throwing an arm around my shoulders and pulling me away from the crowd of waiting workers. His voice dropped to a conspiratorial whisper. "But I was hoping you could make time for me this morning."

I shrugged off his appendage with a mirthless chuckle, not caring how inhospitable I may seem. "I'm afraid that's impossible; I'm extremely busy. But, please, if there's something pressing you have to discuss–"

"There is."

I stopped and met his gaze. Gone was the smile, gone the casual demeanor; in its place, a tension, a suffocating hardness for which I did not care. I cleared my throat.

"Then you can always contact Miss Taylor, and she'll see where I have space in my calendar." The lift chimed behind us, and I backed away from him with a wave. "Now, if you'll excuse me – no rest for the wicked and all that."

"Of course." He bent over in a slight bow and returned my wave with one of his own. "Oh, and give my best to Miss Turing, won't you?"

Blood pounded in my ears and my throat tightened. I froze.

I stared at him as if he had just asked me to do something obscene.

"Excuse me?"

His hand dropped and he slid it into his pocket, voice honeyed with mock concern, as he crossed the space to stand in front of me. "Cadence Turing does reside with you, does she not, Mr. Hale?" Glancing back at his shadow of an assistant, he tugged at his chin with his free hand. "One of the older generations of animanecrons, made just after they'd perfected their production techniques, if I'm any judge." He fixed me with a stare. "And I assure you, after all this time taking them apart, I am quite the expert."

All thoughts of remaining calm vanished from my mind; I lowered my voice, wary of anyone else hearing our conversation. "How the hell do you know–"

"That you're living with a fragger?" He spit the word at me, all semblance of civility stripped away like so much nail varnish. His face, so handsome a moment before, was contorted and cruel, screwed up in a disgusted grimace. "There isn't much about you I don't know, Mr. Hale. I do my research; it's why I'm so good at my job."

He examined me for a moment and then leaned forward, putting his mouth by my ear and whispering, "Did you know that animanecrons are quite capable of feeling pain?" I felt him smile, felt the flesh slide away from his teeth. "Astounding just how much of it they can stand. Superior to humans in that respect I must say. Fascinating to watch."

My eyes widened and my jaw clenched. I became aware of people staring at us, and my skin began to prickle and crawl. I jerked my head towards a small alcove of chairs set off to the left of the bay of lifts and walked us in that direction, even while through gritted teeth I hissed, "Are you threatening me?"

Lech waited until we came to a stop amidst the chairs before answering. "No." He leaned back, but remained mere inches from me, his voice quiet and low. "I'm threatening the overdeveloped pleasure booth you're fucking."

We stayed that way, staring into each other's faces for a few pregnant moments before he straightened, his hand coming up to fondle the knot of his tie. "It's very simple, Mr. Hale – you might be an inane, ungifted pervert in real life, but your position as head of this company gives your words significant weight." He looked down his nose at me. "You will make a public statement coming out in support of the Whiston Offensive, as well as resume your trade with our government. Do so, and all will be well."

"And if I don't?"

He shrugged. "I'll kill your toy myself... after I enjoy her for a bit."

It was at this point that his assistant, Trafford, leaned forward and whispered something into Lech's ear. Lech nodded and rolled his shoulders back. "It's a simple choice, Mr. Hale," he said, voice returning to a normal volume. "I'll wait for your answer. I'm staying at the Helios Hotel. Good day."

He waved at me once again, and then exited out the large automatic doors that led to the PT platform, Trafford following him like a loyal hound.

I wasn't sure how long I stayed standing there in the middle of the lobby. Staring out after Lech, I saw nothing beyond a future where my beautiful Cadence either despised me or was taken from me forever. I had never met a man like Eamon Lech before, and I hoped to God I would never meet another one like him again; I believed without hesitation that he would make good on his horrible promises. I had a decision to make. A decision that was no decision at all.

I stumbled back out onto the PT dock and jostled my way into the first executive PT I could find, getting drenched with rain, and upsetting one or two company executives who were patiently waiting their turn. I slammed the door shut behind me and barked at the driver.

"The Entertainment Market, now."

Moving like a cheap automaton, I fumbled my phone bud into my ear and called my office. Lily picked up with her usual pleasant, efficient greeting, which I quickly cut off.

"Miss Taylor," I said, eyes darting restlessly from one end of the PT's interior to the other, my voice a near whisper. "Mr. Lech was just in the main building."

I heard Lily type something into her computer. "He wasn't scheduled to meet with you. Do you need me to–"

"No." I swallowed hard and let out a long breath through my nose. "No. You just tell security he's not to visit our offices again, alright?"

"What?"

"He's banned." I pointed to the floor of the PT, my finger shaking. "Banned from the main building, banned from the campus. And if he tries to make another appointment with me, you can tell him just that."

Lily sputtered. "But, but you can't just–"

"I just did." I pushed myself back into the plush seats of the vehicle, every muscle in my body screaming with tension. "And clear my calendar for the rest of the day, I'm going home."

"But, why–?"

I hung up the phone and yanked it from my ear, jamming it into my pocket without a second thought for Miss Taylor, or Halcyon Enterprises, or myself.

My head was swimming; I was angrier than I could ever remember being, and at the bottom of it all, a coiled fist of terror sat tight in the pit of my stomach. I don't think I relaxed for the entire thirty-minute flight, sitting on the edge of my seat, hands clenched around my knees, gaze boring into the carpeted floor of the transport. I had no idea it would be like this; that this was what it felt like to have something worth losing.

I didn't remember the PT stopping outside the marketplace, didn't remember getting out into the pouring rain, or making my way through the still crowded streets of people, admirably adapted to living through monsoon season after monsoon season. I didn't remember striding through them all to reach the story sellers. All was a haze until my gaze fell on Cadence once more.

She stood in her stall, watching the rain fall around her. Bent over at the waist, she was resting her elbows on the stall counter, her chin in her hands, looking about as bored as I'd ever seen her, blue eyes half-lidded, unfocused. People milled around the walkway between booths in front of her, but no one was stopping at her store, and it was clear that no one had stopped for quite some time.

The fist of terror in my stomach loosened. I became aware of myself again, aware of the rain pelting against my face and scalp, aware of the rivulets of water running down my neck and under my open raincoat, soaking me to the bone; aware of the people around me, trying to move past me with their umbrellas and shopping bags clutched tight about their persons.

With a sudden burst of self-consciousness, I sidestepped behind the nearest stall, anxious that Cadence should not catch sight of me. Explaining my sudden appearance to her was, at this moment, unthinkable. To communicate in any way the terrible things that terrible man had said to me; I shivered and turned away.

No. This was something I was going to have to deal with on my own, in my own way.

I returned to the PT, and meekly requested to be taken to my place of residence, feeling as worn and thin as sheets in a cheap hotel room. When I got back to the apartment, I fixed myself some food and retired to the laundry room, where I sat on the floor and considered my options, such as they were.

I sat there for hours, turning the Lech encounter over in my mind. It couldn't be a coincidence, him coming to me with his "revelation" the day after our first meeting, the day after the incident at the Entertainment Market. Had someone followed me when I left Halcyon? Did I lead them straight to Cadence? I chastised myself for not being more careful, for not being more discrete. Then I felt ashamed and guilty for thinking that Cadence was someone, something I needed to hide. She wasn't a dirty secret – she was my friend.

A fool, that's what I was. To think that I could keep Halcyon Enterprises – the leviathan that dominated commerce and trade over half the system – and my personal life separate. It was a trick that not even my father had managed to pull off, not that he had ever really tried. No, he lived for the company, ate and breathed the damn thing, while I just played at running it, like a child thinking they could control an exotic pet. The damn thing was going to eat me alive, and it was going to take a bite out of Cadence as well. I had hoped that the anonymity of it all might have lasted a little longer; I wasn't ready for the questions, wasn't ready for our relationship to become the stuff of tabloids and gossip columns, and boardroom whisperings. Still, it was inevitable. I was a public figure now, a captain of industry, and it's not as if I had asked Cadence to keep her life a secret. She came and went as she pleased, which was only right. Sooner or later, someone was bound to put the pieces together, and find that they equaled an animanecron and Chance Hale living together.

And what was so wrong about that, after all?

I heard the beeping of the security system and straightened up against the wall of the laundry room, peering down the narrow hallway. I heard the front door shut, and the beeping ceased. There was the thudding of footsteps, and it wasn't long before Cadence rounded the corner into the maintenance hallway.

"Hello, Cay," I said, drawing her attention to me. "What are you doing back at this hour?"

Unflappable as ever, she didn't startle at my unexpected greeting, but merely skittered to a halt, her socks sliding on the hardwood floors. "Chance? You're home?"

"Not feeling very well." I only half-lied, staring up at her. "What's your excuse?"

Cadence shrugged, avoiding my eyes as she stepped into the

room. "I closed up the stand early – didn't see much point in having it open." She looked around me, taking in my dirty plate from lunch, the half empty bottle of whiskey, and the ashtray I had moved in while I was waiting for the cycle to move from wash to dry. "What are you doing here?"

I gestured to the softly humming machine a few feet in front of me, the soapy water swirling past the glass front. "Laundry."

Cadence stepped over to the machine and placed her hand on top of it, frowning. "You can't possibly be doing laundry." Having confirmed by touch that the machine was indeed running, she crossed in front of me, stepping between my outstretched legs, and moved to the drier, flipping open the round porthole in the side. She reached in and pulled out a handful of warm, but decidedly damp towels. She opened her mouth to speak and shut it again, considering the towels with a confused grimace. She replaced them and shut the door, the tumbler returning to life. "You just did laundry three days ago, a big load of it. Since I don't sweat, and you don't engage in manual labor, I fail to see how we could have dirtied enough clothes in the intervening time for you to need to wash them."

I had come to find Cadence's verbose methods of expression charming, but now listening to her long trill of words made my head pound. I rubbed my temples, leaning my head back against the cool, white wall. "I didn't say I needed to do laundry, I said I was doing laundry."

Cadence considered this for a moment and nodded. She nudged my currently empty glass of whiskey to one side with her foot. "How long have you been in here?"

I shrugged violently. "A few hours maybe." I looked up to

find Cadence staring down at me, her eyes wide. I tried staring back, but I always lost. I threw my hands up and then dropped them onto my thighs with a loud smack. "I like the smell of laundry, alright? Scented soaps, warm water, wet fabric! It calms me down."

I drew my legs up to my chest, wrapping my arms around them and rolling my head over the wall. "I used to hide in the cleaning peoples' baskets when I was a kid – I could stay buried in freshly-cleaned clothes forever." I rubbed my hands up and down my arms, feeling every bit of the 50 degrees in which I had become accustomed to living. "So, when I need to think, I...do laundry. And sit in the laundry room for a few hours."

Cadence nodded again. After a beat, she collapsed down onto the floor with me, her legs folding beneath her so fluidly I thought she was falling. Sitting on the side of her hip, she tapped her familiar rhythm against my knees, deep blue eyes looking into mine. "Is something wrong?"

"It's nothing."

Cadence frowned, both eyebrows jutting up over her dark orbs. "For the sake of our water bill, I think you should talk to me about it."

"It's just more things with work." I reached forward and brushed a few stray strands of hair away from the corner of her mouth. "I don't want to bore you."

She watched me for another quiet moment before leaning forward and brushing a soft kiss against my cheekbone, just under my eye. "You never bore me." Her brow dropped low over her eyes. "Except when you talk about lawnball; I find that incredibly boring." Her face cleared, her eyes widening as they stared into mine. "It's not about lawnball, is it?"

I laughed, placing a kiss of my own on her forehead. "No, Cay, it's not about lawnball! Promise."

I took a deep breath and leaned back against the wall, the burst of good humor she engendered within me fading quickly. "There's this...man. He represents some people who have a certain...interest in the company. Quite a lot of interest, actually. And he's making demands with which I don't think I can comply. But if I don't do what he wants, he's threatened to–"

The truth stuck in my throat. I looked back down at the woman sitting across from me. One of her hands had fallen from her chest to play with the buttons of my dress shirt, picking at the smooth white fasteners as she listened. I didn't want to worry her, and I didn't want to upset her.

I moved one hand over her shoulder, garnering a rare smile from her that made my heart leap in my chest. I returned the smile and shrugged. "Well, he could ruin me and the company in ways from which we'd never recover. I just don't know what to do." I reached down to caress her calf, rubbing over the smooth copper fabric of her trousers with a sigh. "I wasn't built to make decisions like this, Cadence."

"I think you've done a wonderful job so far," she said, squeezing my arm. "I know that whatever is best, you'll end up doing it. I really believe that." Standing with a grace that belied her mechanical manufacture, she held out her hand to lift me up off the floor. "What is this man asking you to do?"

I shook my head, the edges of my eyes crinkling up as I forced myself to smile, my hand gripping hers. "Nothing you need to worry about. I promise."

5

Chapter 5

A happier thought then occurred to me. My smile took on a more natural tilt as I stood, my hand still holding hers. "Here's an idea: why don't I make you that dinner I'm always promising?"

Cadence's face brightened like the sky after the passing of a dark cloud. "Really?" The corners of her mouth rocketed up towards her eyes. "Gav, how exciting! What are you going to make?"

"Well, let's see what we have lying around," I said, taking the lead and heading for the kitchen. I dropped her hand and pulled open both doors of the fridge, taking stock of our ingredients. We didn't have much, but for what I had in mind I only needed a few staples, some spices, and not much else. "How does Anga Stew sound?"

"Delicious," responded my dove with enthusiasm, climbing

onto one of the stools at the kitchen island. "Even though I have no idea what it is."

"Meat, vegetables, alcohol-fortified broth – just the thing for rainy weather like this." I reached into the cabinets under the kitchen island and freed a large cooking pot with a lid from the depths. "Simple enough to make. Very much a 'throw a little bit of everything in a pot and let it cook' sort of dish."

Cadence rested her elbows on the counter, watching me. "How did you learn to make it?"

"Minerva, of course." I coated the bottom of the pot with oil and went back to the fridge to retrieve the package of cubed anga meat. "It's one of her favorites. Passed down by the women in her family."

Cadence started to nod, but arrested the movement, her brow furrowing. She straightened, one hand pushing back through her thick hair. "So...how did you–?"

"I was a nosy young man who liked to know how everything worked." I unwrapped the raw, red cubes and dropped them, one after the other, into the heating oil, enjoying the sizzle of the browning meat. "Now, watch and be amazed by my culinary prowess. I'll make someone a fine domestic partner one day."

Despite it being some time since I'd made a full-fledged dinner, I fell into the comforting rhythm of cooking with ease. I had always liked preparing my own meals, even though my privileged upbringing meant I was rarely in a position where I was forced to do so. It was satisfying to take a heap of random ingredients and turn them into something not just edible, but artful. When we were at university, I had delighted in cooking for myself and Henry in our bachelors' apartments. It was nice to get back to an old hobby.

Cadence watched me for a while with a strange smile on her lips. There was a sadness to the expression that puzzled me. However, I was prevented from asking after her when she rose abruptly and padded into the sunken living room, turning on the television.

Slicing, mincing, measuring, and mixing took the better part of a half hour, but soon I had a large pot of something that looked like it could turn into a delicious meal. "Right," I said, stirring with a wooden spoon. "Almost done with the first stage." I dusted in a pinch of spicy capsis seeds. "It'll take another hour or so in the oven, but then: ready yourself for a feast."

The doorbell chimed, loud and insistent. Cadence and I shared a confused glance.

"Are you expecting–?" I started but was cut off by the doorbell chiming once again. Wiping my hands on a dishtowel, I crossed the flat to the front door, mumbling to myself, "Someone must have gotten off on the wrong floor..."

I swung open the portal to find Henry Davers on our doorstep, dressed in a black tuxedo, freshly shaven, and looking a good deal more put together than he had the last time we had seen each other. Smiling, his face took on a shade of confusion when he saw the utter bafflement written on mine.

"Henry?" I looked down at what he was wearing. My eyes darted to the clock in the entryway, the face proclaiming it to be six in the evening. My entire frame slumped, my memory catching up with me at last. "Oh... damn."

"You forgot." Henry rolled his eyes and sighed. "I'm deeply

wounded, deeply, but I can't pretend to be surprised." Knitting his brow, he smiled a crooked smile, strolling inside. "Something smells wonderful... and familiar; is that my mother's Anga Stew?"

He walked into the kitchen, passing by the living room, where Cadence watched him with astonishment. He stopped in front of the stove and gave the stew a stir, inhaling the scent of it deep into his lungs.

"Henry!" Cadence stood up from the sofa, waving the television off as she rose. "Hello. You look very nice. Are you on your way to a special engagement?"

Henry took another deep sniff of the stew before answering, a smirk on his face. "Yes. Alone, apparently."

A witty retort was on my tongue but, given the events of the day, I didn't have the energy to deliver it. I deflated, my shoulders falling as I rubbed at the back of my neck. "I am sorry, Henry. It completely slipped my mind."

Straightening, he threw his arm around my shoulders, pulling me tight against his side. "Don't worry about it." He released me and regarded my expression. "Are you alright, though? You seem a bit... off."

I shook my head and moved around him to the cabinet where the tumblers were kept. "'Rough day at the office' doesn't quite cover it."

He watched in silence as I prepared him a drink, leaning back against the wide kitchen counters. "Anything I can do to help?"

I shrugged, pushing Henry's drink, a Petrarchan whiskey on the rocks, out towards him. "Extend my apologies to Representative Peyton for missing his party, if you see him."

"Representative Andrew Peyton?" Cadence strode towards us, the excitement in her voice leaving a queasy feeling in my stomach. "He's the pro-Animanecron candidate for Chancellor, isn't he?"

"Yes. Henry and I were both invited to a fundraiser he's hosting tonight. Boring as hell, but it's the kind of thing that's expected of captains of industry and..." My brow furrowed as I considered my lifelong friend. I gestured to him, brows jutting up over my eyes. "Henry, chum, how did you wrangle an invite?"

Henry swallowed down his mouthful of alcohol and smiled. "I work for Ergo Sum, remember? Peyton's a big supporter of ours and invited Simone, Elea, and I to the event tonight to do some gladhanding. I honestly wouldn't have considered going, if it hadn't been a chance to spend time with you and Cadence."

Cadence's eyes were as wide and round as the moons. "Simone Harlow and Elea Cerf? They're going to be there?" Her voice was hushed as if in reverence. "I could meet the founders of Ergo Sum?"

Henry wagged his head from side to side, his brown eyes sparkling. "If you can convince this stick in the mud to come along, I'd be only too happy to introduce you."

"Wea! What an opportunity!" exclaimed Cadence, a smile erupting over her pale face. She leaned forward, gripping me by the forearms. "Oh, Chance, please can we go? It sounds amazing!"

I groaned and tossed my head towards the pot still sitting on the stovetop. "But, darling... the stew..."

Henry was no help, offering: "Put it in the fridge; it'll keep till tomorrow."

"Please, Chance! I don't want to go without you," insisted Cadence, pleading like a child desperate for a new toy.

I couldn't explain to her my real reasons for not wanting to leave the flat. With Lech's threat fresh in my mind, I was loath to expose either of us to the wild, wicked world. But, in the face of her sincere desire, I buried my misgivings, smiling wistfully. "If it really means that much to you, Cay, how can I say no?"

She stared at me, not grasping my meaning. "So... we can go?"

I nodded. She laughed in delight, rocking up onto her toes to kiss my cheek. She released me and began walking backwards out of the kitchen. "I'll go get ready!"

Henry and I watched her hurry down the hall to her room. When she was out of sight, I sighed, picking up my now super-fluous stew and ferrying it to the fridge while querying, "So... what are these two mysterious women like?"

Henry fiddled with his bowtie. "You've actually met Simone before – she published a few of my academic papers a few years ago. Since then, she's become very outspoken about what's happening on Whiston. Her partner, Elea Cerf, has quickly become a leading figure in the animanecron community here on Arrhidaeus."

I turned back to face him, surprised. "Cerf's an animanecron?"

"That's right!" Cadence rushed back down the hall to join us, half in and half out of a floor length golden silk gown. "So young too; only a hundred cycles old and already doing so much for our community! She's an inspiration."

"Sounds like an interesting person," I said, zipping up the open back of the dress, careful to avoid catching her loose black hair in the teeth.

Biting her bottom lip, but still smiling, Cadence turned around to face me again, hands fluttering in front of her face. "Xio, I can't wait to meet her. Do I look all right?"

I smiled at her, warmth blooming in my belly. "As if you have to ask."

Her shoulders and expression fell. "I do. It's the only way to know the answer to the question."

My smile only broadened. "You look stunning, dearest, as always." Giving her a light peck on the forehead, I strode around her, saying, "Well, I suppose that just leaves me. It'll take me a few minutes, but soon I'll be fit to be seen in public. Then we can be on our way."

It took me a quarter of an hour to dress – plenty of time for my mind to fall back onto my personal worries. A party was the last place I wanted to be tonight – and out in public, rubbing elbows with pro-ani troublemakers, was the last place I wanted Cadence to be.

But, as I considered during the PT ride to the Sanctorious, who was I to tell Cadence with whom she should associate? She was a grown woman, with ideas and a life of her own – the real problem was, I just didn't know where I fit into it, if it all. Watching my two closest friends converse easily during the flight, my morose mood only deepened until, by the time we had reached the hotel, I was downright depressed.

The PT driver held open the door, and I exited first, extending my hand back towards Cadence. She took it, bouncing across the now empty seat and leaping onto the dock beside me.

"What is this place?"

"The Sanctorious?" I threaded my arm through hers and

gestured up at the colossal glass structure. "It's a hotel, my dear. One of the most famous in Römer; I'm surprised you haven't heard of it."

She eyed it with suspicion, as if it might collapse at any moment and take the city block with it. "It looks expensive."

"It is," chimed Henry as he stepped out of the PT behind her. "Lucky for us, we're not staying the night."

Cadence hummed in answer before reaching back and taking Henry's arm as well, linking us up in a three-person chain. "Well, I suppose we'd better go inside, haven't we?"

The Sanctorious was rumored to be as old as the town itself, though not, of course, in its current iteration. The landmark structure that sat at 71st and Kragmire was built fifty years previously, and occupied a full city block, housing over eight thousand rooms in its sixty-story frame. The structure was made entirely of multi-colored solar glass, the end effect being that the building resembled a single shattered piece of stained glass. On a rainy night, it glistened like a half-sucked lollipop.

We hurried inside out of the wet and through the lobby, following the flow of well-dressed well-to-dos up the sweeping escalators. As we merged with the crowd, I felt Cadence's grip on my arm tighten, her usual unease around strangers presenting itself. I placed my hand over hers and gave it a reassuring squeeze, glancing over at Henry and seeing him do the same before releasing her and taking up a place behind us.

We bobbed along in the sea of humanity towards the ballroom entrance, until we found ourselves standing in front of a long table, behind which sat several suited women. The one nearest us looked up and beckoned us forward.

"Chance Hale and Miss Cadence Turing," I announced, watching as the woman scrolled down the list of names on her pad. She gave a nod, smiling up at the pair of us before her attention flicked to the man just behind us.

"Henry Davers," supplied Henry, "I'm with Ergo Sum."

Rolling her shoulders back, the woman scrolled up the list of names to the 'd's. "Of course," she said at length, leaning back in her chair. "Welcome, and we hope you enjoy our Victory Fund Gala."

"Thank you," Cadence unwrapped herself from me long enough to make her typical gesture of gratitude before I could stop her, bright eyes roaming over the young lady's face. "I hope you enjoy yourself as well."

The woman blinked, her eyes following us as we meandered into the great hall. It was a breathtaking sight, with everything made from more clear, colored glass, including the large, serpentine chandeliers that hung from the soaring ceilings. The bar, which old habits had me locate immediately, stretched a good quarter of the way down the wall to our left. A series of long tables were set up to our right, with various goods on display for auction.

The largest portion of the ballroom was dedicated to a sea of round tables, all facing a large platform and screen. Playing in a projected-loop, Representative Andrew Peyton's campaign commercials flashed across the stage. Not having had the time or inclination to stream lately, only a phrase or two jumped out as familiar to me: "a better system for everyone," and "embracing our commonalities and moving towards the future". Peyton's was a message of inclusivity – of opening borders, hearts, and minds. It was the kind of message with which people liked to be associated, but the cynic in me wondered: how many of these people would welcome an animanecron into their homes? How many of them called them fraggers when they thought no one was around to hear?

A second stage was set up in the upper right-hand corner of the room, and from it live music coiled its way through the air. The band, a quintet, featured a smooth-voiced tenor, who crooned into the tulip shaped microphone as if whispering sweet nothings into his lover's ear. Dancers swayed and spun in a half circle in front of the bandstand, men and women finding heaven in their partners' arms with an abandonment I envied. When the group began playing the opening chords to *You, Me, and the Moons*, I quite simply couldn't help myself.

"Oh, this is one of my favorites," I patted the top of Cadence's hand, smiling for the first time since we set out that evening. "I insist you dance with me."

"Dance?" Cadence allowed me to pull her several steps forward. "I don't know how, Chance."

"I refuse to believe they don't have dancing on Whiston," I said, my eyes set on the slightly raised dance floor ahead of us.

I came to an abrupt stop, Cadence once again reminding me that she would not be hurried anywhere if she didn't wish to be. I was jerked backwards, and I turned to stare at her, a half-smile spread wide across my lips. "Oh, come along, dove, you'll–"

"Frig, I do not know how to dance!" The sheer terror on her face would have softened any heart. I took a step back towards her, rubbing her arm. She glanced at the crowd around us, leaning forward and lowering her voice. "I will look silly. People are already staring at me."

Henry cleared his throat. He jutted his chin out towards the bar and the crowd that surrounded it. "Chance, shouldn't you introduce yourself to Representative Peyton before enjoying the frivolities of the evening?"

I appreciated Henry's attempt at peacekeeping, but I had grown quite adept at quelling my dear Cadence's fears over the past couple of months. I drew her in under my arm, keeping my smile sure and steady. "I'm sure the honorable representative wouldn't begrudge me one dance first with the most beautiful person in the room." I rested my lips against the side of her temple, giving her arm and hand a squeeze. "That's why people are staring, love. They've never seen a woman as stunning as you."

Cadence bent back in my embrace, taking a more critical look at the intrigued faces that surrounded us. She frowned. "I thought they were staring because I came in with you, since you're so important socially."

"There's that too." I gave her a quick peck on the cheek before drawing away, holding onto her hand while gesturing to the dance floor behind us. "One dance, Cay? You're such a quick learner, you'll catch on before you know it." Her brow was still furrowed, her mouth a firm, tight line. I put on my best puppy eyes, enfolding her hand completely between both of mine. "Please?"

She stared at me before letting out a long breath through her nose. "Reg, very well, Chance. I will try." Her free hand flew upward as we strode forward towards the dance floor. "But only for you, and just one dance!"

"Splendid, that's my girl." I led us to the edge of the dance floor before turning around to face her again. *You, Me, and the Moons* was a waltz; simple enough, but it had been a while since my last formal event. Still, I was confident I remembered the steps. I held her left hand in my right, placed her right hand on my shoulder, and placed my left hand on the back of her shoulder.

"Now," I said, looking into her deep blue eyes with a smile, "just follow my lead."

We took a step out onto the dance floor, and Cadence did exactly as instructed. This landed her heavy foot square on top of my own, and the pain of it caused me to collapse like a rotten piece of fruit.

Cadence's hands flew up to her mouth. "Sorry! I'm so sorry!" She shook her head, her blue eyes wide, locks bouncing against her cheeks. "I thought you said to follow you!"

"Yes," I managed through my clenched teeth, using every bit of willpower I had to keep myself from jumping up and down with my foot in my hand. "An inaccurate and unhelpful turn of phrase, I now realize." I gave the searing pain another moment to ebb away before taking a deep breath and resuming our starting positions. "Everything I do, mirror; alright?"

Gaze still brimming with concern, Cadence nodded. I took a deep breath, checked over my shoulder, and when I was certain I wouldn't be blocking anyone's path, I took a step back into the dancing circle.

We floated around the dance floor like two leaves caught in a stream. The warmth of her, always apparent, flowed into my chest, as if I had just drunk a bracing shot of liquor. She smelled sweet and clean, like fresh spring air. I closed my eyes, abandoning myself to my senses, and dreamed that this moment was all there was, and that nothing else in the world existed.

The sound of Cadence's laughter, bright and rare, like a gemstone unearthed in the desert, brought me back to reality. "This...this is very fun!" Her hand slid over my shoulder, and I opened my eyes. Her smile practically sparkled. "I get to be so close to you; I like that."

I gave a chuckle, squeezing her shoulder. "Me too."

We slowly circled the floor, like gently spinning blossoms falling from a tree. I found myself growing dizzy, but it wasn't from the dance. Holding Cadence near was like grasping a living flame, a tongue of fire that by some miracle did not burn me to cinders. I nestled my cheek against her temple, reveling in the feel of her hair against my skin. With Cadence in my arms, I felt as right and certain as I ever did.

It was only as the song and the dance were ending that I realized: I would do whatever Eamon Lech asked me to do, so long as it kept her safe. The truth of that hit me like a speeding transport, and all of Cadence's warmth, and my own, drained from me. It didn't matter if she hated me for the rest of her long, long life – if she was alive, that was all that mattered.

6

Chapter 6

Something in my face must have changed, something in my body must have grown tense, because Cadence stopped moving with an abruptness that sent me stumbling. "Chance?" she asked, her brow clouding. "Are you alright?"

"Fine, Cay, just fine," I lied, walking us off the dance floor with a pained smile, my hands falling into my pockets.

"Would you like..." Cadence stopped, looking between me and the dance floor we had just left. She gave a small smile, hands coming together in front of herself. "We could dance again?"

I shook my head, and then tossed it back in the direction from which we had originally come. "Let's go find Henry; maybe he'd like to give you a turn."

Leading the way back towards the entrance, I was miffed to find that Henry had disappeared; I needed him to distract Cadence from my sudden downturn in mood. I looked around and spotted him standing just in front of the platform on which, I assumed, Representative Peyton would speak. Ignoring the projected commercials, Henry was instead engrossed in conversation with two women, neither of whom I recognized at the time, but whom I would come to know intimately over the next few days: Elea Cerf and Simone Harlow.

While Cadence was the silky sound of a saxophone spiraling out of an open apartment window in the middle of the night, Elea was a brass band marching through the city center on Foundation Day. Although Henry and Simone were the only people immediately near her, Elea held the focus of every person within a twenty-foot radius. She had a loud, rollicking laugh, audible even over the steady hum of conversation and the undercurrent of music. The sound of it led us to the trio like the setting sun leads wanderers west.

Dwarfed by both Henry and Elea, Simone Harlow was a small slip of a thing. Her bright, rust colored eyes leapt around the room, a smirk permanently smeared across her surprisingly plump, pink lips. The unabashed adoration in her eyes whenever she looked at Elea made it clear to me that the two women were more than just partners in social justice.

Henry turned at our approach, opening his arms to welcome us. "Ah, Chance, you found us." He stepped back to allow me an unhindered view of the woman to his right. "This is Simone Harlow, co-founder of Ergo Sum."

I examined her face with more care from this distance, bowing as I extended my hand. "We've met before," I said. "You've published some of Henry's work, haven't you?"

"Yes, that's right. In *History and Historians*, my old journal."

Simone shook my hand, her smile widening, curly black hair jumping around her almond eyes as she nodded. "I'm surprised you remember me, Mr. Hale. It was an awfully long time ago."

I patted my chest with my free hand and gave her a wink. "Well, the social arena happens to be the only one in which I excel."

Simone gave a polite laugh, her eyes crinkling. She drew her petite hand back, and her gaze fell momentarily on Cadence. She cleared her throat and turned quickly to the woman beside her. I caught a whiff of two competing scents of pheromone spray: one heavy and tropical, the other light and powdery. It was an interesting combination, as I was sure Simone and her animanecron lover must be.

"This is my partner, Elea Cerf. She runs Ergo Sum with me."

Elea leaned forward, proffering her hand. "How do you do, Mr. Hale?"

"Pleasure to meet you, Miss Cerf." As we shook, I took note of her long, red fingernails, painted to match the color of her hair. Elea's strong grip communicated a confidence that was backed up by every inch of her. She was a good head taller than me, her pine green eyes staring down from her tanned face. She brought her other hand up to touch the back of mine, tapping a rhythm across it that I did not recognize. A brow curved up over her high forehead. "Frat, I've been following Halcyon Enterprises' stance on the animanecron issue very closely these past few months. Or should I say, your lack of stance?"

"Elea," cut in Simone, laughing nervously, her short hair bouncing around her cheekbones. "This is supposed to be a party!" She leaned in towards me, smiling. "I'm sorry, she's always mixing business and pleasure."

"Too much to do; too many of my people to look out for." She released my hand and turned to my companion, her polite smile softening into something much more genuine. "You must be Cadence." She reached out both her hands towards Cadence, and Cadence responded in kind. They shook, and both, I noted, tapped out a rhythm on the back of each other's hands. "Henry's been telling us all about you."

"It's an honor to meet you." Cadence beamed. "I saw you speak at the AR rally today; you were very stirring."

"Thank you," Elea pushed a hand back through her heavy sheaf of red hair. "Henry tells me that you came here some months ago. You must have been one of the first refugees to this planet."

I watched as Cadence nodded, swallowing hard. "They had just started the containment camps, when I escaped."

Elea nodded, her brow darkening. "I'm sad to say that the camps are still operating, despite our best efforts. Still–" She shook herself, as if waking from a bad dream, and reached for Cadence again, stroking her arm. "–we must remember: we are here. As long as we stay true to our people, we will live on forever."

"I try to remember the old ways," offered Cadence, coming out of her sadness with a sudden eagerness that surprised me. "But it is difficult here, isn't it?"

"That's putting it mildly!" Elea exclaimed with a laugh, her hands gesticulating through the air. "The climate, the people; everything about this planet is wrong!"

"Henry and I will try not to take that personally," I interjected, snagging a pair of drinks off a passing tray, and handing one to the enthralled Cadence.

"You shouldn't. It's not entirely your fault." Elea's brows danced over her eyes again, her smile widening. "If I'd known so many of us would end up here, I would have designed better cooling systems for us."

"Oh, were you a format architect?" asked Cadence, taking a sip of her cocktail.

"Yes!" Elea took a drink from Henry, who offered a second to Simone. "I understand you were an entertainment installer – I've always thought that must be a fun job."

"What's a format architect?" I asked, trying in vain to follow the conversation.

"It was her old job," Simone supplied, one hand slipping into the pocket of her pantsuit. "She would design bodies for the animanecrons. Not build them, or anything practical like that. It was – is, I suppose – a kind of art form."

"I have to say," continued Elea, as if Simone and I had never spoken, "I absolutely love your PCB." She craned her head around on her neck, trying to look behind Cadence. "What I can see of it anyway. Sinc, you know, something that beautiful, you should really show it off."

Cadence looked about us, her hand coming up and massaging her shoulder. "Oh, I've learned not to have it showing in public. It tends to attract so much attention here."

Elea looked down her nose at Cadence and gave a huff, one arm crossed low over her belly, the other tossed into the air. "Why shouldn't we attract attention? We're well worth celebrating. You're not ashamed, are you?"

"Of course not!" With a thud, Cadence put her drink down on the table near her hip. Then, in a move that made me sputter out the mouthful of Hunyin Gin I had just taken, she turned around and unzipped the back of her dress down to the top of her hips. "Here."

I wiped my lips as Elea bent down, her long fingers pressed against my beloved's back. "A phoenix design; not one of Saoirse's, is it?"

"Yes," Cadence called over her shoulder, one hand holding up her dress, the other holding her hair up out of the way of her skin. "We courted briefly. She made it for me."

Having gotten over the shock of Cadence's near-disrobing, I finally grasped what the pair of animanecrons were discussing. "Cay, your tattoo?"

"Tattoo?" Elea barked out a laugh and straightened, a sneer cutting across her face like an open wound. "You really know nothing about her, do you, Mr. Hale?" Arms crossed, she leaned back on her heels and looked down at me. "Sarc, how could we get tattoos? Our skin isn't organic, and it doesn't absorb dyes. How can you be running a company that specializes in AI technology and know so little about it?"

I forced a thin smile across my lips. "I skate by on charm, mostly."

Elea's gaze refused to leave my face, even as she tossed her head at Cadence. "Tell him what it is, Cadence."

Simone, eyes darting between the three of us, laid a hand on her lover's arm. "Elea, maybe she doesn't–"

"Don't be silly, Simone," Elea cut her off without a glance. "Go on."

Cadence looked over her shoulder at me, and then shuffled closer, her back still on display. "You see, it's a large, multi-layered printed circuit board. I had it installed after I decided to work in the entertainment industry. It has a network interface card for large area network connections, so that I can automatically send my books to customers with similar boards. The wings," she rolled her shoulders back, causing the black arcs to flutter, "are actually expansion boards, which connect with an extra hard drive, on which all my books are stored." She glanced over at me again and, when my face must have shown my complete incomprehension, she said, "I got it so I could upload and download books more efficiently. It was quite useful."

"But..." I reached forward, my hand hovering over her exposed back. "It's skin. Just like...all the rest of you"

"It only feels like skin." Elea pivoted where she stood, mirroring my stance. "It's actually a separate panel, created with the laser-printed resist method. You laser-print onto transparency film, heat-transfer using a modified laminator onto bare laminate, touch up with a marker, etch, add a dash of conformal coating, and voila!" She ran a finger down Cadence's back – it took all my self-control not to push it away. "Same texture as skin." She straightened, pulling the zipper of Cadence's dress back up. "We are much more versatile than you humans – being inorganic has its advantages."

"Though it has its disadvantages, as well," said Simone. Elea gave a dismissive shrug and took a sip of her drink, but Simone continued with confidence. "Ergo Sum believes that by bringing animanecrons and humans together, by learning about and from each other, everyone will end up enriched."

"Here, here," said Henry, raising his glass.

"That's really Simone's half of the business." Elea grimaced. "With the exception of her and Henry, I've had enough human interaction to last a lifetime."

Henry flattened his hand over his chest, inclining his head in a small bow. "You flatter me."

"You've been indispensable to the cause!" A warm smile returned to Elea's face. "Your pieces on animanecron intelligence, your interviews with refugees; they've been instrumental in widening humans' awareness of our struggles."

A pleased flush of color rose in Henry's cheeks as he sipped at his cocktail. "Well, I've done what I can to shine a light."

"Without light, darkness prevails." Elea crossed her arms under her bosom and met my eyes once again, her smile vanishing. "It's not enough to say nothing – you have to stand up and be counted, for good or for evil. Don't you agree, Mr. Hale?"

I met her stare without flinching, lifting my glass to my lips. "Things aren't always that black and white, Miss Cerf."

Elea leaned forward. "Why *has* Halcyon Enterprises remained neutral on the Whiston Offensive? Protecting your bottom line?"

"I'd hardly call terminating our defense contracts with Charcornac remaining neutral," I shot back, a chunk of my cheek held between my back teeth, "and it certainly didn't do much for our bottom line."

I felt a hand close around my arm. "Chance was the first person on Arrhidaeus whom I told I was an animanecron," said Cadence, squeezing me tightly. "He's been nothing but supportive and accepting of me." She turned to look me full in the face, smiling. "I'd trust him with my life."

Her words shocked me into silence. I knew Cadence was incapable of lying, which meant she meant every word of what she had just said, but that thought was inconceivable. Had she forgotten how I had first reacted when she told me about who, and what, she really was? How I had pushed her away? Or had she forgiven me all that? Did she really have such complete and utter faith in me now?

Elea looked Cadence over. "You certainly have." She gave a long sigh, shaking her long hair back over her shoulder. "So, where are you living now?"

"Chance and I lease an apartment together." Cadence was too busy stirring the submerged cherry around her drink to notice the knowing looks the two women shot each other. She began nodding to herself, her brow furrowing as she attempted to spear the small fruit with her swizzle stick. "It's very convenient – I pay as much for my own room as I did before, but now I have someone to help with the other bills, and I'm closer to work."

"Oh!" Simone smoothed back her hair, glancing up at both of us from under her brow, her lips pursed in a barely concealed smile. "So, you two are..."

Cadence finally looked up at the inflection in Simone's voice. Her eyebrows rose slowly over her blue orbs, and she glanced around the group, attempting to discern the expected response to Simone's prompting. "Flat mates, yes."

I drained my cocktail and traded out my empty glass for a full one, sucking at the bruised gin with a grimace.

Elea let out a loud laugh, her hand coming up to her chest. She leaned forward and began conversing in that strange language Cadence still slipped into when she thought I couldn't hear.

Cadence's eyes widened at the sound of the sharp, short sentences. She erupted into a broad smile at the series of trills and clicks, placing her hand over the one Elea had placed on her shoulder. Elea nodded, her red hair bouncing around her face. Cadence caught her breath and responded, gesturing between her and me, and talking a mile a minute.

I took a step back, distinctly uncomfortable at being so obviously discussed – a discomfort that grew exponentially when Simone let out a loud 'oh' of understanding and grabbed her partner's shoulder. She joined in, her tongue stumbling over the harsh sounds, but definitely forming them.

She pulled back after a moment, smiling up at me, her hands crossed over her front. I jabbed a finger towards the still clicking pair of animanecrons. "You speak that language?"

"Animatum? Of course!" Elea and Cadence, having finished whatever matter they were discussing at my expense, turned back to the group with wide grins. Simone gestured between the two of them. "Not all animanecrons are as well rounded as Elea and Cadence – many of them have only the most rudimentary knowledge of Common Tongue. I wouldn't say I'm fluent..." Simone looked over to Elea, reaching down to take her hand. "...but I know enough to get by."

Elea swung their clasped hands back and forth, her smile never waning. "I'm sure Simone could teach you if you'd like, Mr. Hale."

"No. Thank you. I manage fine without it." I took a large mouthful of my drink, swishing it over my tongue, feeling embarrassed by the tangible distaste in my voice.

There was a moment of silence as the group shifted at this

display of ill-temper, Henry moving a little closer to me, while Cadence took the slightest step away.

Elea and Simone released their hands from each other's grasp, the latter clearing her throat. "Living space is starting to be a real problem, but Ergo Sum has some big plans, as far as housing goes."

"Really?" Henry glanced around us. He leaned in, his voice low. "Can they be told, or is it strictly under wraps?"

"Well...." Simone looked to her partner. Elea nodded, still regarding me with a clinical detachment I abhorred. Simone clapped her hands together, her shoulders rising and falling in a sigh. "We're very excited about it, but it's so up in the air right now! A lot of it depends on how these next few elections go. We're hoping to get permission from the city to buy those empty apartment hutches by the docks and lease them exclusively to animanecron refugees!"

"With some time and a little work, it'll be the first animanecron neighborhood in Römer," Elea continued. "A place where we can start to rebuild what we've lost – support each other, comfort each other, keep our customs and traditions alive."

"That sounds fantastic!"

Elea smiled appreciatively at Henry's enthusiasm. "You have no idea. We're going to outfit them just like the living quarters we used to have back home. Power stations, cooling towers, every modern convenience we've missed since the beginning of the war." Elea leaned forward, wrapping her hand around my flat mate's wrist. "You are more than welcome to reserve a space in advance, Cadence."

Cadence lifted her hands to her cheeks, as if she were afraid her smile would run off the edges of her face. "How wonderful! It's been so long since I..." She trailed off, her breathing stilling. She blinked once and then again, her hands falling in front of her.

After a moment, she began rubbing the inside of her arm where Elea had touched her, shaking her head side to side. "I can't say thank you enough, it's very kind." Her mouth hung open for a moment, her mind struggling to find words. She shrugged her shoulders, the tips of earlobes brushing against them. "I'm sure they'll be breathtaking. But I'm happy where I'm living now, thank you."

"Oh, I'm sure your apartment is perfectly adequate–" Elea waved our happiness away like so much noxious gas. "–and I'm sure the company is mildly interesting, for a human anyway. But I do think it's important for us to all stay together as much as possible."

Cadence bit her lip, still rubbing at her arm. "Well...I have–"

"Will you excuse me," I cut in. "I've finished my drink."

"I'll come with you," said Henry, depositing his mostly empty first glass on the table just beside us. "Can I get anything for anyone?"

Elea inclined her head. "We're fine, thank you."

I was already several steps away, chewing vigorously on the inside of my mouth. I didn't care much whether Henry followed me, all I knew was that I had to get away; from Elea Cerf, from Cadence, and from myself, if possible. I made a straight line for the buzzing bar, sidling my way to the front of a group of party goers and impatiently flagging down the bartender.

7

Chapter 7

I felt, rather than saw, Henry move into the space beside me as I ordered a Petrarchan whiskey on ice. Henry ordered xampany. I was deciding whether his presence pleased or annoyed me when he said, quietly, "You alright, Chance? Elea can come on a little strong."

The concern in Henry's voice roused me from my thoughts. I cast him a glance, his apologetic frown cooling my displeasure. I took my drink from the bartender, sighing. I waited until Henry was likewise served before moving us away from the crowd and towards one of the small tables nearby. "I can take my licks. And I can't pretend they're not deserved, in some small measure."

We placed our drinks on the table, taking up positions opposite each other.

I spun the ice in my glass round and round, watching the

perfect cubes bounce off one another. "You don't think Cadence would ever–"

"No," said Henry with a firmness I appreciated. "Why would she?"

I swallowed hard and attempted a nonchalant shrug. "Well, she is her own woman. It's not like I've got any claim to her."

Henry leaned in over his glass, meeting my eyes. "You are in love with her though."

"Henry." It was all I could think to say. To hear the words that had been running through my mind night after night, but protected by the cover of darkness, spoken aloud rendered me speechless. A smile struggled onto my lips, and I shook myself, reaching across the table to pat his shoulder as I gave a dull laugh. "Henry, my dear boy–"

He brushed off my hand, scowling. "Don't give me that 'dear boy' routine," he said, his lips turned down in a firm frown. "You're in love with her. Why shouldn't you be? Cadence is absolutely splendid."

I stared at him for a few moments, a dozen lies and half-truths running through my mind. He settled back against the table, glaring at me from under his brow, daring me to refute it. I leaned back. "I...I don't know what I am with her." Admitting it was like a weight lifting from my chest. I sighed, bringing one hand back through my hair, massaging my scalp. "I guess it's complicated."

"Why?"

I let out a huff of air, pinching the bridge of my nose. I waved back towards the group of ladies we had just left, grimacing. "Listen, you and your chums may be perfectly at home with the idea of mecha-romance, but for the rest of us, it takes a little getting used to."

Henry took a sip of his drink, shaking his head. "Oh, Chance," he murmured, swallowing down another mouthful of liquid. "You really are lost, aren't you?"

I only half heard him. My gaze had focused on Cadence, the soft light of the ballroom making her pale skin glow. "I want her." I dropped my gaze, a wave of sadness pushing me under. "I've always wanted her."

Henry came around the table and stood close to me, bumping his shoulder into mine. "And you do like her, right?"

"She's my friend; one of my closest." I waved at his chest. "Present company withstanding."

"So," he said. "What's the problem?"

"It's just..." I turned to face him fully, my hands outstretched. "How can I possibly relate to her, Henry?" I ran my hand back through my hair, tousling it beyond repair. "We have so little in common, it boggles my mind. She's lived a whole lifetime beyond mine, seen and experienced things I could never hope to, never want to. There are secrets behind her eyes – things she's not telling me."

Henry let out a small laugh as he ran his fingers along the lip of his glass, watching me. "You're not exactly the easiest person to get close to either, Chance."

"With her, I have no armor," I said, taking a drink. Henry's brows shot up over his eyes and then fell back down again. I stared at him, jaw clenching. "What?"

Henry shook his head, shrugging. "If that's the way you see it, that's the way you see it. But consider this–" Turning to face me head on, he slid his arm onto the table and leaned towards me. "When have you ever gone after what you really wanted?"

A quick, ready answer was on the tip of my tongue when I stopped and thought about his question. I swallowed hard; the truth was I couldn't remember the last time I had wanted anything of consequence, to allow myself to yearn for something, to hope. Such things always ended in disappointment. I had learned that at an early age. Better to settle for passing pleasures and momentary discomforts than to strive for anything greater; than to risk the sting of failure.

"All I'm saying is," Henry continued. "Cadence needs to know that you cherish her, not just want her."

I took a large gulp of my drink, wincing as the alcohol hit the back of my throat. "Well, there's plenty of time." Henry shook his head again and I sighed, turning my eyes heavenward. "I'll figure something out, alright?"

"There's nothing to figure." Henry insisted, tossing his head back towards the animated group of women. "Just tell her."

I pushed away from the table, leaving my drink behind. "I'm going to get some air; company's been a bit much for me."

I strode away from my old friend, not caring how my abrupt departure might leave him feeling. I headed for one of the floor-to-ceiling doors that lined the room and slipped out the first one I reached. Several other guests had already found sanctuary out on the covered balcony, away from the hustle and bustle of the main event inside.

I got as close to the railing as I dared, careful to avoid the edge of the awning where the rain fell unimpeded on the city streets below. Freeing my nix case from the folds of my tuxedo, I sparked up one of the thin black cylinders with a twist, discarding the end over the edge of the balcony with a flick of my wrist. I took a long, hard drag and felt not in the least bit better.

I had had just about enough of other people telling me what to do – even well-intentioned friends like Henry. The truth was that no one knew, no one could know what I was going through; the decisions I had to face. I exhaled a plume of smoke and thought, not for the first time since his passing, of my father. I recalled his warnings that one day I would understand why he had done all the things that he had done – why he had ended up hated and alone. Turning away from the edge of both my thoughts and the building, I looked back through the double doors and found myself staring at the man of the hour himself. Representative Andrew Peyton of the 22nd District was blessed with what every politician prays for: an honest face. Small brown eyes, the color of tilled dirt, sat close beneath his narrow forehead and grey hair. It was hard to consider him an attractive man, but he was still somehow pleasant to look at, like a child's drawing. In his early fifties, he looked fairly fit for his age, and cut a fine figure in his simple suit.

He caught sight of me, his perpetual smile widening. He leaned over and whispered something in the ear of the woman next to him, who I could only assume was his wife. For such a thick, stout man, he moved with unexpected grace. He was outside and at my side in a matter of moments, his hand outstretched. "It's Mr. Hale, isn't it?"

"Representative Peyton," I took his hand and was favorably impressed with the firmness of his grip. "How nice to meet you.

I've been hearing so much about you over the past few months. Then again, I suppose everyone has."

"That is what I'm paying my campaign managers for," he rejoined, his smile never wavering. He withdrew his hand, taking in a deep breath as he looked me up and down. "I'm so glad we bumped into each other. I wanted to thank you, in person, for your contribution."

I lifted my brow in question, and Peyton leaned forward, voice lowering. "Towards lifting the ani-immigration ban, I mean. The capital you provided really helped get our message out."

That damn contribution; I might as well have just signed my name on the check and handed it over on system-wide television. I shook my head, attempting to muster a smile. "I didn't–"

"Oh, I know you wanted to remain anonymous." Peyton clapped me on the shoulder. "But I'd hardly be where I am today if I didn't have ways of finding out things like that. But don't worry!" He lifted his free hand to his lips and gave me a wink. "Mum's the word." He took a step back and gestured towards the ballroom. "I appreciate you coming out tonight."

I appreciated the distance between us and took an additional step back, shrugging. "People in my position can't really refuse invitations to these kinds of things, can they?"

Peyton ignored my displeasure, barreling on with good humor. "Yes, yes; heavy is the head that wears the crown, isn't it?"

"From the way the polls are looking–" I said, bringing my still smoldering nix back up to my lips. "–you may find out for yourself very soon."

"We'll see, we'll see," Peyton wiggled his eyebrows, drawing a hand down his chin. "Römerians are a hard bunch to read. One day, you think you've got them, the next day, they're burning your effigy in the streets."

"Oh, we haven't had a good effigy burning in ages; I'll look forward to that." I gave a thin smile, allowing the smoke from my nix to curl out my nostrils.

Peyton tossed his head back towards the ballroom. "Did I see you speaking with Elea Cerf and Simone Harlow earlier?"

I nodded, my eyes narrowing. "Yes, you did. My friend Henry Davers has been working for them over the past few months."

"Inspiring women. Did they tell you about our building project by the Mawson Docks?"

"They may have mentioned something about it." I dropped my nix onto the ground and stubbed it out with the toe of my shoe. "You're risking a great deal with this animanecron business, don't you think, Representative Peyton? Taking a strong stance on such a polarizing issue."

"Gone are the days when politicians could equivocate on matters like this, Mr. Hale," said Peyton, rocking back on his heels. "It's a real hearts and minds type issue. Voters see your stance on this as indicative of your deeper values. I need the people of Römer to know that by electing me Chancellor for our region, I'll bring everyone's issues to the Interplanetary Commission; that I will fight for the little guy, just as hard as I fight for the big corporations." Peyton's cool, brown eyes dug into my face as he looked at me askance. "Speaking of Halcyon Enterprises, what is your take on the Whiston Offensive? As a company, I mean."

I was about to tell him that Halcyon Enterprises' stance could go right up his do-gooding ass when a voice interrupted me.

"Dear, Judge Hynter is still waiting to talk to you."

We both turned towards the low, feminine voice behind us. Peyton's smile turned into a beam. "Ah, Jun! I want you to meet someone." He threw his arm around the woman's small, sloping shoulders and drew her into our circle of conversation, his other hand gesturing towards me. "Jun, this is Chance Hale, head of Halcyon Enterprises. Mr. Hale, this is my wife, Jun Peyton."

"Charmed, madam." I took her hand and kissed the back of it.

"Oh, the same, Mr. Hale, the same." Jun gave a sharp, lighting flash of a smile. Everything about the woman was sharp; her eggshell-brown eyes were almond shaped with sharp corners, sitting just above a sharp, upturned nose, and a thin slice of lips. Brown hair danced around the edges of her pointed jaw and high cheekbones. Finely cut jewels dripped from every part of her; her husband, ten years her senior, obviously doted on her.

She slid her hand out of mine with a sigh. "I'm always so pleased to meet one of our most prominent citizens."

Niceties dispensed with, her face returned to what I could only assume was its normal sour expression. "Andrew, dear, Judge Hynter?"

"Of course, of course," Peyton pointed a finger at me as he backed away towards the doors. "Mr. Hale, I hope we can speak again soon. I'm sure between the two of us, we could get this place running right."

"Any way I can help, Representative Peyton, any way I can help."

I kept smiling until he turned away, and then I let my face fall into a much more comfortable scowl. I glanced around and found that the balcony was empty except for one other guest, who was fixated on a palm sized tablet he held in his hands.

I looked at the man with whom I was sharing the patio, something about him tugging at my memory. Sensing my gaze, he looked up from his pad and gave a thin smile.

"Warm night, isn't it?" He said conversationally.

"Yes, quite. Though it should be cooling down soon," I shook my head, examining him. "Summer can't last forever, I'm afraid."

Everything about the man was thin, narrow, and small. He looked like a scarecrow in a tuxedo, his stick-like arms and legs protruding from the baggy cloth. If he'd been a little paler, I would've assumed that he was ill. Pistachio-green eyes peered out from his small face, his head topped by a ragged mop of short, straw-colored hair.

"Summer man, are you, Mr. Hale?" He asked, returning his gaze back to his pad. He typed out a few more lines before shaking himself, frowning. "Don't care for the heat myself. Prefer cooler climates."

The use of my name gave me the opening I needed to inquire, "Sorry, but have we met?"

"Yes, sir," he said, pausing for a moment to let out a belabored sigh. "In fact, I'm supposed to tell you that Mr. Lech would like a word with you, sir, if it isn't inconvenient."

8

Chapter 8

Like a PT door slamming shut, the pieces of my memory snapped into place. I had barely noticed him before, standing like a ghost in the corner of my office while his boss had threatened the existence of the woman who had come to mean everything to me. Mr. Trafford, a non-entity, and one of the last people I expected to see tonight.

I squared my shoulders. "As a matter of fact, it is inconvenient."

Trafford gave a wave-like shrug, one shoulder rising and falling incrementally before the other. "Mr. Lech thought you might say that."

"And?"

Trafford looked up from his pad once again. "And I was to tell you that he'd like a word with you even if it is inconvenient, sir."

I strode across the patio, closing the distance between us. "Your boss is a real bastard; do you know that?"

There was a moment of silence. Trafford lowered his pad and looked me full in the face, his own visage expressionless. "Mr. Lech–" said Trafford, straightening perceptibly, his voice growing quiet, "–is a great man, sir. He has a great vision. That's a great burden." He looked down his nose at me, light green eyes half-lidded. "Not everyone understands that."

We stayed staring at each other for a few tense moments. Finally, I stepped to one side, my hand outstretched.

"Lead the way, Mr. Trafford."

Without another word, the young man turned and walked back towards the ballroom. I followed him, seething on the inside, but outwardly calm. We cut across the crowded room with relative ease, having to pause now and again whenever a wealthy magnate caught sight of and waylaid me for a moment's gladhanding. Eventually we broke through the throng and made our way towards the silent auction area, where I spotted my tormentor browsing through what was on offer that evening.

Trafford reached Lech first, tapping his employer on the shoulder before stepping to one side to reveal me.

"Mr. Hale." Lech beamed, his hand outstretched towards me. "So good to see you again."

I shoved one hand into my trouser pocket, curling it into a fist where he couldn't see it. "I would never have expected to see you here, Mr. Lech. Isn't this enemy territory?"

"Keep your enemies close, isn't that how the saying goes?" Lech dropped his unshook hand, his smile remaining. He turned to peruse a hologram beside us, which was flashing out an e-dvertisement for the Paraesepisian get-away on auction. "The Charcornacian government has to be prepared for every eventuality, even one in which Representative Peyton's wins the IPC position."

"And how would the Charcornacian government deal with that?"

"We have our plans," he said, strolling up the aisle and expecting me to follow. I hated myself for doing just that, and hated even more the way my stomach curled in on itself when he asked, "Do you have yours, Mr. Hale?" He stopped walking to face me directly, his expression open and curious. "I mean, have you given any more thought to our discussion this afternoon?"

I turned away from him. "I don't care much for being threatened, Mr. Lech."

Lech let out a low chuckle. "No one does, Mr. Hale. No one does."

Closing my eyes, I steadied myself on the tabletop. "When would this statement have to be made?"

Lech stopped to consider this, his eyes flickering towards the ceiling. "Soon. Before election day, certainly." After a moment, Lech stepped towards me, a grin quirking the edges of his thick lips. "I have to say, I was expecting more of a fight from you, Mr. Hale."

"Mr. Lech," I faced him, the muscles in my jaw so tight my whole face ached. "You know if I do this, I'll lose her anyway."

"But she'll still be alive." Lech reached out and squeezed my shoulder, hard. "Has to be better than the alternative, doesn't it?"

I shook him off with a growl. "You'll regret this, Lech."

"I don't think I will, Mr. Hale." Lech waved and turned

to walk away down the aisle. "Enjoy the rest of your evening, won't you?"

I pivoted on my heel and stomped back towards the bar, once more intent on getting a proper drink. Part of me, an old part of me that I had not paid heed to in some time, desired to get raucously and thoroughly drunk, but instead I limited myself to another small whiskey, with copious amounts of ice, before winding my way back through the crowd to where I had last seen my flat mate, needing to see that she was safe.

I found her right where I'd left her but was relieved to see that Elea Cerf was nowhere in sight. Henry had rejoined her as well and was speaking to Simone Harlow about his latest academic project – a treatise on the effectiveness of the IPC in matters of armed conflict – when I stepped up to the group.

Cadence did not turn to look at me until Henry had finished his explanation of the current state of his research. When he was silent, she glanced at me, her face clouding.

"Urio, are you alright, Chance?" Cadence tapped out a fast rhythm on the back of her hand, her gaze roaming over my face and body. "You were gone for some time."

I tried out a smile, but it felt thin and rubbery. In the end I let it slide away, settling for a shrug as I said, "People to see, things to discuss, I'm afraid."

"Were they not pleasant things?" Her brow furrowed. "You don't look very well."

I patted her back. "I'm fine, Cay. Thanks." I inclined my head towards the empty space beside Simone. "Where's Miss Cerf?"

"She had to go; work." Henry took a sip from his xampany

glass, his eyes narrowing. "You really look rough, Chance, are you sure you're alright?"

Pushing my hand back through my hair, I pressed my tongue against the back of my teeth. "I am fine, alright? Just fine."

Cadence glanced between the three humans in the group before taking a step back towards Simone, as she observed, "He's lying." She sipped at her drink, her eyes never leaving me. "And lying badly. I never know what to do when humans get like this."

I sighed, rolling my eyes. "Humor us, Cay; isn't that right, Miss Harlow?"

"That's usually for the best." Simone smiled, toying with the earring dangling from her lobe. "I find these events awfully taxing myself, Mr. Hale. I'm sure no one would think less of you if you cut out a bit early."

"Yes, we could do that, Chance." Cadence stepped over to me, wrapping her free arm around my own.

At the very thought, relief began seeping into my tense muscles. I looked into her dark, inky eyes and asked, "You sure you don't mind?"

"Sinc, of course not." Cadence turned to place her drink down on the table behind us. "I'd much rather know you were alright, then spend more time at a party with strangers."

I turned to Henry, but he was already waving away my questions. "Don't worry about me. Simone and I have a few more contacts to make, and then I'll make my own way home."

"Henry." I untangled myself from Cadence and embraced my oldest friend.

"Chance." He patted my back and then released me, smiling.

I extended a hand out to Simone, which she took and shook once again. "It was very nice to meet you, Miss Harlow."

"Likewise, Mr. Hale."

9

Chapter 9

Neither of us spoke during the PT ride back home. Cadence, never one to chatter, seemed content with my silence, though she watched me with an intensity that bordered on uncomfortable. I soon realized it was because she had ceased to blink, a sure sign that she was thinking about something important.

I let her think without inquiring what problem occupied such a large section of her neuroprocessing. I stared out the window, watching the city fly by, and tried to let my own mind go blank.

More and more over the last few months, our apartment had begun to feel like my sanctum sanctorum. As I stepped over the threshold in front of Cadence, I breathed a sigh of relief. At least here, no well-meaning politicians would ambush me with questions about animanecron independence, no activists would make snide remarks about my relationships, and no slimy interplanetary ambassadors would seek me out to ruin my life. After hanging up my raincoat on the automatic coat cleaner, I trotted down the stairs into the living room, a tired smile beginning to work its way onto my face. Here there was no unpleasantness. Just me and Cadence.

"Elea asked me to be a speaker for Ergo Sum."

My fingers froze over my necktie. My eyes widened. "What?" I turned on my heel to face Cadence, my mouth falling open in a grimace. "At rallies and events and things?"

Cadence shook her sleeves down her arms, allowing her coat to pool on the ground behind her. Smiling with all her teeth, she ran her hands down her neck. "Yes! She thinks since I've been living with humans for so long, I will have a unique perspective to offer."

Closing the distance between us in a few long strides, I stopped on the entryway's bottom step and looked up into her eyes. "You're not actually considering taking her up on this, are you?"

"Of course." Cadence walked down the steps, breezing past me and through the living room as if I weren't even there. "It would be incredible to be a part of the ani-rights movement in such a way."

"Incredibly dangerous, you mean!" I followed her progress with my eyes, shoving my hands into my pockets before finding they were too agitated to be confined in such a fashion and removing them again. "Everyone would know that you're one of them!"

She glanced up at me, frowning, and pulled the zipper down on her dress, shrugging the straps off her shoulders before disappearing down the hallway towards her room. "So, what if they did?"

I let out a rough, unfriendly chuckle, my arms spinning out at my sides. "You can't actually want people to know," I called after her.

A long moment of tense silence hung in the air like a missile hanging at its apex. After a minute or two, Cadence remerged from the hallway, her golden gown changed out for what I imagined was a far more comfortable pair of thin cotton pants and bright blue tank top. A deep frown cut into her face, and she stared at me. "Why shouldn't they?" She pressed her hand against her collarbone, glaring up at me from under her raised brows. "I'm proud of who I am. What I am is a part of that."

"It doesn't have to be!" My hands clenched into fists at my sides, and I followed her over to the long couch underneath the windows. "Why is it so bloody important now? When you first came here—"

"When I first came here, I thought I was alone. I'm not." Collapsing into the cushions, Cadence pushed herself back against the sofa, crossing her arms high over her chest. "Things are bad out there for my people. Would you have me just sit on the sidelines and be a coward?"

Her offense only encouraged my exasperation to morph into rage. I clenched my jaw, the words squeaking out from between my teeth. "I'm not asking you to be a coward; I'm trying to keep you safe, Cay."

She scoffed loudly, bouncing up and down in her seat as she resettled herself, her legs crossing over each other. "By lying about who I am?"

"Yes, alright? Yes." I sat down beside her, perching on the very edge of the cushions. "If someone comes up to you on the street and asks, 'hey, are you one of those animanecrons?' your answer is going to be, 'No, no I'm not!'"

Cadence recoiled, shaking her head violently from side to side, disgust dripping from her voice. "I can't do that. How could you ask me to do that?"

I met her disbelieving gaze with my own. "You have completely lost your mind. Don't you see what's happening out there? Things are boiling over, and you can't let yourself be caught up in that! I can't let you get caught up in that." I stood up, a decision firm in my mind. I gripped her arms, my eyes never leaving her face. "Don't ever go to one of those rallies again, alright? Just work at the shop and come home, that's it. No more going off on half-baked political adventures, not for you."

With a slowness that belied her true feelings, Cadence wrapped her hands around my wrists, squeezing them so hard I thought they might break. I released her, chomping down on the inside of my mouth to keep from crying out as she shoved my arms down to my sides. Eyes filled with the acid, the look she poured into me stung. "You are in no position to tell me what I can and cannot do, Chance Hale."

She turned and strode out of the living room and into the kitchen. I followed her, my blood pounding in my ears. "Like hell I'm not."

It took all my strength to latch onto her shoulder and spin her round to face me, but I had counted on that and put my back into it. The glass she had been reaching for clattered onto the counter with a resounding crash. "I've been living with you for the past five months. I've put up with all your bizarre quirks, your complaining – I did my best to take care of you, and now you tell me I don't have a say in your life?"

She shrunk back from me into the countertop, even though there was no place to go. Cadence's hands were gripping the counter behind her, her body still aside from the slight quiver that rippled over her face; I was frightening her.

I loosened my grip, trying fruitlessly to return to a more civilized tenor of conversation. "Can't you think about me, just for once?"

"About you?" Cadence took the opportunity to shake my hands fully off her. "What has any of this got to do with you?" She stared up at me, the corners of her mouth pulled down in a sharp frown. I was about to respond when her eyes widened. Her mouth fell open and her tongue came out to wet her bottom lip. She straightened against the counter. "Or do you not want people to know about me because–" her eyes flickered away from my face and came back, like a bee to a flower. Her brow furrowed. "–because it will reflect badly on you." Her hands fell to her sides like they were made of lead weights. "Are you ashamed of me?" She began breathing again, her chest heaving up and down, her volume ticking upward with every word. "Are you embarrassed by me?"

The accusation ripped through my heart like a blade. I backed away from her, a tense sneer curling my lip up away from my teeth. "You're being ridiculous."

But she was not to be silenced, the idea worming its way into the very core of her. She drew her hands up to her throat and slashed them down her body as she shouted. "Would it not do to have the head of Halcyon Enterprises associated with a fragger?"

The apartment phone's ring cut through the air like a siren. It was not until its second or third ring though, that I drew my stony gaze away from Cadence, my entire body ramrod straight as I struggled desperately to keep myself in check.

I glanced at the palm-sized handset on the living room table. It blinked at me, its green light flashing on and off. I turned back to her, my hand coming up to puncture the air in front of her chest with a pointed finger. "We are not done with this conversation."

I didn't wait for a response, pivoting and jogging into the living room. I skimmed the caller ID as quickly as I could before snatching the set off its charger, relieved that I didn't have to bother concealing the agitation in my voice. "What is it, Henry?"

A flood of words engulfed me, none of them in the least bit intelligible. I held my free hand up to my other ear and shook my head. "Wai–...Hen–... Henry, slow down, slow down, I can't understand you!" I caught the sound of sobbing in the background and my stomach clenched, as did my hand around the phone. "Henry, are you alright? What is it?"

"That's what I'm trying to tell you, Chance, it's not alright." Henry's voice was high pitched yet muffled, as if he had one hand over his mouth. "It's Elea. She's...She's dead, Chance. She's been killed."

"What?" I swung around and locked eyes with Cadence, who had taken a step towards me, the vehemence in her gaze tempered by concern.

"Is Cadence there with you?"

My mind whirred, jumping from thought to thought. I had to shake myself to force the answer out of me. "Yes, yes, she's here."

"Could you both come, please? I'll give you the address, I just..." There was a rustle on the other end of the line and Henry's voice dropped to a plea-filled whisper. "Simone is so upset...I don't know what to do, Chance."

The desperate tone of his voice snapped something into place for me; I straightened, my mind clearing. "What's the address?" He rattled off the street listing for a place in the 16th District. I nodded and repeated it back to him before saying, "We'll be there as soon as we can. You must try to stay calm. You've called the Enforcement Office?"

"Yes, they should be here any moment now."

"Alright, good. Just stay there." I looked back at Cadence and swallowed. "We're coming."

Hanging up the phone, I let it clatter back onto the living room table. Cadence, our earlier fight seemingly forgotten, placed a hand on my shoulder.

"What is it?"

I licked my lips and shook my head. "Cadence, I...I'm not..." I closed my eyes and steeled myself to deliver the news. "It's Elea Cerf. She's been...killed."

I felt Cadence slip away from under my hand. I opened my eyes to find her standing a little way away from me, her dark eyes wide. "Impossible." She shook her head, slowly at first and then faster and faster. "Impossible, she – this isn't–" Her hand dropped to her side and clenched into a fist. "What happened?"

"I don't know." I held my hand out to her. "But if you come with me, there's a chance we can find out."

Without a moment of hesitation, Cadence bypassed my hand and made a straight line for the door. "We'd better hurry."

10

Chapter 10

District 16, mostly residential, sat nestled in the undergrowth of the urban sprawl of Römer. The buildings there didn't rise beyond ten or twenty stories, and they were all at least one hundred years old, made of brick and mortar rather than the preferred steel and glass. The PT dropped us near the edge of the district, as there were no PT hubs within that section of the city, and we soon found ourselves walking down dark streets that glistened with grimy rainwater.

By the time we arrived on the scene, a crowd of inquisitive passerbys had already gathered in front of Ergo Sum's building. After excusing and shuffling our way to the front of the group, it was easy to see what had attracted everyone's attention. The rest of the buildings on the street were dark, but it appeared that every single light inside Ergo Sum was turned on, the whole place blazing like a lantern. The front door was propped open, and EO officers walked in and out, going from the building to the three EO PTs blocking the street. Several officers were stationed between each transport, eyeing the curious crowd suspiciously, ready to turn away any that pushed too close; Cadence and I ended up directly behind one of these EO PTs.

I craned my head back to see over the top of the humming transport in front of us, my hands clenching and unclenching at my sides.

"Blast! How are we supposed to get past all this?"

Cadence lifted herself onto the tips of her toes, swaying gently like a cattail in the wind. "Can't we just say we were invited?"

I turned back to stare at her. "Somehow I don't think walking up to an enforcement officer and saying, 'Sorry to bother you, but we were invited to this murder, so do you mind terribly if we head in?' is going to work."

She returned my glare. "You could try, instead of just standing there."

I had had enough of Cadence's remarks upon my ineffectiveness, and was about to say so, when the jostling and shuffling of the crowd behind us captured my attention by way of a carelessly applied elbow between my shoulder blades.

"Hey, watch it!"

The crowd was forced to either side of the street to make way for an EO PT, inching its way ever nearer to the office building. Enforcement officers lined the makeshift lane, struggling to keep the interested onlookers back from the PT's propulsion jets.

"Bit late, isn't he?" I observed.

Cadence gave an unladylike snort beside me.

We watched as the PT slid into the empty space diagonal to

two of the EO transports already on the scene. An Enforcement Officer stepped out from behind the wheel, uniform looking black in the weird shadows cast from the building behind him, and a second, smaller figure exited from the back of the vehicle.

Had we been any further away, we wouldn't have noticed anything familiar about the man as he stood, talking to a pair of officers who had rushed up to the transport to meet him. But there was something about the way he was standing; something about his coiffed brown hair and slim, sharp shoulders. When he turned around to gesture at the crowd of which we were a part, the sight of his face, even in shadow, was enough to make me remark:

"Is that–?"

"Inspector Brisbois!" Cadence was already waving, her entire body swaying back and forth as she swung her arm back and forth. "Inspector, over here!"

We had met Inspector Oliver Brisbois of the Enforcement Office several months earlier, when he had overseen the investigation of my father's murder. He and Cadence had gotten on rather well, both being in possession of sharp, analytical minds and dry senses of humor. Intelligent as they both may be, however, Cadence had outfoxed the man and solved the case, whilst also escaping detection as an animanecron at a time when her presence on Arrhidaeus had been illegal. I wondered, as I watched the Inspector turn to seek out the source of the shouting, what he would think of my friend if he discovered her true nature now.

As it was, when he spotted her in the crowd his eyes widened, and his mouth fell open. "Miss Turing?" he shouted back. He walked over, cinching closed his raincoat. When he was within a few feet of us his brow furrowed, and he repeated, "Miss Turing. And Mr. Hale. What are you doing here?"

Cadence smiled wide and clasped her hands in front of her bosom. "We were invited."

Taken aback, Brisbois opened his mouth to respond, but I cut him off, reaching forward to grab his hand in a firm shake. "What she means to say, Inspector–" I pumped his arm up and down several times before releasing him, "–is that it's lovely to see you. And it'd be rather easier to explain if we could go inside."

Brisbois stepped back, lifting an eyebrow. He let out a laugh. "I'm terribly sorry, but now isn't a good time–"

"I can imagine, Inspector." I pointed at the building behind him. "But you're going to see another friendly face in there, and it may be best if we accompany you."

He cocked his head to one side and considered me for a moment before shrugging. "I suppose you two had better come along then."

"Thank you, Inspector," I said, extending my arm back out towards Cadence and ushering her in front of me.

Keeping close to Brisbois, we picked our way through the crowd of Enforcement Officers and walked through the open front door. The lobby of Ergo Sum was spacious and modern, reminding me of a run-down version of my own offices at Halcyon. An oval reception desk protruded from one wall, behind which sat three computer terminals, each demarcated with privacy screens that stretched over the desk and to the floor. The lobby itself was peppered with plush chairs and low square coffee tables, and the smell of fresh flowers permeated the room.

Screens bolted to the walls were playing a loop of Arrhidaeus travelogs. As we entered, a quiet, male voice was saying, "–today, the city of Römer is divided into more than fifty unique districts, each with its own history and vibrant cultural background."

Pausing to get his bearings, Brisbois then headed for the spiral staircase tucked in the back of the room. Seeing no sign of Henry or Simone, Cadence and I followed. Winding our way up the stairs, we stepped out onto the second floor and in the middle of a suite of offices. The brown carpet beneath our feet was threadbare, and the stained wallpaper was beginning to pull away from the drywall in bits and pieces. None of the offices had actual doors – just gaping portals with hinges, where a plank of wood had once been attached. From the initial trio of offices surrounding us, two hallways broke off, stretching down the length of the building. From the one to the left, sobbing echoed.

The three of us followed the sound, stepping with care past the open doorways. The first thing I saw was an EO officer standing on the left side of the hallway, her blue uniform standing out like a smear of something unmentionable against the wall. She was standing guard, so it seemed, over two people huddled together on the opposite side of the hall. One was curled up tight into a ball, crying into her knees. The other was kneeling over her, rubbing her back and murmuring. At our approach, the second figure rushed to his feet, stepping in front of the crying person as if to protect her from further harm.

In front of me, I heard Brisbois let out a long sigh, but watched as he lifted his hand up in greeting all the same. "Mr. Davers – what a surprise to see you again."

Henry shook the hand extended to him. "Inspector Brisbois."

He blinked in surprise, but his face flooded with relief when he looked over the man's shoulder and laid eyes on us. He stepped around Brisbois and moved towards us, arms open wide. "Chance, Cadence, you made it."

We both embraced him in turn, and I was about to ask him how he was holding up when Brisbois cleared his throat, reminding us of his presence.

"Right, well–" Brisbois rolled his shoulders back and shoved his hands into his coat pockets, "–much as I'd love to catch up with you all, I was led to understand there was a body somewhere here for me."

Henry stepped forward, but the enforcement officer beat him to it, extending a hand out towards the door beside her. "She's in here, Inspector," said the woman.

With a nod, Brisbois stepped forward and entered the room. Cadence and I shared a glance and then followed behind him as far as the door frame, needing to see for ourselves what had called us here in the middle of the night.

A tawdry scene assailed us; the small office sat in total disarray. Two chairs, which had once sat in front of the desk, were tossed onto their sides and flung to the far corners of the room. A potted plant was ripped from its home; the dirt scattered across the carpet in great, blood-like swathes. A pair of cheap, biodegradable cups lay crumpled in one corner. Cracked optrics hung crooked on the walls, staring down on the scene with jittery, pixelated eyes. Every drawer of the desk laid open and ransacked, and various file folders and discs lay strewn about the floor.

In the middle of all the chaos, lay Elea Cerf, splayed

belly-down across her desk. Her marbled dress pulled up around her knees, heeled shoes dangling off the balls of her feet, her face turned towards the doorway. Her eyes screwed shut, her mouth was open in a terrible scream. Her entire body was rigid, frozen in the moment of her death – a death that could have only been caused by the gaping hole in the back of her head. The wound opened so wide that one could clearly see the intricate matrices of wire, silicon, plastic, and shiny, synthetic material that made up the inside of her head. The skin and skull were popped back, like a hatch, and hung beside the gaping wound, tendrils of fiery red hair dangling in contrast to the mechanical wreckage.

Hand to my mouth, tearing my gaze away from the horror in front of us, I sought out Cadence. She stood beside me, wide, unblinking eyes darting from detail to detail with such rapidity that I wondered if she was taking any of it in. Her fists hung at her sides and her jaw was clenched. She had ceased breathing some time ago.

I reached down for her fist. Cadence flinched at my touch, pulling her hand away, but her gaze remained fixed on the room.

Brisbois hummed to himself, standing on the edge of the gutted room. After a moment he took a deep breath, undid his coat, and dug his palm pad out of his suit jacket. Using his stylus, he jotted down a few quick notes, and then exited the room past us once again, nodding to the dazed figure still sitting on the floor opposite him. "And this is?"

"Simone Harlow," supplied Henry from behind the group. "Miss Cerf's partner."

Brisbois nodded, stylus flying across his pad. "Business partner?"

My voice was quiet and filled with pity as I answered, "Among other things, yes, Inspector."

He didn't look up, but I saw the surprise register, ever so briefly on his face, his eyebrows undulating once before he nodded again. "I'm going to need you all to wait downstairs in the lobby for me, please. I'll need to talk to you all when I'm done up here."

"Of course, Inspector." Henry wedged his way forward to the front of us, the narrow hallway making navigating through the group a challenge. Balancing on the balls of his feet, he bent down and placed a hand on the crying woman's back. "Simone..."

As if afraid of what she might see, Simone very slowly raised her head from her knees. I was astonished by the change in her; it was hard to believe this was the same woman with whom I was speaking only a few hours before. Her entire face shined with sweat and tears, the makeup around her eyes and lips smeared across her cheeks and chin. Her skin had grown pale, except for the areas around her nose and eyes, which were pink and raw. She looked out just past the tops of her knees as Henry spoke, with no other sign that she was hearing a word that he was saying.

"Simone, this is Inspector Brisbois; he'll handle Elea's case." Henry rubbed her back once and then again. "He needs us all to wait downstairs."

Simone looked up, slow and halting, as if every movement hurt. Her eyes drew up and up and up until they met Brisbois', who looked down at her without expression.

Struggling at first, Simone eventually stood in stockinged feet, her high-heeled shoes abandoned on the floor beside her.

Tears still ran down her olive face, every blink unleashing a drop or two more from her reddened eyes. She took a step forward and then stopped. I don't think she was even aware that Cadence and I were there, her gaze so fixated on Brisbois, her mouth a thin, tight line.

"You'll find who did this, won't you?" she whispered at last.

Brisbois, a man who I knew liked to turn a phrase, remained silent and looked away from Simone's pleading eyes. When it was clear he was not going to respond, Henry took Simone by the shoulders and led her away towards the stairs. Cadence and I followed.

We made our way back to the lobby in silence. Henry sat Simone down in one of the chairs and then stood and looked around, at a loss for what to do next. I went to him, taking him by the arm and pulling him a little way away from the distraught woman.

"Henry," I said, brow furrowed. "Are you alright?"

"I'm fine, I'm fine." Henry cast about himself, his quivering hand stroking his chin. "It's Simone I'm worried about. She has a daughter at home, Ayla; I need to call through to the sitter and let her know what's going on, but my phone's gone dead."

"Here, use mine," I dug into my pocket and held my mobile out to him.

He grabbed the device with both hands like it was a lifeline and he a drowning man. "Thanks." He took a step towards the windows and hesitated. "Would you and Cadence stay with her? I don't want her to be alone right now."

I swallowed and shook my head. "Of course, of course. You go. Take your time."

Henry gave a tight smile before turning away, fitting the mobile in his ear. I looked back at Simone. She sat slumped in her chair, staring down at her hands, shoulders trembling.

Steeling myself, I stepped over to her, stopping just in front of her seat. "Miss Harlow? Is there anything I can get for you? Anything that you need?"

Simone jumped at the sound of my voice and stared up at me. She sniffed and blinked several times to clear her vision. "Mr. Hale," she said, surprise clear in her tone.

I nodded and gestured behind me. "Cadence is here as well."

"Hello, Simone." Cadence stepped forward, much bolder than I, and took the seat next to the bereaved woman. Without hesitation, she reached over and tapped a simple beat against Simone's arm before gripping it tightly. "Sinc, I am so, so sorry this has happened to you."

Gasping, Simone brought the back of her free hand up to her lips. "Thank you," she managed, her voice breaking. She swallowed several times, shaking her head from side to side. "Oh, Cadence, this can't be happening. It can't be happening."

Henry came over to me, mobile held out. I took it from him without a word and the four of us waited without speaking, only the occasional sob from Simone breaking the silence.

The change in atmosphere was subtle. I don't think any of us noticed when the first few EO officers stepped outside. But when they began leaving in groups of threes and fours, when the sound of them loading up into EO transports outside reached our ears, and it was clear that they would not be returning, all of us began to wonder what the hell was going on.

Henry and I were at the window, watching the first EO PT

pull away when Brisbois came down the stairs with a heavy, plodding tread, one hand pressed against the side of his face.

"Yes, sir," he said, speaking into the mobile nestled in his ear. "Yes, sir. But don't you think–" He stepped down onto the first-floor landing with a thud, his mouth gaping open mid-sentence, eyes tracking backwards and forwards as he listened. "Respectfully, sir, I disagree! This is still a–" His jaw clenched shut, and his hands fell to his sides. "Yes, sir. Oh, I understand, sir. Goodbye."

Simone stood up from her seat, wiping her nose. "What is it, Inspector? What's going on?"

Brisbois stared at her for a moment, and then cleared his throat and crossed the room. "Miss Harlow," he said, stopping a few feet in front of her. "I'm sorry to inform you that the EO will not be looking any further into this matter."

"What?" Henry was beside Simone in seconds, hands already clenched into fists at his sides.

Brisbois ignored Henry's outburst and continued, gaze fixed on Simone's confused face. "You see, there was no sign of a break-in, and in the absence of any evidence of illegal activity–"

"Illegal activity? You have a dead body upstairs, Brisbois!" I shouted.

"There's some question about that," he shot back, glaring at me. He returned his attention to Simone, clearing his throat. "The Chief Superintendent has cited current assault laws surrounding animanecrons and feels that, given the nature of Miss Cerf's existence, we can't treat her destruction as a murder."

"Inspector," Cadence asked, folding her hands in her lap as she looked up at him. "What exactly are you saying?"

Brisbois looked from me to Henry to Cadence, taking in a deep breath. At last, he shrugged, his hands spreading in front of himself. "You can't murder what was never technically alive."

The slap rang out like the clang of a bell. Brisbois' head snapped to one side, his eyes wide. Simone, standing on tip toe, let her hand remain in the air, frozen at the point with which it had contacted his cheek. "How dare you," she hissed. Eyes blazing, she sucked in a lungful of air and wound her arm back for another swing, shouting, "How dare you!"

But Brisbois was ready this time, catching her wrist as her hand came towards his face. Undeterred, Simone swung her other hand at him. Brisbois scrambled to take hold of that one as well, wrestling with the woman until he could get both of her arms under his control. When she finally stopped struggling, they were face to face.

"I'm sorry." Brisbois lowered their hands, staring into Simone's eyes with an earnestness that made my heart ache. "But my hands...my hands are tied." He released her wrists from his grip and took a step back from her, his own hands still up at his chest, ready to fend off another barrage if necessary. "Unless you'd like to seek a charge for destruction of private property–"

"She wasn't my property, damn you, she was my life!" Simone shouted, curling up into herself. "Someone took her away from me. Someone came in here and ripped her to pieces, and you're just going to stand there and do nothing!"

"I'm trying to help the only way I can, Miss Harlow," said Brisbois, taking a step towards her.

"You did notice the scratches on her neck, Inspector?"

Cadence stood at last, sweeping her arms behind her and holding them there.

"Scratches?" interjected Henry, lost as the rest of us at this sudden change in conversation.

Brisbois turned to Cadence with a huff, his jaw clenching. "Yes, I did, Miss Turing, but may I remind you what happened the last time you interfered in EO business?"

"Yes." I shoved my hands in my pockets and rocked back on my heels. "She solved your bloody case for you."

"What?" Simone's head jerked up.

I nodded. "It's true. If it weren't for Cadence, my father's killer would have gotten away, free as a bird."

"And my father would've been convicted of the crime instead." Henry sneered at Brisbois.

"That is a gross mischaracterization of events–" cut in Brisbois, color rising to his cheeks.

Cadence waved her hand through the air, cutting off Brisbois. "I have to agree with the Inspector. Henry – the evidence against your father was purely circumstantial, I doubt very much that it would have garnered a conviction, and Chance – I'm sure the Enforcement Office wouldn't have let the case sit cold forever; eventually the guilty parties would've been apprehended."

"Cadence." Simone turned to face her fully. "Do you think you could find out what happened to Elea?"

"Yes." Cadence answered without hesitation, but then glanced at Brisbois. "But the Enforcement Office–"

"The Enforcement Office can go to hell!" Simone grabbed Cadence's arms, pulling her in close. "Find out who did this to

Elea, I'm begging you. I'll hire you, officially, as – as a private investigator if that's what it takes."

"Simone..." Cadence gripped Simone's arms in return, a small smile on her face "You are my friend. All you have to do is ask." The smile disappeared and she gave an abrupt nod. "I will take the case."

The tension in Simone's frame visibly slackened. She released Cadence with a sigh. "Thank you, Cadence." With narrowed eyes, she surveyed Brisbois once more before collapsing back into her seat. "Inspector Brisbois, you can go now."

Brisbois stood for a moment, hands flexing at his side. He looked around the room and then shrugged. "I truly am sorry for your loss, Miss Harlow." He turned to the three of us and nodded to each of us in turn, mouth a firm line. "Miss Turing, Mr. Hale, Mr. Davers." He lifted a hand in farewell. "Stay safe."

Turning on his heel and buttoning his coat closed, Brisbois exited through the door. The last waiting EO officer followed him, and the four of us were left quite alone inside Ergo Sum.

11

Chapter 11

"Right." Simone crossed her legs and looked up at us all, tossing her hair back from her face. "Where do we begin?"

Henry, Cadence, and I looked at each other. Feeling oddly parental, I sensed the burden was on me to say something. "Well, first things first: we get you home." Simone opened her mouth to protest, but I cut her off with a slice of my hand. "No, no arguments; you need to rest, you need to see your daughter, and you can do no more good here, for now."

Henry stepped forward and rested a hand on Simone's shoulder. "I'll take her." He smiled. "I have the feeling I'll just be in the way otherwise."

Simone stood, leaning against Henry, the anger which had given her a moment's vitality fading. "Thank you," she said to Henry as he helped steady her. Then she turned to Cadence, reaching out her hand. "Thank you, Cadence. I know I can count on you."

Cadence gripped the woman's hand and gave it a squeeze before releasing it. With care, Henry ushered her to the front door, knocking the stone out that was holding the portal open, and allowing the door to swing shut behind them.

A distant rumble of thunder broke through the momentary silence that had settled over the room. Cadence turned to me. "You should return home too, Chance." In a perfect mimicry of me, she sighed and ran her hand back through her voluminous hair. "It's very late, and you have work in a few hours."

"Oh, I'm not going anywhere, Cay." I placed my hand on her shoulder. "I can't even imagine what it's like for you to look at that scene up there, and there's no reason you should have to do this alone." I took a step back from her, holding my arms wide. "You're the brains here – it's your case – but whatever I can do to help, even if it's just someone to talk to when things get too much, I'm here for you."

"Sinc, thank you, Chance." She leaned forward and caressed my arm, her gaze meeting mine. "I'm sorry about earlier. I know you are only concerned about my safety."

I held her hand against my skin, sighing. "I'm sorry too. You're a grown woman. You can take care of yourself, can't you?"

She nodded, and I closed my eyes, aware then how little she really needed me. Shaking away my own self-pity, I squared my shoulders and threw my hand out in the direction of the staircase. "Well, shall we?"

Without a word, Cadence turned and headed back towards the stairs. I followed suit. We made our way up the rickety staircase, our shoes clanging against the grated metal as I contemplated why death seemed to follow my Cadence around wherever she went. I wondered if she thought the same as we moved down the hallway to the scene of the crime, or if other reminiscences consumed her.

When we turned into the room, I paused on the threshold, allowing Cadence to move several steps in front of me. All was silent. Cadence stood just inside the doorway, her gaze intent on the scene in front of us. I wanted to touch her, but I was wary of breaking her concentration. Instead, I settled for asking, "What do you see?"

"Death." With a shiver, Cadence wrapped both arms around herself, shaking her head from side to side. "Frig, Chance, I..."

I stepped closer behind her, hoping my presence alone would soothe her. "It's okay, Cay. I'm here."

With halting steps, Cadence walked over to the body spread across the desk. She lifted her hand and touched the back of Elea's arm. I heard her sharp intake of breath.

"She's so cold." She drew her hand back sharply. "That is stupid to say. Of course, she is cold."

I examined the body from a distance, doing my best to stop imagining that it was Cadence lying there instead of Elea. I swallowed, wetting my dry mouth, and half-whispered, "What happened to her head?"

"Her main processing board has been removed." Cadence brushed strands of Elea's hair away from the opening. "Probably destroyed in the incinerator over there."

I looked around the room and saw the incinerator to which she was referring. Industrial grade, it was most likely used for destroying confidential discs and chips. It was larger than something one might expect to see in an office of this size; it took up the whole back right corner of the room, a tarnished, squat square with a hinged opening.

"Destroying the main processing board is one of the only ways to truly kill an animanecron," continued Cadence, moving away from the body, her eyes intent on the wreckage surrounding it.

"You've seen it before." It wasn't a question. I could tell, had been able to tell since the first moment we investigated the room with Brisbois, that the scene was familiar to my friend.

She nodded. "On Whiston. Many times."

"How would someone even do that?" I leaned over Elea's head as far as I dared, trying to ignore the smell of hot plastic mixed with her pheromone spray. "I mean, if I tried to pry off the back of your head, I'd imagine you'd have something to say about it."

"I imagine Elea did." Cadence gestured around the office. "Hence all this." She paused in her surveying of the floor and desk to look up at me, concern apparent in her face. "Not many people would know how to do this."

I straightened, watching as Cadence carefully stepped around the room. "But what human could overpower an animanecron?"

She knelt behind the desk. "None, unless they came prepared to do so. They could have had an EMP gun or were specially modified themselves."

While Cadence searched through the debris, I returned, almost against my will, to Elea's body. From this angle, I could see the full column of her throat and neck and spied the angry red lines that had caught Cadence's attention. I pointed to them. "Are these the scratches you mentioned to Brisbois?"

"Yes." Standing, Cadence moved to join me by the body. "The rest of her appears to be relatively unscathed. That is an interesting place for an attacker to scratch, don't you think?"

I stared at the scratches, rubbing my chin. "You know what we really need? A doctor."

Cadence glanced at me. "Hm?"

"You know, a doctor; someone who could do a postmortem, tell us a little more about how she died."

Cadence crossed her arms over her chest and looked down her nose at me. "We know how she died – her main processing board was removed and incinerated." Her eyes flickered heavenward. "Still, a postmortem is standard procedure in cases like this. But what would a doctor know about animanecrons?" A moment of silence passed as we considered the question and then, suddenly, Cadence snapped her fingers, grinning. "A reczec!"

"A what?"

"A reczec – they are like doctors but much, much better. I wonder if Simone knows of any in Römer?" She started for the door. "We should go ask her."

I scrambled for her arm and caught it just as it swung past me. She pulled me along for a step and then stopped.

"Let's give Simone a few hours, okay?" I said. "She really does need time to rest." I let go of her arm and gestured around the room. "Is there anything else we can do here?"

"Yes." Cadence looked over her shoulder, her smile fading. "The body."

I followed her gaze, her meaning dawning on me slowly. "Are you sure we should move it?"

She stepped back towards Elea, her hand outstretched. "We can't just leave her like this."

I nodded. "Alright. I'll go look for something to cover her up."

I headed out into the hall and turned right, towards the spiral staircase and the cluster of offices we had first seen when we stepped onto the second floor. I glanced inside each room, finding nothing of use until I investigated the last. When I poked my head inside, a motion-sensitive light flashed into life, and I found myself staring into a storage closet. Metal shelves crowded the room, and plastic bins stuffed full of miscellaneous items jutted out into the space.

I pawed through a few boxes at random, uncertain of what I should find, until one several inches above my head caught my eye. It overflowed with fabric. When I pulled the bin down for closer inspection, I found that it was the home of several green and blue tablecloths; each emblazoned with stark black letters that read, "ERGO SUM: THINK -- FEEL -- FIGHT".

It seemed as fitting an epitaph for Elea Cerf as any; I hoped Cadence would agree.

By the time I returned to Elea's office, Cadence had re-arranged Elea's remains into a more dignified position. I entered the room to find her holding the woman's hand, the body laid face up and flat on top of the desk. Elea's face, however, was still a mask of terror, painful to look at.

I proffered Cadence the half-folded tablecloth, my eyes downcast. "This was all I could find. I'm sorry it's not more... more..."

Cadence took the cloth from me, her fingers brushing against my hand. "Thank you, Chance."

Gripping the tablecloth by the short edge with both hands,

Cadence walked to the end of the desk, standing next to Elea's feet. She closed her eyes and began to hum. A low, quiet sound, like the vibration of servers, it soon gained intensity and volume, rising and falling into a mournful dirge. Cadence swayed to the sound, her brow furrowing, her lips firming into a thin line. She took the cloth and drew it up slowly over the body, pausing every step to rock in place. When the cloth covered Elea up to her neck, Cadence dropped the fabric, folding it like the top of a blanket.

I watched as Cadence drew in a deep breath. She opened her eyes and, looking not down at Elea but directly ahead, began to speak in Animatum. The words clicked and tripped off her tongue and from between her teeth in rapid succession; I understood not a word. But the reverence with which Cadence pressed her thumb to the hollow of Elea's throat, then the woman's forehead, and then to her own lips, told me everything I needed to know.

She stood there for a long moment, her thumb pressed hard against her full lips, and brows drawn as if in pain. With a final release of breath, she looked down at Elea, took up the edge of the tablecloth, and covered the woman's contorted face.

She stepped backwards until she stood a few inches in front of me and reached back for my hand. I took hers without hesitation.

We had talked about death before – it was difficult to avoid when meeting over a corpse the way we had. But all I had known about how animanecrons dealt with death, is that they didn't. However, what I had just witnessed, and what I now knew was happening to them on Whiston, indicated something to the contrary.

"Cay," I said, my voice a whisper as I squeezed her hand tighter. "Do animanecrons..." I struggled to ask the question to which I was certain I already knew the answer. I swallowed and tried again. "What do you think happens when—"

"Nothing happens, Chance." Cadence let go of my hand, turning to look at me for the first time since she took the table-cloth from me. "We are created from nothing, and to nothing we return." She took in a deep breath through her nose, and let it out through her mouth, her eyes flickering shut. "When you are gone, you are gone. There is no coming back from nestati quru-maq. No more adventures; no more anything. You are done."

"Then...why?" I gestured to the covered body that still lay before us. "Why say all those words? Why the ceremony?"

"Because what was, deserves to be honored, even if it is no more. Because, although she may be gone, she lives on in our memories." Cadence tapped her lips with the front of her thumb, meeting my eyes. "Because we are still here."

"Yes." I attempted a smile. "I suppose we are, aren't we?" Breaking her gaze, I let out a deep breath of my own, my hands falling into my pockets as I looked around the ransacked office. "Well, what now?"

"Now perhaps we should go home."

I began to protest, but Cadence put up her hand, shaking her head. "I don't need sleep, but you and Simone do, and there's little more we can do tonight. And..." She gave a small smile and reached forward, tapping her signature tattoo against my cheek. "You look tired, Chance."

It had been a long night. With a sigh, I extended my arm out behind me towards the office door, ushering Cadence out of the room in front of me.

As we clattered down the rickety staircase into the lobby, the recorded, hushed male voice still echoed in the deserted space, but it was mixed with another sound: a muffled, booming patter of words that reached us, even in the back of the room. My first thought was that the EO was still attempting to control the crowd outside, but then I remembered that they were no longer on the case. Brow furrowing, I strode forward to see the flash of lights and cameras pouring in through the front windows, and an unmistakable crowd of people with recorders jostling for position. They were focused on something off to the right of the building's front steps. It was from this direction that the muffled voice was emanating.

"What's going on?" said Cadence, looking to me for answers. "I thought the EO had gone?"

"They have." I scowled, shouldering open the front door. "This is something else."

12

Chapter 12

We went largely unnoticed as we exited the main doors of Ergo Sum. A couple of people turned to look, casting glances over their shoulders, but most of the crowd was fully occupied with what was happening down on the sidewalk.

The EO had indeed cleared out, and with them most of the spectators. Those who remained were those who turned misery, tragedy, and violence into a lucrative business: journalists. They clustered together like a swarm of ants, swaying and moving as one body, silent as their palm sized drones floated above them, capturing live footage of the scene, each one emblazoned with a company logo.

Set up at the bottom corner of the front steps was a hastily thrown together cluster of recorders, shielded from the rain by biodegradable plastic sheaths. Behind them, the collar of his rain jacket flipped up against the drizzle, was Andrew Peyton. Jun stood beside him, her sharp face upturned as she gazed at her husband with pride, holding an umbrella over them both. The usual cadre of bodyguards and assistants stood respectfully to one side, all eyes on their leader, who was mid-address when Cadence and I stepped out of Ergo Sum and onto the street.

"Elea Cerf was one of the finest people–" Peyton paused and looked around pointedly, raising both hands into the air. "–and yes, I will say people – I've ever had the pleasure of knowing. Her work with Ergo Sum helped hundreds of refugees rebuild their lives on our fair planet." He clasped his hands in front of himself, shaking his head. "But her work was more than that – what she did was bring people together. She showed us that we were strongest when we celebrated our unique heritage and embraced the wider world around us. She was a beacon of hope to many who had lost all hope. And now–" His volume increased, a scowl cutting across his face. "–because of the backwards and outdated laws of our planet, her death is not going to be investigated." At a momentary loss of words, whether real or manufactured, the representative pinched the bridge of his nose and stuttered. "If-if-if that isn't a miscarriage of justice, folks, I... well, I just don't know what is."

With a deep sigh, Peyton let his arms fall to his sides. He reached out and drew his wife closer to him, nodding. "I will not let all that Elea Cerf stood for be forgotten. We can be, and we will be better than this. And we'll do it together. Thank you."

There was a smattering of applause, but it was immediately drowned out by a cacophony of shouted questions, the flashes from cameras lighting up the street like bolts of lightning.

"Representative, is it true that you support the unionization of Ani workers in Römer?"

"If elected to the Chancellorship, will you press for more inclusive laws that recognize Ani rights, Representative Peyton?"

"How do you respond to those planets that feel that Animanecrons represent a clear and present danger to the human race?"

But Peyton merely smiled and waved, the questions bouncing off him like balls against a brick wall. Like a well-oiled machine, his entourage swung into action, bodyguards moving forward to keep the crowd of journalists at bay while Peyton and his wife moved through them, accompanied by their assistants. A sleek, expensive looking PT waited at the corner behind us, a minor miracle – the mind boggled at the thought of how much the representative must have paid to persuade a professional transport vehicle to wait around in this part of town.

I positioned myself in front of the PT's passenger door and made no effort to hide the judgment on my face when Peyton appeared from the dispersing crush of bodies.

"That was quite the speech, Representative Peyton," I said, arms crossed high over my chest.

"Mr. Hale." Peyton blinked at me once, then again, and then remembered to smile. "How nice to see you again so soon." He buttoned his coat with one hand, his other outstretched towards me. "What brings you out to District 16 on a night like tonight?"

"The same thing as you, actually." I shook his hand once. "Elea Cerf."

His brows shot up over his small eyes. "Oh?"

"Like you said..." I looked up to the sky as a roll of thunder

echoed through the dark streets. "For her death to go uninvesti-
gated would be a miscarriage of justice."

I took an instant dislike to the amused tilt of his smile. "And
you're going to do the investigating, Mr. Hale?"

"No, I am." Cadence stepped forward, her hand outstretched.
"Cadence Turing. I've been asked to investigate this matter by
Simone Harlow." She pumped the man's hand up and down
several times, maintaining eye contact all the while. "You are
Representative Andrew Peyton of District 13."

Peyton's chest swelled as he straightened. "Yes, ma'am, I am."

"What are you doing here, in District 16?" She released him
and took a step back, looking him over appraisingly. "You don't
belong here."

"On the contrary." Peyton's smile didn't even waver. "I belong
anywhere that the citizens of Arrhidaeus need me to be and
tonight, they need me here. Someone in power had to say something about Elea's death, and call it what it was: a murder, plain
and simple."

Cadence shook her hair back out of her face. "In my experience, murder is rarely plain or simple, Representative Peyton."

Peyton's smile dimmed at last, but rather than taking on an
edge of annoyance, his eyes narrowed in suspicion. "And you
have a lot of that do you, Miss Turing? Experience with murder?"

Cadence opened her mouth, doubtless ready to fully explain
her credentials, but Peyton held up his hands, rolling his eyes.
"Look: I'm anxious to help anyway I can. Elea wasn't just a
supporter or a colleague; she was a friend. If you get any leads,
please–" He dug into his breast pocket and produced a small
black card, proffering it to Cadence with earnestness. "Get in

touch with me at my office. I'd like to be kept apprised of things. Now, if you'll excuse us; it's been a long night."

Peyton gestured his wife forward and, having no real reason to further impede their progress, Cadence and I retreated far enough for him to open the passenger door and disappear behind the tinted windows of the PT.

Watching as the PT hummed into life and slid off and up into the dark night, Cadence stood akimbo, a frown twisting her lips. "I don't know that I trust that man."

I pushed my hand back through my rapidly dampening hair, scowling. "Politicians, Cay – I wouldn't trust them to tell me it was wet when it was raining."

Cadence turned toward me, still frowning, but this time more in thought than with displeasure. "Representative Andrew Peyton is of importance in the current political landscape of Arrhidaeus, is he not?"

I nodded. "He's running for Chancellor; has a very good chance of getting elected too."

Her brows drew up to a point. "I'm not sure I understand."

"You see–" I put my hand between her shoulder blades, leading her farther away from the dispersing band of journalists. "Every district on Arrhidaeus is represented in the Parliament of Peers by a representative, elected by residents of that district." We stopped just past the Ergo Sum building and I turned to face her fully. "The Parliament crafts legislation, confirms judges, so forth and so on, but ultimately, the leader of Arrhidaeus, the person who represents us on the Inter-Planetary Commission, for example, is the Chancellor."

She began to nod slowly. "And everyone gets to vote for this Chancellor position?"

"Every seven years, yes." I flinched as a few larger drops of rain splashed onto my face and glared up into the sky.

"So, it's a popularity contest?"

"We prefer to think of it as a meritocracy but, yes, sometimes it devolves into a popularity contest." I wiped my face dry, only to have it shiny and wet a moment later. "How do they do things on Whiston?"

She smirked, a touch of pride in her voice. "It's far simpler. We all work together for the common good."

"But surely someone is in charge," I pressed. "Otherwise, how do decisions get made?"

"Well," she said as her smile wavered, and her shoulders fell. "If there is a disagreement amongst the general populace, it is taken to the Coders. Their decision is final."

I leaned in, cocking my head to one side. "The Coders?"

"The wisest and oldest animanecrons among us. They're never wrong." Before I had a chance to comment on this pronouncement, Cadence had turned back around to stare off into the darkness. "Would Representative Peyton have a reason to harm Elea?"

"She was one of his allies; I don't see what he would have to gain by her death, aside from a photo opportunity. Still, it's probably worth a closer look at him and his campaign, if we can manage it." Hunching my shoulders against a gust of wind and rain, I turned up my collar, trying to do what I could to avoid getting drenched by the increasing deluge.

Cadence hummed contemplatively and returned her attention

to me, her mouth open. She shut her jaw with a snap when she saw my soaked frame, looking me over with concern. "You're getting very wet, Chance."

I smiled at her, hugging myself. "So are you, darling."

She looked down at herself in surprise, as if noticing the rainwater suffusing her clothes for the first time. With a sigh, she strode past me towards the corner of the street. "I'll attempt to find a PT to take us home. I'll be back – wait here!"

I watched as Cadence disappeared around the corner, rain dripping down into my eyes.

I loved her so madly.

The thought appeared as soon as she left my sight, as if to keep me company in her absence. Sighing, I closed my eyes, leaning back against the brick wall behind me and turning my face up into the falling rain.

She deserved better than me; I knew that like I knew my own name. She deserved a partner in life who was unafraid – adventurous – passionate – who would never hesitate to put her happiness before their own.

But, as I opened my eyes and looked across the street, I was reminded of the unhappy truth of our present circumstances.

Lurking under an umbrella held by his assistant, Trafford, Eamon Lech took a long pull on his nix. He smiled, smoke curling up from his nostrils as he nodded in greeting.

The truth was this: Cadence may have deserved better than me in the long run; but I was all she had at the moment.

With images of Elea's terrified face and destroyed body still fresh in my mind, a rage flared within me, deep and hot. Shaking with anger, I pushed myself away from the wall and strode straight towards Lech and his companion.

I stopped so close to the ambassador that Trafford had to move the umbrella higher, lest I knock it out of his spindly hand. I pointed at the now dark Ergo Sum building. "Did you have anything to do with what happened?"

Lech waved off my accusation like it was so much foul air. "No, of course not." His free hand fell into his coat pocket, and he shrugged. "Even if I did, though, what would you do? What could you do? We both know the EO aren't investigating what happened to Elea Cerf, because there was no crime committed." He leaned forward, grinning. "Animanecrons aren't people, Mr. Hale. Not in the eyes of the law."

"The law is wrong." My short nails began to dig into the palms of my hands. "And laws can change."

Lech laughed. "And who's going to change them?" He shook his head, nose wrinkling. "Don't put too much faith in Representative Peyton. He's a politician, after all. They're not known for keeping their campaign promises." Reaching forward, he clasped my shoulder, squeezing. "But ask around, Mr. Hale: I am known for keeping mine."

"Chance?"

I spun around; it never failed to amaze me how something as substantial as Cadence could move so silently. She stood behind me in the street, her eyes wide with concern. She stepped up onto the sidewalk, and was about to say something, when she caught full sight of my conversational companion. Her inky blue eyes widened, and she froze.

"You're Eamon Lech," she said, her voice hushed. "The Charcornacian ambassador."

Lech examined Cadence with obvious glee, his smile widening as he leaned forward, his hand outstretched. "Pleasure to–"

Cadence's fist connected with Lech's face with a resounding crack. Letting out a sharp yelp, the man folded in on himself as if all the bones had just been pulled from his body. Cadence stood above him, her face impassive except for a light in her eyes that could have ignited ice.

"Mr. Lech!" shouted Trafford, dropping the umbrella to steady his employer.

"Cay!" I exclaimed, my eyes wide, mouth agape.

"Ira, that–" shouted Cadence, drawing herself up to her full height, her fist held out in front of her like it was a deadly weapon, "–was for Bunker 1202, you chestat fertal con tekker!"

"You bitch! My nose!" Still doubled over, Lech swung round towards his assistant, one hand trying and failing to staunch the blood gushing freely down his face. "Trafford!"

Trafford dug a dry handkerchief out of his back pocket and started to move his hand towards Lech's face. "Sir, let me–"

"Give me that!" The injured ambassador ripped the handkerchief out of Trafford's hand and pressed it to his face, straightening and snarling even as he scurried backwards. "Control your toy, Hale, or I'll break it!"

Cadence stalked after the retreating man, her teeth bared. "Come on and try it! Try it, you coward!"

I stepped in front of her and attempted to hold her back. "Cay, Cay, Cay–!" I might as well have tried to hold back the tide. She pushed against me, and we stumbled several feet down the sidewalk after the retreating Charcornacians. I finally managed to get her attention with a final shout of her full name. "Cadence!"

She blinked down at me and stopped walking, some of the fire dying in her eyes. I rubbed her shoulders and met her gaze. "Let him go, just: let him go. He's not worth it."

Cadence's chest began to heave as she sucked in large breaths. Her eyes darted around the street for a moment before settling on me, her brows furrowing. "What the hell was Eamon Lech doing here?"

I sighed, looking over my shoulder in time to see the pair of men disappearing around the corner. "Following me, probably."

I could have sharpened knives on the look Cadence shot me. She grabbed my hand, squeezing it tight. "You? Why?" She shook her head and gritted her teeth. "Sinc, Chance, that man is evil. A killer."

I nodded. "I know it, Cay; I know it." I looked back at her from the corner of my eye, the ghost of a smile playing around my lips. "Good punch, by the way."

She rolled her eyes, but I saw a sickly smile pass over her features. "Thank you." She tapped a rhythm against the back of my hand. "It was my first."

13

Chapter 13

It was four in the morning by the time we made it back to our apartment, and even my concern for Cadence couldn't keep me from yawning. Upon manifesting this physical sign of exhaustion, Cadence was most insistent that I head for bed.

It was after eleven the next morning before I dragged myself out to the kitchen, only to observe that Cadence was nowhere to be found. I did a quick check for her in the living room, but as she was also absent there, I could only assume that she too had taken to bed. I took advantage of her absence to brew up a fresh pot of dark black coffee and, after retrieving the holo-puck from my bedside table, decided to see how my old friend was faring on this rainy morning.

I dialed Henry's holo-puck and waited for the technology to connect, placing my own puck flat on the marble kitchen island.

Within moments, the puck buzzed and flashed into life, and my friend's tired face lurched into frame.

I leaned against the kitchen counter. "Henry, love of my life," I said, examining his fuzzy holographic features. "How are you holding up?"

He ran his hand through his brown hair, doubtless attempting to bring order to the chaos. "Not too badly, for not having slept."

I shot him an incredulous look, my brows knitting together. "Did you stay with Simone all night?"

"I couldn't just leave her," he said, sighing as he sat and reclined back against the headrest of his bed. "And there was her daughter, and then today I've been handling things for Ergo Sum the best I can – making sure everyone knows what's happened and, of course, what's not happening." The sour purse of his lips gave way to a curious, hopeful smile. "Speaking of, how did you and Cadence fare last night?"

I drew a hand down my face, rubbing at my stubble. "Early days yet, but we didn't uncover much beyond the obvious."

Henry grew serious once more, lowering the volume of his voice. "Is Cadence alright? I can't imagine seeing... I don't imagine that was easy for her."

"You know Cadence," I said, resting my forearms against the countertop. "She says she's alright, but who knows what's really going on inside those processors of hers."

"You always seem to."

I swallowed and looked away, avoiding his pointed stare. "Yes...well..."

Cadence walked around the corner and into the kitchen,

cream-colored shorts slung low on her hips, her hair a curled and messy halo around her head. She glanced at the projection hovering above the counter and mustered a smile. "Good morning, Henry."

"Morning, Cadence." Henry inclined his head in greeting.

With her usual disregard for my personal space, Cadence draped herself against my back, her arms dangling limp in front of my chest while her chin rested on top of my shoulder. "Do you think Simone would be up to answering a few questions today, Henry?"

Henry licked his lips, trying and failing to suppress a tired grin as his eyes flickered between Cadence and myself. "When?"

Cadence rolled her head side to side, humming, before answering: "An hour or two?"

Nodding, Henry heaved himself back into an upright position. "I'll send Chance the address and let her know you're coming. I'm sure she'd welcome the company and the distraction."

"Wonderful, thank you."

Cadence slid herself off me and the sensation was not unlike the removal of a heated blanket. The sudden cool made me shiver, and I shot her a glare which she completely ignored.

The amusement in Henry's voice was clear. "Well, I'll let you two get ready. Keep me updated. And if you need anything..."

"We'll let you know." I nodded, finger hovering over the 'end' button on the holo-puck. "Goodbye, Henry. Get some rest."

"Will do. Bye."

Henry's visage flickered out of existence. I stood up, rolling out the muscles in my back and shoulders.

"Chance."

I turned to see Cadence standing in front of the open re-frigerator door, shiny silver spoon in one hand, open rose hip yogurt in the other. Facing me, her foot was holding the door open, letting out a steady stream of chilled air. But it wasn't half as cold as the look in her eyes as she stared at me. At last, she spoke again, the words tight and clipped as they shot from her lips: "Why was Eamon Lech at Ergo Sum last night?" Her frown deepened and she stabbed the spoon into the yogurt cup. "You said he was following you."

I fell back against the kitchen island, gazing heavenward. "I'm sorry; I shouldn't have said anything. I should have just ignored him."

Her eyes narrowed. "But you couldn't. Why?"

I chewed the inside of my mouth for a moment, crossing my arms over my chest. "Charcornac is – or rather was – a client of Halcyon Enterprises. They were heavy users of our DAT products."

"DAT?"

I met her eyes. "Defensive Application Technologies."

Cadence blinked. She looked down at her breakfast, stirring her yogurt around its biodegradable cup. "I... I didn't know Halcyon Enterprises sold weapons."

Squirming against the hard marble, I shook my head. "Nei-ther did I. Certainly not on the scale..." I heard the excuse on the tip of my tongue and hated myself for it. I licked my lips and rubbed compulsively at my unshaved face. "Suffice to say, I stepped in and put a stop to the Charcornacians' supply of DAT. They sent Lech to persuade me to reconsider, but he's been extremely aggressive in his negotiations."

I watched as Cadence's grip on her spoon became a stranglehold. "Frig, he's a monster."

There was a tremor in her voice that I had never heard before. I pushed myself off the counter and stared at her, my mouth going dry. But her focus remained on her food, her jaw tight, her shoulders stooped. She took in a deep breath and shook her head. "The way he talks about my people, about what's happening on Whiston – you can tell he thinks his cause is righteous. That our destruction is necessary. But more than that..." She looked at me from under her brow, her eyes glowing like lanterns. "I think he enjoys it."

"I don't doubt it." I reached out for her, but then thought better of it, my outstretched hand balling into a fist. "I banned him from the Halcyon Enterprises building, so I think he was trying to get my attention on neutral ground."

She lifted her head and shook her hair out of her face. "Do you think he had something to do with Elea's murder?"

I shrugged. "He said he didn't, but I don't have a reason in the world to believe him."

With a sharp exhale of breath from her nose, Cadence took up her spoon and popped another helping of yogurt into her mouth. "We'll have to look into it," she mumbled. Spoon still held on her tongue, she walked past me and patted my shoulder. "Don't worry about Lech, Chance. I'll keep you safe from him."

Sitting in companionable silence on our way to Simone's abode, I silently berated myself for not telling Cadence the whole truth about my entanglement with Eamon Lech. As we rode up the elevator to Simone's apartment, I watched Cadence from the corner of my eye, chewing the inside of my mouth, lost in thought. I didn't like keeping secrets from her, but I couldn't know how she would react to learning that Lech had threatened her. On the other hand, if I did what Lech was demanding, and didn't explain to Cadence that it was all to protect her, she would never forgive me.

It was an impossible situation – but it paled in comparison to the hell Simone Harlow was facing.

When the elevator doors opened, Simone was there to greet us, standing in the entryway in the same clothes from the night before. If she had gotten any sleep, it didn't show, but she managed the smallest, welcoming smile as we stepped out of the lift.

"Morning, you two." Simone stepped to one side, her hand sweeping out behind her. "Won't you come in?"

"Thank you, Ms. Harlow," I said, following Cadence out of the lift. "We appreciate you taking the time to see us."

Shaking her head, Simone rolled her eyes and started forward into the apartment, hands balled into fists at her sides. "Don't be ridiculous – you and Henry are the only people doing anything about what happened. I want to help in any way I can."

The apartment was spacious but done in a more old-fashioned style than our ultramodern suite. The walls were painted a light, robin's egg blue, and the light fixtures were all made of white ceramics. Floor lamps were scattered down the main hallway, and all of them appeared to be turned on, desperately fighting back the oppressive gloom of the rain clouds outside. The signs of a child were also visible here and there, if one looked closely: a discarded toy car in one corner, gathering dust; a small sippy cup on the edge of a coffee table; a well-worn square of blanket thrown over a chair.

Simone stepped over a pile of coloring sheets just inside the living room, pushing her hair back from her face. She shook her head, one hand falling to massage her shoulder. "I'm sorry everything is such a mess!"

"Please, don't think about it." I gestured between Cadence and myself. "We're the ones who are intruding."

She gave us a weak smile, but it couldn't blot out the puffy redness under her eyes, or the rumpled state of her clothes. "Well, I've–" Her smile fell abruptly, her stare intensifying somewhere near my left leg.

I glanced down and was met by a pair of wide, hazel eyes at the level of my thigh. I blinked at the small child and tilted my head to one side. She mimicked the movement, one hand stuck in the corner of her mouth. But being more top-heavy than I, the motion seemed to throw her off-balance. She bumped gently into me and wrapped an arm around my leg to steady herself. I had to spread them a little to make room for the ridiculously fat plush dog she was also clutching.

Simone moved towards the little girl, one arm outstretched. "Ayla, what are you doing out here?"

The child regarded the hand with distrust for a moment, pulling back into me. She looked back up, a spit-slicked finger sliding out of her mouth as her jaw dropped open. I smothered a smile and gave her a shrug. Finding no answers with me, she finally waddled towards the embrace of her mother, holding onto her hand tightly. The plush dog's feet skittered over the ground as she walked. She brought it up to her chest when she spoke, wrapping an arm around its neck. "Bernard is hungry. He wants cookies and milk and ice cream."

This at least elicited a genuine chuckle from Simone, who leaned down to wrap her arms around the child, heaving her up into her arms with a sigh. "Oh, does he?" The child nodded emphatically, her curly black hair jumping all around her head. Simone curled a finger into Ayla's chest, tickling her affectionately. "Sweetie, you just had your lunch an hour ago."

The child was not to be dissuaded, and she twisted away from her mother's prodding fingers, leaning out of her arms, throwing her head back dramatically. "I know I did! But Bernard didn't! He didn't have any!"

Simone was preparing a rebuttal when a loud chime rang out from the next room. It trilled on and on, and I assumed it was her incoming call tone. She looked back towards it with a tired frown, placing her daughter onto the floor with a huff. She ran a hand down her legs and began backing out of the room. "Excuse me for a moment, won't you?" Cadence and I both nodded. Simone gestured to the sideboard just before she rounded the corner, putting on another brave smile. "Please, help yourself to a drink if you'd like."

Swinging her arms behind her back, Cadence wandered over to the sideboard. I was about to follow her when I realized that someone else had already beaten me to it. Ayla shuffled after Cadence energetically, the hem of her pink dress sliding over the carpet. Cadence seemed unaware that she had picked up a devotee, mixing herself a small glass of scotch and amaretto with her usual efficiency. It wasn't until Ayla had pressed herself against the sideboard, pushing herself onto the very tips of her toes to try to see what lay on top of it, that Cadence finally took note of the small lifeform next to her.

I don't mind admitting that I was very interested in seeing how my dear friend would react to the lovely little thing. I leaned back against the doorframe, running my thumb over my bottom lip and grinning.

Cadence stared down at the child unblinkingly. The child returned the stare, the calmness of hers marred by the constant huffing and grunting she was making as she attempted to reach the top of the sideboard. Cadence leaned back to get a full view of the child, her eyes trailing over the pink dress, curly hair, and stubby red feet with scientific detachment. After a moment, she bent down sharply at the waist, her own uncouth mane falling into her eyes as she politely inquired, "Would you like a drink?"

Ayla nodded emphatically. Cadence handed her the drink she had just mixed, which the child was forced to grip with both hands and reached for another glass to make a second for herself.

I was across the room in a heartbeat, snatching the glass away from the child even as she was struggling to lift it to her lips. "Cadence!"

Cadence turned to me sharply, clutching her half-filled glass to her chest. I glanced down at the child, checking my language as much as I could, and lowering my voice lest her mother become concerned. "What the hell are you doing?"

Cadence's brow furrowed, her mouth pulling down into an offended scowl. "What?"

"You can't give alcohol to a child!"

She drew her head back, eyes flicking between my face and Ayla. "But she asked for some?"

Ayla pounded a foot onto the floor. I turned around to look

at her. Her bottom lip was sticking out, her hands akimbo on her hips. "I'm not a child. I'm six."

I raised my eyebrows, but nodded at her before turning back to Cadence, who was now taking large sips of her drink. "You can't just give children whatever they ask for, especially not alcohol. Alright? It's very bad for them."

"Oh?" Cadence considered this. "I can see where certain properties of alcohol could lead to slowed neural development and stunted growth in most youth."

"One day, I'm going to be ten bajillion feet tall."

Cadence leaned to one side to see around me, meeting Ayla's gaze evenly and nodding in encouragement. "That would be very impressive."

The little girl was twisting the bottom of her dress around her hands, clutching and pulling at the fabric like it was a constant discomfort to her. She bit into her bottom lip as Cadence walked past her to the couch, settling into it with a quiet sigh.

I was staring after Cadence in frank amazement and had forgotten about the other lady in the room until I felt a tugging on my trouser leg. Ayla took a step or two back once she had procured my attention, so she didn't have to crane her neck quite so much.

"Do you know where Elea is?" There was a matter-of-factness in the tone of her voice that greatly endeared her to me. Ayla dropped her hands to her sides, her dog ending up face first on the carpet. "She hasn't come over. She always comes over for breakfast, but she didn't come over today."

My heart seized in my chest, and I bit into my own bottom lip at the question. I glanced around for help and found none. I crouched down to Ayla's level, rubbing the back of my neck. She stared at me expectantly, the edges of a displeased frown on her face. I moved my lips over several beginning words and found all of them wanting before I alighted upon a happy deflection. "Have you asked your mummy?"

Ayla sighed, rolling her eyes, and turning away. "She wouldn't say, she just cried."

I cinched my eyes shut and rolled my lips over my teeth. When I opened them again, Ayla had made her way around the front of the couch and was peering at Cadence suspiciously. In a sudden panic, I crossed to the pair, fearful that Cadence would unleash her cool truths upon the impressionable child.

"Do you know where Elea is?"

Cadence straightened in her seat, her eyes widening and flicking up to meet mine. I slashed my hand across my throat, hopeful Cadence would correctly interpret that as a sign to stay silent, but I don't think she ever saw it. She became preoccupied with assisting Ayla in scaling the couch. Ayla was halfway onto the cushion, her legs kicking in the air. "I need another person for my tea party."

Cadence sat her drink down on the table in front of her and lifted the child up the rest of the way onto the couch, placing her down on the adjacent cushion. The little dear's chest heaved at the effort she had exerted. Cadence's own breath stilled when Ayla crawled into her lap. Her hands hovered awkwardly over the small figure. Ayla, having thus adjusted herself, stared up at Cadence, her fingers returning to her mouth to be chewed on. "She has to come." Ayla's eyes drifted down to the couch. "She promised."

I held my breath. Cadence was staring down at the child the way lionesses sometimes looked at wounded animals – that is, with devouring interest. After a beat of silence, one of her hands came down on Ayla's stubby legs.

"I'm sure she'd be here if she could." A small smile flitted over Cadence's face, but it vanished when the same could not be seen on Ayla's. Cadence began rubbing her legs absentmindedly, her mind whirring. She took a deep breath. "I could come to your tea party?"

Ayla slid off Cadence's lap in an instant, absolutely beaming. She grabbed Cadence's hand and pulled at her until the older woman realized she was meant to follow. I laughed at the sight of Cadence being dragged determinedly from the room by a six-year-old who was chanting, "Yay, yay, yay, yay!"

Simone entered the room at the same moment, catching the tail end of Cadence's ignominious exit. She stared after her, a grin blooming over her face. "Oh no!" Simone walked to me, shaking her head. "Ayla hasn't wheedled another person into one of her tea parties, has she?"

I nodded emphatically, slipping my hands into my trouser pockets. "It would seem so, yes." There were the sounds of clattering plastic and furniture moving from down the hall. I glanced towards it, my heart feeling dangerously light in my chest. "Ayla's a darling girl."

"Yes," said Simone, her smile trembling and beginning to fade. She sat down on the couch Cadence had just vacated, her legs crossed, her hands clasped tightly together. "I'm very lucky the courts gave me full custody." She tapped the bottom of her hands against her knees over and over again, attempting to rally her smile, but ending up with a shambling grimace. "Not that I think her father really wanted her. I don't like to imagine what a man like that would do with a child."

"Oh!" I took a step back, shaking my head. It had never occurred to me to think of Ayla as blood-related to the woman in front of me. "I'm sorry. I just... assumed Ayla was adopted."

Simone shifted to face me, brows raised over her dark oval eyes. "Because of Elea and I?"

I nodded, shrugging.

Simone smacked her lips, shaking her head. "No." She haltingly leaned back into the couch, casting quick, sharp glances at me from under her eyelashes. She cleared her throat, her voice quieting. "You have to understand, it's not women I'm attracted to, it's just – just Elea." Tears stuttered on the edges of her eyes. She lifted a hand to her lips. She swallowed. "Or it was." She shook her head again, this time sending the captive water sliding down her cheeks. "She was special to me in every way."

I shifted where I stood, hands clenching and relaxing in my pockets. "Miss Harlow–" The formality hung in the air like an unpleasant odor. I pursed my lips, walking towards her and taking up the seat beside her. I placed my hand over her own. "Simone. I'm so, so sorry."

Both of her hands gripped mine, her long, blue fingernails digging into my skin. The tears were running down her face freely now, but no sound came from her for several minutes. At last, she tore her eyes away from mine, saying simply: "I don't know what I'm going to do."

There was emptiness in the thought, in her voice, which hurt more than all the sadness she could have mustered behind it.

She shook her head, turning away from me. She brought her hand up to her face, wiping away the trail of her tears as she sniffed. "And Ayla's asking questions. What do I tell her? How do I tell her?" Her hand massaged her temple and her eyes flickered shut. "The world doesn't make any sense anymore."

I knew the way she was feeling all too well; the hopelessness, the helplessness when someone was taken from you so suddenly. I took a deep breath, patting her hand. "We – Cadence and I – we're going to do everything we can to help it make sense."

"I just keep thinking..." She released my hands to bring both of her own up to her face, wiping the tears off her cheeks. "...that if I hadn't let her go back to the office alone, none of this would have happened."

"You can't think like that." I reached over to her and placed my hand on her shoulder. "If you'd gone with her, who knows? Neither of you might be here right now, and then what would happen to Ayla?"

"You're right, you're right." Shaking her head, a long sigh stuttered out of her as she collapsed back into the couch away from my hand. "I have to think of Ayla now."

I looked down the hall towards where her daughter and Cadence had disappeared, and then back to Simone. I thought about what I would do if Cadence were taken from me and shivered, turning away from the thought with an abruptness that left me nauseous. I forced myself to focus on the case at hand, to do what Cadence would do if she were in my shoes, and I found myself asking Simone, "What was Elea doing back at the office so late?"

Simone shrugged. "She received some kind of emergency

message on her tablet asking for a meeting. She didn't give me the details, just that she had to go."

"Did this happen often? Emergency meetings, urgent messages?"

"More often than you might think" The tremulous smile returned to Simone's lips as she rubbed her hands together on her lap. "There was no problem too big or too small for Elea to handle; not for one of our clients."

"The refugees you mean," I interjected.

She wiggled her head from side to side. "Mainly, yes."

"How many refugees is Ergo Sum currently supporting?"

"We have sixty animanecrons staying with us at the moment, but we've provided aid and information to well over five hundred individuals." Simone's tired eyes met mine and she shook her head. "I know what you're thinking, but none of them could have done this."

I stretched my arm over the back of the couch, facing her openly. "How can you be so sure?"

"If you want suspects," she said, heaving herself off the couch with a grunt, "I can give you suspects: any member of the A.F.O; the Charcornacian Government; hundreds of normal, everyday humans wandering around this city who just didn't like the thought of living next door to an animanecron, and finally decided to do something about it." Arms crossed high over her chest, Simone shook her hair out of her face. "Elea was putting her life on the line to help get people off Whiston and other Charcornacian controlled planets; we receive death threats every day."

"We should start there."

Simone and I jumped at the sound of Cadence's voice. I looked up to find my dark-haired companion peering at us from around the corner of the hallway, her intense gaze softened by the spirals of sparkling tinsel which hung from the plastic tiara I could only assume Ayla had placed atop her head.

Cadence stepped back into the living room, her focus on Simone. "Where would these death threats be? Did you keep them?"

Simone craned her head around to check that Ayla was not likewise hiding behind the hallway corner before continuing, her volume low. "We did as a matter of fact. They're all back at the office, on my computer. Here." The bereaved woman walked out of the living room and into the kitchen. She wrestled a lanyard loose from a pile of hard copy keys and walked back to us, holding a dangling plastic rectangle out to Cadence. "Take my key card. My office is right off the second-floor landing - the one farthest to the right. Look through whatever you like. I can't... I can't go back there right now."

"Of course," I said, hoping that Cadence would have the emotional intelligence not to push her on this issue.

Cadence took the keycard, lanyard and all, with a nod. "There is something else. Do you know a reczec here in Römer we could contact?"

"A reczec?" Simone repeated the word as if she hadn't heard it quite right. Her eyes narrowed in a squint, and she blinked, rubbing the back of her neck before answering: "Ah, yes, there's one who's done work for us at the center. But, why?"

"We think it would be best if Elea's body was... examined," I explained, finding no more delicate way to put the truth.

Simone frowned. "Is there some question as to how she died?"

"We won't know for certain until someone qualified has taken a look at her." I stood as well, reaching up to place a hand on Simone's shoulder. "We just want to be absolutely sure we're not missing anything; you understand?"

Jaw tight, Simone placed her hand over mine and squeezed before nodding in assent. "I'll give Bartholomew a call. Let him know to meet you at the center."

"Cadence..."

We turned as one body to find Ayla standing in the mouth of the hallway, her arms limp at her sides, her own plastic crown crooked atop her tiny head. She stared up at us, her gaze passing from adult to adult before settling on the animanecron woman she had initially addressed. "Are you leaving?"

"I have to go to work now," said Cadence, removing the plastic tiara from her head with a flourish. Kneeling to Ayla's level, she presented the crown to the child with a bow, looking very much like a knight pledging fealty to a young queen. "Thank you for the tea, your highness. It was delicious."

Ayla's bottom lip pooched out in a pout. She took the tiara from Cadence's hands, picking at the tinsel that decorated its points, and stared into Cadence's eyes with unabashed misery. "But I don't want you to go."

Cadence frowned and pushed her feet back under her body, rising to her full height. "I'm sorry; I have to."

Ayla sighed. She looked away from Cadence to the floor. "Will you come back?"

I watched as Cadence blinked once, slowly, and then her eyes widened in what would have been a comical flash of panic had it not been so sincere. It seemed she grasped the implications of making promises to a child of this age, and she jerked her head round to stare up first at me, and then turned to Simone, swallowing hard.

Simone stepped forward and swept the small child into her arms, lifting her so her bottom rested just above her hip. "Of course, she'll come back, my love!"

She rubbed the tip of her nose against Ayla's, which sent both child and mother squirming and giggling. It was good to see a smile on Simone's face, however threadbare. Having placated her daughter, Simone returned her attention to us, her smile losing none of its shine, but gaining a hint of desperation. "Please, do come back. You're both welcome here any time. Anything you need, it's yours."

"Just leave it to us," I said. "We'll get everything sorted."

14

Chapter 14

District 16 appeared cozier and quainter in the grey daylight than it had in the rainy night; I found myself appreciating the charm of the ramshackle buildings and archaic streets as we walked to Ergo Sum. Simone's keys granted us access to the building's lobby, but somehow it felt wrong to switch on the blinding overhead lights, so the pair of us stood in the dim room, staring around at the quiet space by the light of the weak sun, the only sound the murmur from the travelogues, which still played on loop around the room.

"Right," I said, hands on my hips. "Shall we have a better look around while we wait for this chap of Simone's to show up?"

Cadence rolled her eyes in a rare moment of cheek, chiding: "He's not a 'chap', he's a reczec." She strode past me into the lobby. "But, yes – we may as well be productive."

I made a face at her back before striking out in the opposite direction, heading for the large oval reception desk. Behind the desk, I found a paper logbook, filled with tallies, names, and dates of which I could frankly make neither head nor tails. At last, I determined that it was a general accounting of the busyness of the space, who was at the desk, and when.

I flipped through the logbook and glanced up at Cadence. "I thought you did very well with Ayla, by the way."

Cadence turned away from the wall-bolted screen she was watching. "It turns out that children are not so different from adults. Except I think I might prefer them. They're more... honest."

I quirked an eyebrow and refocused my attention on the endless list of names and dates in front of me. The logbook went back months, and people's penmanship often left something to be desired. "They certainly don't hesitate to let you know what they're thinking."

"I like that," said Cadence, crossing to one of the low square coffee tables. She picked up one of the complimentary readers that sat there, turning it on and flipping through its contents. "I'll admit, sometimes I don't have the slightest idea what's going on in your head."

"Me? I'm an open book," I lied with gusto.

"You're a mystery," she looked up and met my gaze with her customary boldness. "One I don't think I'll ever quite figure out."

I almost told her then. Maybe I should have. Maybe things would have turned out differently if I had just admitted that, if being a mystery was what was keeping her with me, I wanted to be uncrackable. Because I never wanted her to leave.

Instead, we both turned at the sound of the front door

opening and closing. In the lobby, a tall, lanky man stood partly in shadow. He sported a large puff of bouncy black hair and carried a bulky messenger bag slung diagonal over his chest. Even from this distance, I could see that the man's arms were covered, from wrist to elbow, in cascading triangles, geometric tattoos that were reminiscent, but not identical in style, to Cadence's. The starkest difference between the two markings were the colors that danced beneath his skin. I remembered Elea laughing at my assumption that Cadence's phoenix was a tattoo rather than what it was – a printed circuit board, a piece of technology, an inorganic part of an inorganic machine. Where Cadence's PCB was easy to mistake for a human tattoo, this animanecron's tech was obvious by the way electronic light in rainbow colors flashed up and down the sigils, illuminating him even in the unlit room.

I admit to staring openly as he walked towards us, my eyes following his arm as he raised his hand in a wave.

"Hello," he said in an airy voice. "Are you the people I'm supposed to meet?"

Cadence returned the wave, oblivious to my discomfort. "Are you Bartholomew?"

The man stopped just in front of Cadence, formed a complex pattern with his hands, and shook them at her, bowing his head. "Bartholomew Grange, at your service, miscisk." He smiled at her, his brown eyes bright in his dark face. "You must be Cadence Turing. And this–" He turned to me, bowing his head once more. "–is your young man, yes?"

"Yes," said Cadence, answering before I could correct the inaccurate, if flattering, turn of phrase. "This is Chance Hale."

"A pleasure to meet you, sir." He extended his hand to me, and

I noted the long, delicate fingers. "I wish it were under happier circumstances. But life is not often so accommodating."

I shook his hand firmly, clearing my throat and forcing myself to look him in the eye. "Simone explained then?"

"Yes," he said, nodding. "You wish me to look at Elea. Where is she?"

"She's upstairs, in her office," Cadence moved towards him, an arm outstretched as if to help him move. "Here, let us show you–"

He waved away her concern, but took her arm all the same, patting it congenially. "I know the way well, miscisk."

I allowed the animanecrons to lead the way, trailing behind them as we headed towards the stairs that led up to the offices above the lobby.

"So," I said. "You knew Elea. Did you know her well?"

"I did, I did. She helped me get my papers to come here. I was in the visa pool on Khalaman. It looked like it was going to take years, and the Charcornacians were closing in on the moon. I sent a communique to Ergo Sum. Elea helped me get out before it was too late." He relayed his story with such calmness, such matter-of-factness, that it almost took the sting out of the true horror of his circumstances. He lifted his hand to his chest and patted himself as we climbed the rickety spiral staircase. "I owe her my life. This is the least I can do for her." He turned his head to Cadence as we reached the second-floor landing, and asked, "And where do you come from, miscisk?"

Cadence kept her gaze focused on her feet, but her grip on the man's arm tightened. "Gav, Bunker 1202."

I watched in fascination as Bartholomew's face fell. "Ah." He stopped in the hall and turned to stand in front of Cadence, holding both her hands in his. "I am sorry for you, miscisk. But I am glad you are here with us still."

She squeezed his hands tightly. "Thank you, reczec."

The man mustered up a weak smile and released her, walking down the hall towards Elea's office, stopping in the doorway. If the sight inside affected him adversely, he was skilled at hiding it. His tongue flicked out to wet his lips as he worked his messenger bag up over his head, brown eyes taking in everything.

"I will let you know what I find," he called out to us. "If you have other work to be getting on with, don't let me stop you."

With that, he disappeared inside the room. Cadence shifted her weight from foot to foot, unusually, but understandably, ill at ease. She was scowling, looking as if part of her wanted to follow the man into the room, while the rest of her wanted to do anything but. I ghosted my hand over her shoulder blades and leaned towards her, my other arm stretched down the hallway in the opposite direction.

"Shall we investigate Simone's office?" I asked. "Give Bartholomew space and time to work?"

"Yes." Cadence shook herself before heading down the hall. "Yes, that's a good idea."

We made our way back to the landing, and the trio of offices that could be accessed from there. We walked into the third as Simone had told us, the lights flickering to life as we entered. The room was small and sparse, filled to bursting with little more than a tiny desk, two file cabinets and a chair. Cold and damp permeated the space, and I shivered despite myself, shoving my hands deeper into my coats' pockets.

Cadence set to work right away. She scooted behind the cramped desk and began pulling out the drawers of the arcane file cabinets, her fingers flicking over the labels and papers.

I followed her, my steps slow, and my mind turning over the exchange I had witnessed between her and Bartholomew. The man had spoken so freely of his past, of the tragedy that had brought him here. Cadence, on the other hand, avoided talking about her flight from Whiston – of what had driven her from her home, of what she had done to survive, and of how she had come to be here, with me. I wondered if she worried I would judge her, or if she simply wished to leave the past behind – as if any of us ever could.

I watched as she pulled a stack of files out of a drawer and placed them on the desk beside me. I picked up a stack of discs that lay piled on the edge of the desk, labeled with an incomprehensible series of numbers and letters. "Cadence?"

"Yes?"

"Why don't you ever talk about Whiston?"

The folders she had begun to lift from the bottom drawer dropped back into place with a thud. She stayed stooped over, her back to me.

I could feel a heaviness in my chest being lifted, the relief of setting loose words too long unspoken. I could only pray the weight of them were not now crushing her. I swallowed, tapping the discs in my hand against my opposite palm. "Why don't you ever talk about your family, or how you came here, or...or...?" I shrugged, brows rising and falling in time with my shoulders. "Or any of that kind of stuff?"

Cadence stood slowly. "Why?" She turned to one side, and the puzzled expression stamped over her features told me that the question was not directed at me, but at herself. She leaned back against the cluttered desk. Her chest rose and fell once with a single labored breath before stilling. "Why? I...why? It's..."

The rain pattering against the windows became deafening in the silence that followed. I waited, licking my lips, trying to ignore the growing thought that I never should have let the question slip past them in the first place.

I was about to tell her to forget it, to just keep looking for clues, when she turned around to face me fully. She avoided my gaze, her eyes flitting round the room like leaves in a gust of wind. "I..." Her hand closed into a fist. She pushed it into the top of the desk, gritting her teeth. "I do not talk about it because it is painful."

"But you know you can, don't you?"

She looked at me at last, her brows drawing up in confusion. She seesawed back and forth, her fist the fulcrum point of her movement. "You...want to hear me talk about it?"

I let the discs fall onto the top of the desk. "Well... no, I guess, not really."

Cadence blinked, frowning. I stepped towards her, waving my hands. "No, no, I didn't mean–" I let out a sharp breath and bit down hard on the inside of my mouth. Sighing, I looked out the window over Cadence's shoulder. "I...I care about you, Cay. Deeply. So, I can't say that I would particularly enjoy hearing about some of the...the horrible things I know you must have gone through. Knowing you've been hurt..." I brought a hand to my chest and squeezed the flesh over my heart. "It hurts me too."

I felt her fingertips, warmer and softer than anything else

on the planet, brush against the back of my hand. The precious rhythm I had memorized so long tapped against my skin.

I opened my eyes, my breath catching in my throat to find her mere inches from me. Her ink-blue eyes stared balefully into mine. She gave a small nod, clicking her tongue off the back of her teeth. "Tris, I don't want to hurt you."

I shook my head. "I know. But, sometimes, for humans, anyway, when something bad has happened it makes us feel better to talk about it." I reached up, taking her hand in mine. "And if it will help in any way, I want you to know that you can talk to me." I smiled and brushed my lips against her knuckles. "About that or just...anything."

Cadence gave a single, slow blink. She pulled back from me and turned to resume her work. "Sinc, I shall have to think about it, Chance."

"Oh, sure, yes!" I shoved my hands into my trouser pockets, shoulders coming up to brush the bottom of my earlobes as I babbled. "I didn't mean – we don't have to, of course. And not, not here. Or if you need–" I cleared my throat, grateful her back was to me, and she couldn't see the miserable expression on my face.

At a loss for how to contribute to our search in a meaningful way, I focused my attention on the desk beside me, pulling out the battered, rolling chair and dropping down into it. The computer set up was a touch archaic, the screen bulky, resting on top of the desk on a tower of plastic, the drive itself a four inch by six-inch rectangle fastened to the side of the under desk. I depressed the 'on' button and, while it struggled to life, busied myself with looking through the drawers.

In the top drawer was an array of writing utensils, fasteners, extra holopucks and data chips, and one fresh, yet full address book, its pages bulging. I thumbed through the hand-sized tome with a frown, my brow furrowed as the pages fluttered. "There's an awful lot of paper records here for an organization that dealt with beings as advanced as animanecrons. You'd think we were back in the dark ages."

"I imagine that was for security's sake." Cadence let out a deep breath through her nose. "The Charcornacians and people like the A.F.O. have been known to hack into pro-ani organizations and steal data to better target animanecrons. You can't hack this," she said, flapping a file folder at me over her shoulder.

"Smart," I responded. I sighed and picked up the address book, sliding it into my jacket pocket. "If a bit annoying now." I opened the bottom desk drawer and groaned as the sight of even more hanging file folders. "It's going to take forever to get through all this."

I shoved all the folders towards the back of the drawer to go through them one at a time. The shifting of the papers revealed the bottom of the drawer and, sitting there, a long, dark shape.

My head falling to one side, I reached in and took hold of the object. My fingers closed around something solid but covered in velvet. I knew what I was grasping the moment my hand brushed against it, and my heart began to plummet towards my stomach.

Taking the jewelry box out of the drawer, I placed it on the desktop in front of me. With a swallow, I flicked the case open.

The necklace which sat nestled inside the black velvet lining was elegant and beautiful. A thick golden chain held a series of fourteen square cut emeralds, separated from each other by flower-shaped, dangling diamonds.

It was a piece that would have looked exquisite laying across Elea Cerf's throat.

"Cadence..." Her name escaped my lips in a hushed whisper.

She was at my side in an instant. I looked up at her over my shoulder. Her wide eyes met mine. "Is that...?"

Nodding, I looked back at the bauble held in my fingertips. "A betrothal necklace." I sat back heavily in the desk chair, my hand coming up to my mouth. "Oh lord. Simone was going to ask Elea to marry her."

"Would that have even been possible?"

My eyes remained fixed on the necklace in the rectangular case in front of me, even as I shook my head from side to side. "Legally? I have no idea."

"Sinc, what a beautiful sentiment, though."

I swallowed, my mouth suddenly dry. I thought of the little family we had left earlier that morning; thought of Ayla and Simone and how Elea must have fit with their day-to-day existence, making them happy, making them better.

Just like Cadence did for me.

My lips firmed into a hard line. "I'm going to find those death threats Simone mentioned."

I swiped Simone's keycard against the computer drive; the machine, powered up at last, flashed into life. What greeted me on the desktop was a well-tended collection of clearly labeled folders. I selected one folder titled simply 'Holomessages - Threats', my scowl deepening as the screen flooded with holomessage files. Pushing air through my clenched teeth, I sat back, prepared myself for the worst, and waved for the computer to play all.

The holoplayer at the edge of the desk lit up, and a litany of hate spewed forth from the computer's speakers, as holo after holo played. Most were only a few seconds long, their images either distorted, masked faces, or simply hands making vile gestures at the camera as their owners screeched or growled out their objections to Ergo Sum's very existence. After a few minutes I had had my fill, my chest aching with rage. I was about to tell Cadence that the death threats, while horrible, were too numerous and too vague to be of any real use to us, when a man's face flickered onto the holoplayer, snarling, mask-less, and addressing Elea by name.

"Cerf! Listen here you fragger bitch – you stay out of my goddamn business, or I'll put you on the fucking scrap heap where you belong! Get between me and mine again and I'll rip your goddamn head open and piss on your innards! Fuck off, fragger!"

"Charming," I muttered.

"And specific. Unlike the others." Cadence leaned over me, her hand warm on my shoulder. "Any identifying information on that holo?"

I called up the relevant file on the computer and scanned the information attached to it. "Just that the message was received three days ago from a...well, looks like a burner puck, if I had to guess."

"Hm." She turned to look at me. "Is there any way we can save this and take it with us?"

"Sure..." I rifled through the top desk drawer for the holopuck I had found there earlier. With a few well practiced movements,

I attached the puck to the computer, dragged and dropped the file onto the device and watched as it uploaded.

"Here we go." I unplugged the holopuck from the computer and tossed it up and down in my hand. "Don't know what good it'll do, though. We're not the EO; it's not like we can run it through any kind of Facial Recognition System."

Cadence caught the puck in midair and examined it with a wrinkled nose and furrowed brow. "Oh, I'm sure we'll think of something."

"Miss Turing! Mr. Hale!"

Bartholomew's voice echoed in the otherwise empty building. Cadence and I moved quickly out of Simone's office, not bothering to put things back the way we found them, a certain urgency to the man's shout drawing us into the hall. We found Bartholomew leaning around the lip of the doorless office, beckoning for us to join him. Sharing a look, Cadence returned the holopuck to me and we followed the reczec back inside the ransacked room.

The office was just as much of a mess today as it was yesterday. Today, however, grey light poured in through the open blinds of the office window, illuminating everything with an additional gloomy glow. I entered first, pausing as I took in the sight of Bartholomew's gear spread over the top of a table. On it, several datapads flashed and hummed, while a collapsible microscope sat unfolded and powered on, the illuminator blazing.

Bartholomew stood over Elea's body, the tablecloth with which I had covered her drawn down to her waist. I admit I was relieved to see that he had turned her on her side, her face to the wall, her back towards us. He looked up as we entered, one hand on Elea's shoulder, as if comforting her.

"I have found something very interesting." Bartholomew gestured to the deep gouges in Elea's skin. "These scratches on her neck..."

Cadence nodded, craning her head around my shoulder to get a better view. "Yes, we noticed those as well."

He grasped his delicate hands in front of his hips. "I believe she caused them herself."

I started. "What?"

He nodded and lifted Elea's hand up for our examination. "I found synthetic skin under her fingernails that matches her own. But that is not all." He replaced the limb gently, his voice quiet. "There is... a virus present."

Her eyes widening, Cadence jerked back, pulling her hands to her sides as if she had just touched a hot metal coil. "A virus?"

Bartholomew crossed over to his equipment, talking all the while. "With her main processing board destroyed, I have had to examine her sub tissue matrices for signs of additional damage. When I did, I found indicators that a virus had been introduced into her system sometime immediately prior to her death." He paused with his hand on the head of his collapsible microscope, turning to face us. "In fact, I believe the virus is what caused her death."

I shook my head, looking between the two somber animanecrons. "You are talking about a computer virus, aren't you?"

"Yes, naturally. This one takes the form of nanobots." He tossed his head to some discarded pads and chips that he had piled up to one side. "They nearly destroyed my hardware before

I had a chance to isolate them." He waved Cadence and I forward, indicating the eyepiece of the scope. "Here, take a look."

I gestured for Cadence to precede me, and she leaned over the eyepiece, tucking her hair behind her ear. She stilled and then, with a sharp huff of breath, she withdrew, her face blank as she drew her hand down it.

Glancing at her in concern, I mimicked her previous posture, pressing my face against the scope. The viscous material on the slide was a murky mixture of oil and blood, translucent black and greyish bubbles dotted with clumps of pinkish circles. But within this amalgamation of fluids, something else became visible as my eye focused. Floating between the bubbles, flitting like silverfish, were stark white bulbous-headed creatures, with thin legs trailing behind them. They would attach themselves to a blood vessel, digging their legs into the cell, and after a moment or two, release, and zip back into the oil.

I pulled away from the lens. Bartholomew rubbed at the back of his neck and sighed. "I believe they have been programmed to target inorganic material, infiltrate said material, and then eat away at the structures that keep the material intact. This would destroy her inner systems, wiping her matrices and programs."

I swallowed hard. "How long would an animanecron live with this virus inside them?"

The man shrugged and shook his head. "Minutes at most."

"Frig, I didn't think technology like this existed," said Cadence, her wide-eyed gaze intent on the body beside her.

"Neither did I," admitted Bartholomew, his airy voice heavy with sadness. "But I am here, looking at it, and so are you."

"So," I said, doubtless catching up to the two faster minds in the room. "Her main processing board--"

"Would have been defunct before being incinerated," confirmed the reczec.

Cadence turned away from Elea with a shudder, closing her eyes. "How would this virus be introduced into her system?"

With great care, Bartholomew leaned down and took the slide off the scope's stage. "Like any poison: taken internally somehow, injected or ingested."

Frowning, I dropped my gaze from my companions to the floor, scanning the edges of the room; something about what Bartholomew had just said tugged at a memory. A few feet from the latched door of the incinerator, I located the two crumpled cups I had seen before. Cheap, biodegradable coffee cups, the kind you would find at any convenience store on Römer, they lay against each other, one caved in at the middle, the other ripped down one side.

Reaching out to touch Cadence's back as I passed, I walked towards the discarded coffee cups, taking them up gingerly with my fingertips. Something in the bottom of the caved-in one sloshed as I moved it, and I handled it with even greater care as I returned to the side of my companion.

"I noticed these earlier," I said, offering them to Cadence with a grimace. "But I thought they were just trash that didn't make it to the incinerator."

"Let me see, please?" said Bartholomew. I turned to him, and he took the cups from me.

He handled the crumpled cups as if they were bombs, swiveling around to place them beside the microscope. His long fingers skittered along the tabletop until they alighted on a hand-sized black case, which he flipped open. He withdrew a large eyedropper from the interior and, slowly and carefully, inserted the tip into the caved-in cup. Squeezing the rubber end of the dropper and releasing it, a small amount of brown liquid was sucked into the tube. Bartholomew grabbed a fresh slide from his bag and gingerly pipetted a drop of the liquid onto the glass. He squashed the droplet flat with a square of thin plastic, latched the slide beneath the microscope's objective lens and peered down the eyepiece.

I looked between the two animanecrons and swallowed, discomfited when I noticed that both had ceased breathing.

"Yes, yes," said the reczec at length. "The same nanobots are present in this cup." Bartholomew straightened and took up the cup, holding it out to Cadence with a nod. "This was definitely the delivery device."

Cadence took the biodegradable cup between two of her fingers, holding it up to the buzzing electrical lights above us. Turning it this way and that, she sighed. "And it just so happens to have Elea's shade of lipstick on the rim."

15

Chapter 15

"You needn't worry, miscisk," said Bartholomew, leading Cadence from the room and out into the hallway. "I will see that she is taken care of. You have your work to do, and I have mine."

"Yes," Cadence nodded. "We do have some new leads to follow." She folded her hands together into a complex shape and shook them at the lanky man, bowing her head reverently. "Thank you, reczec. For everything."

Smiling, the man returned the gesture. As Cadence moved towards the stairs, I followed behind her, pausing for a moment on the threshold of the doorway to turn and shake the reczec's hand. "It was very nice to have met you, Bartholomew," I said, putting on a weak smile. "Despite the circumstances."

The tattoos on his arms rippled through a rainbow of colors and he returned my smile with a nod. "You as well, Mr. Hale.

It is good to see an outsider taking an interest in something like this."

I squirmed under his gaze and withdrew my hand. "Yes, well... we all have to do what we can."

"Yes." Bartholomew nodded, his eyes never leaving my face. "Yes, we do."

I bit down hard on the inside of my mouth. Was he asking me to do more? He must have known who I was, what I represented. I had to admit, it was far easier to make the argument about neutrality on the "Ani-Issue" from a 200th floor corner office, than standing in front of a person directly impacted by my company's actions, or lack thereof.

I started to stutter out a response, but Bartholomew was already turning away and heading back into the office, his hand waving behind him. "Goodbye, Mr. Hale. I hope we will speak again."

Disquieted in the extreme, I swallowed down my ill-formed excuses and turned to find Cadence watching me from the landing, a curious quirk to her brow. I moved quickly to her, starting down the stairs in front of her. "Shall we, Cay?"

She nodded, allowing me for once to take the lead without an argument. Moving down the rickety metal steps at a steady pace, I was about to ask Cadence just what our next moves were, exactly, when a sound from below silenced me.

I closed my mouth and my steps slowed. Head quirking to one side, I continued down the spiral staircase, when, once again, a loud rustling reached my ears.

Cadence and I froze on the steps and shared a look. Almost to the bottom of the staircase now, I broke away from her gaze

and peered out into the dim lobby, cursing myself for not thinking to turn all the lights on when we first arrived. From the
darkness, there came the unmistakable sound of a shoe brushing
against carpet.

"Hello?" I called out, my hands curling into fists at my side.

Cadence stepped around me on the narrow stairs with her
usual boldness. "If you're the murderer," she said loudly. "You've
picked a very bad time to return to the scene of the crime."

"In all my years with the Enforcement Office," rang out an
all-too-familiar male voice, "I've never once arrested a murderer
who had returned to the scene of their crime. I think it's a myth."

Brisbois emerged from behind a pillar and into the grey light,
a roguish smile playing over his lips.

Cadence's serious face brightened in a way that made my
stomach twist. She stepped off the bottom step of the staircase
and walked towards Brisbois, smiling for the first time all morning. "Behind every myth is at least one true story, Inspector."

Releasing the inside of my cheek from between my teeth,
I clomped down the stairs. "What the hell are you doing here,
Brisbois?"

He met my glower with a cold stare. "Very nice to see you
too, Mr. Hale." His expression warmed considerably as he lifted
his hand towards the approaching Cadence. "Miss Turing."

"Please, Inspector," Cadence leaned forward, squeezing his
hand tight before shaking it. "After everything we've been
through, I think you can call me Cadence."

Brisbois mimicked her stance, grinning as he met her gaze.
"Charmed."

Quickening my pace, I reiterated my question with more emphasis. "What are you doing here, Brisbois?"

He released Cadence with palpable reluctance and turned to me. "Investigating."

"Investigating what?" I stood next to Cadence and sneered at the slight man. "According to you, no crime has been committed."

"A decision was made by those higher up the food chain than me, Mr. Hale," he answered, frowning. "That doesn't mean I have to like it."

Cadence reached forward and placed her hand on his shoulder. "That is comforting to know, Inspector."

The ghost of a smile returned to his face, and he pressed his hand to his chest. "Oliver, please."

Dropping her hand from him, Cadence tilted her head to one side. "But doesn't that mean you could be reprimanded for looking into this affair?"

He nodded, glancing around the empty Ergo Sum lobby with exaggerated care. "I could. So, I'd appreciate it if you didn't mention to anyone that you found me snooping."

"Of course," said Cadence. "Have you found out anything enlightening, Oliver?"

"Sadly, no." Brisbois sighed, perching himself on the arm of one of the waiting room chairs. "I can't remember the last time I worked a case with such a plethora of suspects. One hardly knows where to begin. I was hoping to find some direction here. What about you two?"

Cadence and I looked at each other. I shook my head in the

negative, but Cadence flicked her gaze between the Inspector and the puck I had stashed away in my pocket.

"If we gave you a face," she asked at length. "Could you run it through the EO FaRS?"

Brisbois blinked. The man looked her up and down before answering, "Our Facial Recognition System? Possibly. It might raise questions, though."

She proffered her hand to me. With reluctance, I dug the holo-message puck out of my trouser pocket and slapped it into her palm. Without looking down at the device, she ran her finger along the appropriate buttons on the bottom and pulled up the message, pausing it before it could play. She held out the hologram between herself and Brisbois. "We're trying to find out who this man is."

With the grainy, enraged face floating in the space between us, I watched as Brisbois' head fell to one side. His brow furrowed and his jaw tightened. At length, shaking his head, he spoke. "No FaRs required, Cadence. I know that man very well."

"You do?" Cadence made no effort to hide the excitement in her voice.

"That," said Brisbois, pointing at the holo-message, "is one Noll Hudd; fancies himself an entertainment entrepreneur, but really, he's just a drogan-dealing thug with delusions of grandeur. I arrested him a few years ago for manslaughter, but he made a deal and only served the minimum. Now, he owns and operates several clubs in District 68."

Cadence's brows furrowed. "Clubs?"

"Nightclubs," explained the Inspector. "Bars. Dives, most of them, but one or two are almost passable."

Cadence retracted the holo-puck and examined the face of the now-identified man. "Do you know what he would have against Ergo Sum?"

"The organization as a whole? No." Brisbois leaned back against the top of the chair on which he was reclining, smiling in that self-satisfied way of his. "But Elea Cerf did steal his wife away while he was in prison."

Breath left my lungs in a shocked huff. My mouth gaped. "What? Simone?" I shook my finger at the angry face suspended in Cadence's hand. "That is Ayla's father?"

Brisbois nodded, running a hand down his chin, chuckling. "Bit of an underworld scandal when the divorce happened – quite the embarrassment for Mr. Hudd, losing his family to an animanecron."

Cadence's gaze flicked heavenward. She shut off the holo-puck with one hand before fixing Brisbois with a pointed stare. "Why would that be embarrassing, Oliver?"

The flatness of Cadence's tone and the challenge in her arched brow couldn't be missed. Brisbois, much to my delight, floundered immediately, standing up from his recumbent position, the words tripping out of his mouth as he tried to backpedal from his casual bigotry. "Well, I only meant – I didn't mean to say–"

Realization, when it dawned on the Inspector, brought a deep pink blush to his face, his sharp green eyes turning into flat saucers. "Miss Turing, are you... an...?"

"Cadence," prompted my flat mate, crossing her arms over her chest. "And yes, Oliver, I am."

I watched with glee as the full enormity of what Cadence

was, what she had always been, washed over Brisbois like an unexpectedly large wave at the beach. He attempted a chuckle, but it must have sounded hollow even to his ears; his hand came up and covered his mouth.

"Where could we find Mr. Hudd?" I pressed, immensely proud of myself for staying focused on the task at hand, and not rubbing the man's nose in his ignorance.

"There's one place in particular: *The Nest*. He practically lives there," mumbled Brisbois. He shook himself, glancing over at me at last. "But I wouldn't recommend going there alone."

Cadence clapped me on the shoulder and smiled. "We're not going alone. We're going with each other." She shook her head. "I'd invite you along, Oliver, but I think an EO officer would set Mr. Hudd on edge, so it's best you let us handle this." Wiggling her fingers, she turned and walked towards the front door, a spring in her step. "Thanks for the help!"

"Brisbois." I nodded a goodbye, trying my hardest not to grin.

Brisbois waved vaguely at me, one hand still covering his mouth, his eyes fixed on Cadence's retreating figure. "Mr. Hale."

Outside the rain had abated, if only for a few minutes, and a shock of blue sky split the dark clouds like a tear in a piece of clothing. By the time I exited the Ergo Sum building, Cay was already at the base of the stairs, staring up into the sky with a familiar, thoughtful expression. I watched her for a minute from the top of the landing, letting the doors suction shut behind me. Taking in a deep breath, I went over all we had uncovered in the last hour. Watching the woman whom I cared for so deeply, one detail stood out among the others as particularly heartbreaking. I shook my head, my chest tightening.

"So... Simone and Elea were going to get married." I dug my nix case out of my breast pocket and selected one, taking the steps down to street level. "Just when I thought this whole mess couldn't get any more tragic."

Cadence waited for me to light my nix, keeping a steady pace with my long strides, before inquiring, "Do you find it tragic that they were going to wed, or tragic that now they don't have the opportunity to do so?"

I enjoyed these questions from her, if only because her curiosity was an honest one – a child's curiosity, free of the weight of social convention, even though the queries centered on potentially thorny topics.

I took a long drag on my nix, pinching the fragile black tube between my thumb and forefinger. I exhaled the pungent smoke through my nose, enjoying the warmth as I considered my response. "A little bit of both I suppose."

I shrugged, running my thumb over my bottom lip. "To be honest, I've never really understood the point of matrimony in this day and age. People can live with whomever they want, for however long they want, and in whatever way they want – I don't see why such relationships need to be sanctioned by the state." I perched the nix in the corner of my mouth before turning to Cadence, my head tilted to one side. "Archaic, don't you think?"

"I believe to most people, marriage provides not only a stable life for any future progeny – with at least the tacit assurance that their home life will remain intact – but also a state of peace and certainty between two people who deeply care for each other." A broad smile broke across her face, lending her next words a vibrancy the others had lacked. "The value of marriage lies less in the official sanction of a government, and more in the promise it represents between two people to build a life together and persevere through hardships. It's a sign of devotion, as much of a sacrifice as it is a gift."

My nix dangled listlessly from between my lips while I gaped at her. I shook myself, blinking. "My goodness, Cay," I said, withdrawing the nix with a smack. "I hadn't realized you had thought so much about it. The way you're going on, you'd think you were talking from experience!"

"I am."

I scoffed aloud, the bridge of my nose wrinkling. "What?"

"I've been married. I found it an extremely rewarding experience." Her head vacillated from side to side. "On the whole."

She continued up the sidewalk, oblivious that I was no longer following her, but had, in fact, frozen in the middle of the path. Disinterested pedestrians moved around me like I was roadkill – unpleasant and somebody else's problem. Ash from my still burning nix fell from the limp tip and onto my white dress shirt, jolting me out of my stupor as I frantically brushed at the hot material. I hurried after her, jogging to make up for the distance and stepping in front of her to bring her to a halt. "You–" I pointed a finger at her. "–have been...married?"

Cadence's eyes narrowed. She crossed her arms high over her chest and slowly arched one brow. "I'm almost a hundred and fifty years old, Chance. What do you think I've been doing with my life up until this point? Sitting at home, alone, recalibrating and defragging my hard drives?"

"I just..." I pulled the nix from my lips and dropped it to the ground, snuffing it out with the heel of my shoe. "I guess

I never thought of you like that." Cadence began to frown, her brow furrowing in confusion. My mouth flapped on its hinges as I struggled to express my thoughts. "I mean, I didn't know your interests..."

What I was trying to say was that I was equal parts relieved, confused, and disturbed to have discovered that she was capable of romantic attachments at all. It was a confirmation that all my efforts to spark an affair between us were not in vain, while at the same time an indictment of how truly unsuccessful I had been thus far. Her confession gave me the first concrete glimmer of hope that we could one day be together in the sense I so desperately yearned for. In the end, I settled for saying nothing; a desire not to offend her and a desire not to embarrass myself helping me swallow down the truth.

I slid my hands into my pockets, stepping back to her side and gesturing us forward. "Who was he? Or she?" I compulsively ran my tongue along my dry lips. "You're not still married, are you? I haven't been living with a married woman all this time?"

"We separated a long time ago."

"I'm sorry to hear that," I said with a smile, pushing my hand back through my hair and surreptitiously wiping the perspiration off my brow.

Her eyes were drawn upward by a roll of thunder, her arms crossing over her chest as she rubbed her shoulders. "It was perfectly amicable. We stayed good friends."

I brushed a lock of hair away from her neck and behind her shoulder, playing with the tip of it. "Why did you split up? If you don't mind me asking."

Her head fell to one side, her gaze focused on the horizon.

Her lack of an immediate response began to worry me, and I was on the verge of telling her to forget the query, when she drew in a deep breath. "We just weren't quite what the other one needed. It happens sometimes. I was young when I met her, barely sixty, and she was a good deal older than me. I suppose I was attracted to the aura of worldliness and wisdom she expressed." She sighed and looped her arm around mine, bringing her hand up to caress my bicep as we strolled down the rapidly darkening streets. "But we were at two distinct parts of our lifespan – I was just getting started and wanted to explore, she was tired and wanted a rest. We didn't match each other at all."

I watched the movement of her hand with absorbing interest, my lips pulled taut in something between a smile and a wince. "Do you think you'll ever marry again?"

"I think so, yes." She looked up at me, beaming like the sun, shaking her hair back out of her face. "Life is too wonderful to spend alone, don't you think?"

I stopped walking, turned to her, and leaned in to kiss her, the hand that was playing with her hair coming up to cradle the back of her head. I couldn't help myself, couldn't stop myself – I needed her, in that moment, to know how viscerally I agreed with her sentiment. That yes, life was too wonderful to spend alone, as long as she was the one I was spending it with.

The heavens choose that exact moment to begin dumping fresh sheets of rain on the city. It was not unlike jumping fully clothed in the deep end of a pool, and in a second, we were drenched to the bone, the cool water shocking me into stillness, my closed eyes snapping open.

Cadence laughed in delight and pulled away from me, leaving

me breathless and unsatisfied, as always. I watched as she spun in the deluge, her arms stretched up to the heavy black clouds above us.

"Weather – amazing!" She gave a loud sigh, dropping her arms to her sides, but keeping her face upturned, her eyes flickering shut. "Rele, the rain feels so damn good."

I looked her over head to toe as she stood there, her summer smile shining like a searchlight. I didn't think that I would ever get tired of moments like these, ever tire of her ability to find joy in a world that had long ago lost its glitter for me. I turned my collar up against the pounding rain, an ache in my chest. I both envied and admired her stubborn optimism – and the more I learned about what she had gone through on Whiston, the more miraculous she appeared to me.

How could I ever hope to be worthy of sharing a life with such a woman?

Cadence turned back to me, opening her eyes as she pivoted on her heels. She glanced at me and promptly burst into laughter, a hand covering her mouth.

"What?" I demanded, shivering as a rivulet of rainwater snaked its way down my spine.

"You don't seem to enjoy it very much," she managed after a moment, laughing all the while. Shaking her head, she gripped her shaking sides. "Hila, you look half-drowned!"

I glared at her but couldn't smother a rueful smile as I wiped water out of my eyes. "That's because I am, you little vixen." I strode towards her and slung my arm across her shoulders, jerking my head up the street. "Come on, let's get to a place where we can hail a PT. We'll need to dry off and change before we head to this club of Hudd's."

"Really?" Cadence finally ceased her giggling, allowing herself to be led up the street and around the corner. "We can't go now? Every minute may count in catching Elea's killer."

"It's not even midday, Cay. Places like *The Nest* don't open until late," I explained. "And we'll want to look like we belong."

16

Chapter 16

We made it back to the flat without incident, squelching our way inside. Cadence began stripping her wet clothes off her body as she walked back to her room, leaving me to trail behind her, picking up her discarded garments while keeping my gaze fixed on the floor.

"I'm going to take a quick shower, love," I called to her from the laundry room, tossing her sodden clothes into the dryer. "Get myself warmed up before changing for tonight."

"Alright," she shouted back.

I waited until I heard the door to her room click shut before disrobing myself, throwing my clothes in with hers and turning the dryer on before walking naked to my own quarters.

The warm spray of the shower pelted my skin and the steam curled around me like a gossamer curtain. I breathed in the thick vapor and closed my eyes, pushing my hands back through my hair and down across my shoulders. Cadence had been married. How had I not known that? *Well, idiot, you never asked.* I shook my head and gritted my teeth. Truth was, as much as I might accuse Cadence of being reticent about herself and her past, I hadn't exactly shown myself to be very interested in the subject either. What was the old Earth saying? Ignorance is bliss?

What if Cadence wasn't who I thought she was? What if it turned out I was just a footnote in her life, a convenience rather than a necessity? What if I couldn't live up to what had come before?

Before I knew it, a half hour had passed and I was still standing in the shower, brooding. A sound broke through my musings, a persistent humming. My brow furrowed and I leaned out of the cascading water, pushing back the curtain to see my mobile flashing and buzzing on the bathroom counter where I had thrown it. Frowning, I stretched my arm out as far as it would go, just managing to grasp the bud with my fingertips. I fitted the device into my ear, careful to remain outside of the shower's spray. "Yes?" I said aloud.

"Chance!" Lily Taylor's voice half-hissed and half-shouted my name into my ear, making me wince. "I've been trying to reach you all morning! Where are you?"

I hurried to switch off the water with one hand, the other scrambling for a towel. "Oh, I'm home at the moment, but I was...out."

Lily gave an exasperated groan as if I had just punched her in the gut. "You can't just – not show up to the office, Chance. You're the boss! You have meetings, work; people are depending on you to –"

"Look –" I stepped out onto the heated floors, swinging my towel low across my hips, and tying it in place. "– something came up; something personal."

"A hangover is not personal."

I scowled at myself in the mirror. "I didn't go on a bender, Miss Taylor, I'm – I can't explain, but I'm going to be out of the office for at least a few days."

"But your schedule –!"

"Clear it." Turning away from the sink, I leaned back against the cool marble, crossing my arms over my bare chest. "What is the point of being the boss if I can't take time off when I need it?" Staring out into my bedroom, a thought occurred to me, and I straightened into a standing position. "Miss Taylor, is Solomon Davers in today?"

There was a pause and then a disdainful sniff from the other end of the call. "I'd assume so; most people come to work when they're supposed to."

I ignored the barb and remained focused on my current train of thought, wandering from the bathroom into my sleeping quarters. "Can you transfer me to him? I need to ask him something."

Lily sighed, but I could already hear her fingertips flickering across the pad on her desk. "Yes, sir."

While I waited for the call to connect, I toweled myself dry, tousling my thick mess of hair with the cotton. Pulling out clothes from my wardrobe and laying them out on the bed, I was on the verge of dressing when a familiar, friendly voice finally picked up on the other end of the phone.

"Hello?"

"Solomon, Chance here," I said, pulling an undershirt down around my torso. "How are things in Research?"

I could hear the muffled sound of whirring machinery, clicking keyboards, and murmuring voices in the background. "Oh, ticking along," answered Solomon, a touch of confusion coloring his words. "Don't we have a meeting tomorrow afternoon? I thought I'd update you on all our projects then."

I shook my head, slipping a dark red dress shirt up over my arms and across my shoulders. "I won't be making it; something's come up."

"Oh?"

Chewing on the inside of my mouth, I looked at myself in the floor length mirror inside the walk-in closet. I knew what I had to ask, but I dreaded the potential response. "Solomon, do you know anything about nanotechnology?"

"Not my field of expertise," said Solomon. "But I know enough to get by."

As I finished getting dressed, I described in as much detail as I could the substance we had found in Elea Cerf's blood – from the effect it had had on her inorganic components, to the appearance of the nanobots themselves. When I'd said all I could, I paused, letting Solomon absorb the information, before querying: "Have you ever come across anything like that?"

Solomon gave a hum of thought before answering. "No, no can't say that I have." His voice brightened. "I'll tell you what; let me do some digging, talk with some people who might know more than I do. Sounds like an intriguing concept."

"If you find anything out, let me know, would you?" I finished running a comb through my hair and sat down on the foot of my bed.

"Will do."

We exchanged goodbyes and I ended the call, pulling the mobile out of my ear and into the pocket of my black suit jacket. Rolling my shoulders back, I stood, looking over myself one last time. Deeming my ensemble acceptable, I headed out into the flat to find Cadence.

I very nearly tripped over my own feet as I stuttered to a halt at the edge of the living room, catching sight of my room-mate. Cadence was standing in front of the TV, facing the large windows that looked out over the city. She turned when she heard me stumble, one brow raised in question.

My heart pounded loud in my ears.

I had seen every piece of clothing she was wearing before – but this particular combination of them was quite simply stunning. Her hair, usually pinned and piled up off the back of her neck, was loose and long around her shoulders, the twists and curls of the dark tresses kissing her pale cheeks and throat. A long-sleeve, sheer black silk cardigan sat open over a spaghetti-strapped lacy white half-corset with a plunging V-neck, her abdomen completely exposed. Baggy, worn jeans hung low on her round hips and I could just spy the bottoms of sharp heeled boots on her feet.

I was aware that my mouth was hanging open. I was aware that I must look like an idiot, staring at her like she had grown a second head. But I could do nothing about it. Blush spreading across my cheeks, I was struck dumb by the sheer seductive appeal of her.

I finally found my voice, and gestured to her with an almost steady hand while querying, "Is that what you're wearing?"

"Yes..." Cadence looked down at herself with wide eyes. "Does it not suit?"

Blinking, I shook my head. "Actually, it's... perfect."

She picked at her sleeves, shaking them out. A smile crept onto her face. "I looked up appropriate nightclub attire on the vertex. I didn't want to look out of place." Her smile faded, her brows drawing to a point. "I'm still a little unclear as to what to expect at such a venue."

I crossed the room, drawn to her inexorably, like a passing asteroid drawn into the gravity of a moon. "It's not so different from the fundraiser: there'll be music, dancing, drinks, lots of people..." Now mere inches from her, I could smell the soft scent of the pheromone spray she had spritzed on herself. Pleasant as it was, it was also entirely unnecessary – my body needed no artificial encouragements to reach the heady heights of arousal where Cadence was concerned. I reached out and brushed my fingertips against her cheek without thinking. "I bet you'll like it."

Quite unexpectedly, Cadence responded to my touch by leaning her face into my hand. She lifted her arms and rested her hands on my hips, her grip firm, her thumbs caressing me through my tucked in shirt. Her inky blue eyes looked up into my own green orbs. "When should we go?"

Delighted by her reaction, I stuttered out a laugh, starting to step even closer to her. "Not until later, I told you. Well after dark, anyway." I stopped when I remembered a thought that had occurred to me while showering. I let out a sharp sigh and drew back from her, pulling my mobile back out of my jacket pocket. "Which reminds me, there's something I want to try..."

Crossing towards the living room couch, I fitted the bud into my ear once more and said aloud, "Call *The Nest* nightclub."

Cadence started to say something behind me, and I shushed her as my mobile searched for the appropriate number. Finding it within seconds, it connected me to the establishment in question.

A bored, older female voice answered the call after a loud click sounded. "You've reached *The Nest*."

Sitting down on the couch, I unfastened the button of my suit jacket, crossing my legs. "Yes. Chance Hale for Noll Hudd, please."

"...excuse me?"

The disbelief was palpable in those two words. I smirked. "Chance Hale? Head of Halcyon Enterprises? I'm trying to reach Noll Hudd; I was told to try here."

There was a long pause. I could just imagine the person on the other end examining the name on their caller ID, checking it once and then checking it again, not believing what their device was telling them.

The voice was decidedly breathier when it spoke again. "Just – just a minute. Hold on."

"Sure." I brushed a piece of lint off my trouser leg, wincing a little as the tinny hold music kicked in.

It didn't last for long.

"Noll Hudd's office." This woman's voice was soft and smooth, like a fur pelt, and slid into my ear with such sweetness it made me shiver. "How can I help you?"

"Yes, hello." Uncrossing my legs, I leaned forward and clasped my hands together. "I wanted to set up a meeting with Mr. Hudd. Tonight, if it's convenient."

"Certainly," answered the woman, who I could only assume was some kind of assistant, if criminals had such things. I heard the faint click of fingers against a keyboard and then: "Mr. Hudd would be happy to see you at the club at one."

"Lovely, I'll be there. Thank you." I hung up with a tap, and removed the mobile from my ear, smiling up at the confounded expression on Cadence's face.

She crossed her arms over her chest slowly, her eyebrow lifting. "Why?"

I shrugged, relaxing back into the cushions, and spreading my arms out over the back of the couch. "My clout's got to be good for something. Now we don't have to wheedle our way in when we get there."

I watched as Cadence considered this. With a sigh, she glanced up at the clock that hung in the entryway, disappointment scurrying over her features. "One is a long time away." Her face cleared and brightened, like a summer sky after a sudden rainstorm. "Oh! I know! We can watch a flicker!"

She collapsed next to me and waved the television on. At the same time, I stood and waved the set off.

"No," I said, my hands falling akimbo. "No flicker."

"What?" Cadence stared up at me, aghast. "Why not? Flickers help me think."

"Because tonight, I thought we might try something different." I paced into the kitchen and retrieved two wine glasses from the cabinets. Selecting what I hoped would prove to be an amusing cabernet, I placed all three items on the counter and looked back at my companion, my brows dancing over my eyes. "Talking."

Cadence, one arm slung over the back of the couch, stared at me from the living room, smiling and blinking. "Sarc, we talk all the time. Or haven't you noticed?"

"I meant about each other."

Cadence stared at me from under a hooded brow, her lips curled downward in a slight frown. I gave a frustrated grunt, setting the corkscrew device to work on the bottle before leaning against the counter, palms flush against the stone. "Cay, for God's sake we've known each other for more than half a year, and sometimes I feel like we're still strangers."

Cadence heaved herself out of her seat and meandered towards me, letting out a long breath through her nose. "Dis, I know plenty of things about you, Chance."

"You helped solve the murder of my father; you had an unfair advantage." I could tell I was beginning to upset her. I had sensed this wall before; behind it was a great horde of things and unpleasant memories. I could see her face fall, replaying scenes to which I wasn't privy.

The cork came free from the bottle with a pop, and I looked away from her, pouring out two liberal glasses of wine for us. "You're my friend, Cadence. I want to know who you are."

I could feel her gaze boring into me, her fingers tapping up a storm against the kitchen island. "What do you want to know?"

"Well," I said as I slid one of the glasses over to her. "Why don't you tell me about your family?"

"I don't have one." She shot off her answer like a bullet. She cleared her throat, folding her hands on top of the counter, leaving her wine pointedly untouched. "Satisfied?"

"Everyone has family, Cay." I swirled the wine around the glass and swallowed down a mouthful before continuing. "A mother, a father – siblings?"

Cadence brought her hands down flat onto the marble countertop with a bang.

I recoiled. But before I had the opportunity to fully react to this outburst, Cadence was gone, disappearing around the corner of the kitchen at a run.

"Cay?" I'd known personal details weren't her favorite topic of conversation, but I didn't expect her to run away to her room like a petulant child.

This is exactly what I thought she had done for a moment, the sound of shuffling and closing drawers emanating from her room down the hall. But soon I heard her heavy footfall pounding back towards me.

She rounded the corner into the kitchen in a stiff-legged run, a hand held out in front of her. I put down my wine and took several quick steps backwards, hands held-up in front of me in defense. "Cadence, I'm sor–"

"This!" It was a shout, an explosion of a word. She shook her outstretched hand at me, her head hung low. "This was my family!"

I realized that thrust out at me was the unframed optric I hadn't seen since that first weekend we spent together. She sat at the center of a group of people, all smiling and touching.

Her other hand came up and pointed to the figure on her right. "This is Iago." Cadence's face remained perpendicular to the floor, her expression a mystery, loose bangs hanging down like icicles. Her finger slid around the edges of the optric till it rested on top of the figure at her left elbow. "And this is Cassandra. We were all developed in the same batch of code."

"Cadence..." The dead tone of her voice frightened me. I took a step towards her, shaking my head. "You don't have to–"

"This is William and Zachariah," she barreled on, speaking so quickly I could barely understand her. "They wrote us; they embodied us, reviewed our code, updated our drivers – there were others before us, but we were the last. My parents–" her finger flew back to the bottom of the picture. "–my brother. My sister. My family. And they're dead now." Her shoulders shuddered. I took a step back despite myself, completely at a loss for what she might do next. "I saw them. They're dead."

Without warning, she threw the optric to the floor with both hands. The thin piece of plastic and metal shattered like a chipped glass, the force of Cadence's rage embedding smaller shards in the wooden floor. I had to jump back to avoid being hit by the jagged projectiles.

The silence was deafening. I lowered my arms from my face slowly. Every inch of Cadence was quivering now, like an arrow pulled back on a bow string. "I hid. I hid like a coward." Her hands disappeared under her loose black hair, pulling and pushing at her face. "There was a fight. I hid under some rubble. I didn't fight for them. I just let them go. I saw them go into the shop with fifty others. And I saw them get carried out of the shop with the back of their heads ripped open."

Cadence slowly collapsed onto her knees, hands moving down to squeeze her arms. "They piled them up in the center of the camp. Like trash. All of them. So many bodies. The furnaces were running all day and all night just to melt them down."

With infinitesimal slowness, Cadence reached forward, her fingertips brushing over the fragments of the optric. "Why?"

It was the voice of a child speaking. The Cadence I thought I knew was stripped away, leaving this shaking, broken figure in her place; foreign, yet heartbreakingly familiar.

Her head craned up. Her face was drawn, her blue eyes wide, pupils so dilated the orbs looked almost black. She found me with those empty eyes and shook her head. "Why me? Why did I live? I shouldn't have lived."

I carefully lowered myself onto my knees across from her, avoiding as much of the ruined optric as I could. "Do you think they would have wanted you to die there?"

Cadence put her hands up to her shaking face. "No."

"No." I repeated it back to her, reaching forward. I tried to still my own trembling hand before I touched her. "I'm sure they loved you. Very much. They'd want you to be here. Helping people." I brushed her shoulder, trying to keep my voice steady. "Helping me."

"I..." Cadence curled further into herself, face shielded by her knees. "Tris, tris, tris, I miss them so, so much."

I didn't know what to say to that. This had all gone so wrong, and I felt so stupid that I hadn't thought it would. That I thought I could somehow casually open and sift through the box of her memories and only the good things would come out.

I started to pull my hand away, tears pricking at the edges of my eyes. How could I possibly make any of this better? Relate to her, try to heal the wounds of the atrocities she'd suffered and witnessed? I really was a stranger to her, a stranger in a strange, unfriendly land.

I let out a heavy breath. To be so impotent, so unable to comfort her after all the times she'd comforted me. Then, a thought stayed my hand over her skin.

I swallowed and closed my eyes, desperate to remember the exact sequence of beats she had tapped against me time and time again. I lowered my hand back down to her arm, hesitating for one moment longer before clumsily patting out the code for affection and attachment against her skin.

"Cay, I am so sorry."

Silence reigned. I left my fingers against her skin. I tapped out the beat again, the inside of my cheek gripped tightly between my teeth.

Then, with a slowness which gave me goosebumps, her tremors receded, leaving behind a faint humming sensation on my fingertips.

I opened my eyes when I felt Cadence's hand wrap around my wrist. She stayed hunched over herself, sitting against the counter, the top of her head resting against her knees.

She drew my hand towards her, pulling it into the valley her body created between her legs and torso. My breath caught in my throat as she kissed the top of each one of my fingers, lingering over every digit for a few pregnant moments before moving to the next.

Her lips were soft and warm, fitting over my skin like a velvet glove; the inside of her mouth just wet enough to leave a thin film of moisture behind. I shifted towards her, barely breathing. She likewise drew herself closer to me and before I was fully aware of what was happening, I found her mouth a hair's breadth away from my own trembling lips.

"Cadence..." I breathed her name like the final word of a prayer and felt a confession heavy on my tongue. With my free hand cradling her against my body, I lowered my face to hers. "Cadence, I lo–"

Fate, depending on how you look at it, was on my side. In my rush to put down my wine glass, I had left it a little too close to the edge of the counter. Gravity worked its will upon it and sent the fragile object hurtling to the ground with a crash, at which we both jumped. Even Cadence, who was so hard to surprise, started, her head flying up, her chest heaving with quick sharp breaths.

It was the breathing that comforted me more than anything; seeing her reinitiate her basic programs meant that whatever I'd done had worked, and the worst of the storm had passed, for now.

Cadence was still quicker to recover than I was, bringing her free hand up to her forehead and relaxing back against the counter. She sighed, running her hand back through her knotted hair. "Fytaq Dukuark."

I couldn't help but give a small laugh at that, the corners of my lips twitching up into a smile. "Was that an animanecron curse word you just let loose?"

A rough huff of air passed her lips, the curvature of which suggested that it was indeed a laugh. "Yes. Yes, it was." She straightened, her hand coming down to pat my own, still caught in her grasp. "If you do decide to learn Animatum, I will not be teaching you those."

"Aw, but that would be the best part!" I smothered the vague flare of disappointment I felt in my chest when she released my hand at last. "You know Common Tongue curses. It would only be fair."

Cadence's only response was a shake of her head. She struggled to get to her feet. "I'm sorry about the wine glass."

"Nonsense." I grunted as I stood, brushing fragments of optric off my trousers. "Easy enough to replace." I moved to the spilled wine and cracked glass, surveying the damage with a sigh. I didn't trust myself to look at her as I said, "Here's an idea: how about I finally finish cooking that Anga Stew for us while you find a flicker for us to watch? How about that?"

"Alright."

I nodded and, after carefully picking up the pieces of glass and mopping up the wine, I turned on the oven and went to pull the large pot out of the fridge. I thought Cadence had already left long ago, when I heard a tiny laugh from behind me. I looked over my shoulder to find Cadence standing on the step that separated the kitchen from the living room, her hand pressed to her lips. The laugh surprised me half as much as the small smile I glimpsed behind her fingertips.

"Iago used to cook for us all the time."

Her happiness was a balm to me, and I managed a smirk amid my own misery. "Would never have thought of cooking as a hobby for animanecrons."

"It isn't really. Iago was a little strange." She laughed again, her eyes widening as if she was startling herself with the reaction. "And he was terrible at it. He burned everything." Her eyes found my face and her smile wavered. She pushed a hand back through her tangled hair. "He would have liked you."

I looked away from her, rubbing my chin. "I wish... I wish I could have met him. All of them."

We stood there in silence for a few moments, the oven ticking next to me as it warmed.

She stepped back towards me, halting at the edge of the optric destruction zone still to be tidied up. She leaned over the pieces, cupping my face in her hands. I closed my eyes and let her pull me in closer. Her lips pressed against mine with all the tenderness of a flower being pressed between two pages of a book. She rested her forehead against mine, tapping her attachment over my skin. She released my mouth with a sigh of words in which my name was the only thing I could understand.

"Janisti plysta Chance plysta unisti."

I had no idea what she was trying to say, but it sounded soft and sweet, and I smiled. She stepped back after a beat, striding into the living room with her customary certainty. She left me in a tumult of emotions; I felt guilty for asking about her past, felt aroused by her affections, pained by her loss, glad all the same that she had started to talk about it, and selfish that I was glad. After depositing the stew in the oven, I rubbed my lips and closed my eyes. I sighed before moving to the far wall to activate the sweeping robots.

My hand hovered over the control panel, another thought seizing me.

I wished I could give her something back.

I stared down at the broken optric. The remains glinted back at me temptingly. Without having any real plan, I knelt onto the floor, grabbing a small bowl I had intended to use for serving the stew. Carefully, I gathered up every single piece of optric I could find and placed it in the bowl. When I was certain I had all of it, I placed the bowl in the refrigerator, behind several bottles of milk. I knew Cadence would never touch that area of the fridge, due to her aversion to the idea of drinking "liquid which came out of an animal."

That done, I poured myself another glass of wine before joining Cadence in the living room, leaving the stew to cook.

17

Chapter 17

I worked hard to hide my nervousness from Cadence as we sat in the PT, bound for *The Nest*. I had never met a bonafide criminal kingpin and would've quite liked to keep it that way; I was keenly aware that money and influence would only get me so far in Noll Hudd's world – but it wouldn't keep a knife out of my back.

For Cadence, however, this was the next logical step in the case and, therefore, no great cause for concern. I wondered if she really had any concept of the type of man we were going to meet – if she understood that he wasn't some cartoonish villainous archetype, but a dyed-in-the-wool killer.

There was nothing for it, of course; Hudd was our most likely suspect, and talking to him was the surest way to determine his guilt or, unlikely as it may be, his innocence.

The PT dropped us in front of *The Nest*. I stepped out onto the dingy District 3 walkway, screwed my courage to the sticking place, and put on my most charming smile.

As busy as I was with Halcyon Enterprises, my social activities had fallen to the wayside; it'd been quite some time since I'd seen the inside of a nightclub. *The Nest* was a several-story tall, nondescript steel building, with opaque sliding glass doors and no indication of what entertainment one might find within. Clearly, if you had to ask, you weren't in the right place.

A quick flash of my ident card got us past the large heavies guarding the entrance, and we proceeded down a long, low-ceilinged corridor. The hallway ended at a booth, where I explained the nature of our visit to the young man stationed to collect any cover charges. Pushing his loose blue hair over his shoulder, he put a finger to an earpiece, murmured a few choice words, listened to the response, and then nodded.

Turning back to face us, he smiled, tapping the thin screen that unfurled on the counter in front of him. "Ever been here before?"

"Never," I said with conviction.

"Cool, cool," he responded. "Well, there's a big elevator on the far side of the dance floor. Someone should be there to let you up to see Mr. Hudd. You want the top floor." He stopped his tapping and glanced down at the pad. His smile widened. "You have time for a drink at the bar if you like. Compliments of the house, of course." He waved a hand over the screen and, with a well-oiled woosh, a door to our right slid up and open. "Welcome to *The Nest*."

A large, round dance floor was sunk deep into the center of the club; a writhing pit of bodies illuminated only by flashing lights and the occasional flicker of someone recording a holofeed. Every other part of the club radiated out from this like the twisting tendrils of a spider's web. Exotic dancers of every gender and ethnicity slid their way around poles on raised platforms throughout the bar area, listless expressions on their faces as they gyrated hypnotically to the music.

There were no booths or tables on the first floor of the club, but a quick glance at the upper levels revealed a plethora of private rooms and VIP spaces. These looked down onto the club from large windows sealed with tinted privacy glass, allowing the occupants to look out, without others looking in.

The only lights in the club, aside from the strobes and colored spots employed on the dance floor, were fluorescent globes of purple, giving everything the appearance of being dunked in ink.

Anxious to appear as if this was just another night out on the town, I waited to order a drink from the bartender, a grizzled-looking older woman covered in tattoos, but with a pleasant enough smile. When I turned to look back at Cadence, she had both hands clamped over her ears, elbows jutting out on either side of her head. A pained scowl was grooved into her face, exaggerated to clownish quality by the flashing lights. I smothered a laugh with my hand, but not soon enough. Cadence's scowl deepened. She shook her head and shouted, "This is nothing like the ballroom!"

"It's a little like it," I said, stepping closer to her, pitching my voice above the noise. "There's the music and the dancing, just like I said!"

Cadence's face dropped. She peeled one hand away from her head, and winced, her mouth clicking shut before quickly re-covering her ear. "That is not music!" She turned towards the dance floor, her brow furrowing as she took in the sight of so many grinding, heaving bodies. "And that is not dancing!"

I rolled my eyes, turning back to my light blue drink, frothing and bubbling in front of me. "You sound just like Henry."

She gave a violent nod. "We both have good taste!"

I chuckled into the sweet liquid before swallowing it, grunting at the familiar burn. Cadence moved closer beside me, still wearing her hands like fashion accessories. She elbowed my shoulder, jutting her chin towards my glass. "What is that?"

"A double Yarin Twist." I lifted the glass to her. "Would you like some?"

"If it's alcoholic, I think I need some," she said, releasing one hand from her head to snatch the drink away from me.

In her enthusiasm, some of the drink sloshed onto my hand. I grimaced and sucked at the inky stuff, already staining my skin. "Don't pretend that alcohol affects you in the slightest; we both know I'm not that lucky."

If she heard my quip, she ignored it, downing the rest of the drink in one go and earning impressed looks from the other, less-enlightened bar patrons. The taste hit her as soon as she swallowed, and she rattled her head from side to side. She stuck out her tongue and made a disgusted noise, bringing the empty glass down onto the bar with a thunk. "Rus, how can you drink that, Chance? It's like licking window sealant!"

I pulled my mouth away from my hand and sighed; the stain remained. I brushed my hand over her shoulder and jerked my head towards the other end of the bar, where a stack of towels sat. "I'll be right back, okay?"

A nod was her only response as she returned her hands to her ears.

The rags at the end of the bar were covered in a sticky, red substance I didn't dare guess at, forcing me to avail myself of scratchy low grade paper towels, one step up from tree bark, and thick pink soap in the men's room. As I struggled against the stubborn stain, an additional ten minutes had passed before I realized it.

I wound my way back across the crowded club, worried that Cadence had gotten bored and wandered off to find me. However, when the bar finally came back into view, I realized that something far worse had happened.

I don't know why it hadn't occurred to me the second I stepped away from her; heaven knows she had a figure that would attract the eye of anyone with an appreciation for beauty. In a place like this, people really weren't that picky, of course. Hell, if I had breasts and a skirt, some man would be trying to chat me up within five minutes – and I'd given them double that for Cadence.

My head began to pound when I first caught sight of them: three pathetic excuses for men huddled around my dove like she was a campfire on a wintry night. Two members of their little trio had taken up on either side of her, boxing her in for their leader: a wiry, greasy thing, with needle marks on his arms. They were laughing, jostling each other, creeping ever closer towards their captured treasure.

I pushed my way back to the bar, teeth grinding together like rusted gears. I was almost there when a thought occurred, which slowed my jog to a cautious walk. Given that Cadence was made of one of the strongest metal alloys known to man, and capable of crushing a stone to dust, her unpleasant suitors couldn't physically harm her in any way. In fact, the thought of them even trying to lay a hand on her – and the inevitable consequences thereof – brought a smirk to my face. I slid my hands into my trouser pockets. I wouldn't mind seeing them bleed – not in the slightest.

I caught the very end of their conversation as I came up behind them, Cadence's face peeking out from the ring of muscled flesh and tattered clothes.

"...even if I did perform such acts," Cadence was saying, her face blank, the slightest thoughtful wrinkle folding her brow. "It is very insulting of you to assume that I do, given that we have been unacquainted until now."

"Aw, don't be like that girlie, it's a fucking compliment!" The man on her left leaned back, throwing his hands up into the air. "We want to have a go with you because you're fit, a'right?"

"Some bitches don't know how to take a compliment, right, Davo?" said the man on her right, compulsively tugging at his bottom lip, making his grin even more distorted and grotesque than it was otherwise.

"Some bitches don't know how to take anything." The thin man in front of me leaned forward and dragged his hand from Cadence's shoulder down to her forearm, tongue flicking out to wet his bottom lip as he spoke. "What say you and my friends go upstairs, and we teach you how to take us, huh? Bet you'd like that."

"You have nothing I want to take." Cadence looked from his face to the hand he had wrapped around her wrist, and back to him. "Please remove your hand from my arm, before I remove it for you."

The thin man's face clouded faster than muddied water. I watched as his grip tightened, the skin under his fingers twisting and reddening. "Here, girlie, are you fucking threatening me?"

"The lady asked you to take your hands off her," I spoke at last. The three men turned to face me, the thin man, Davo, dropping his hand from Cadence's arm as I had hoped he would. I inclined my head towards my friend and smiled. "Quite politely too, under the circumstances. I would've told you to get the hell off her, unless you have an intense interest in finding out what your testicles taste like."

"Oi, you want to have a go at me, you limp-wristed shithead?" Davo stepped forward, bringing himself mere inches from me. The stench of his overpowering, knock-off pheromone spray made me want to gag, but I merely looked up into his bloodshot eyes and grinned wider, removing my hands from my pockets.

"I want to knock your teeth down your throat," I said brightly. "But there's a lady present, and not being a supreme ass like yourself, I will restrain myself." Keeping my feet planted, I leaned around the thin man and extended a hand towards Cadence, ignoring the other two who had closed in on either side of me. "I believe Mr. Hudd is ready to receive us, Cay. Shall we?"

The mention of Hudd's name had the effect I had hoped it would. The man on my right blanched visibly, his eyes widening. He tugged at Davo's shoulder, his gravelly voice low and insistent.

"Come on, Davo, leave it. It's not worth it, leave it..."

Davo, teeth clenched and bared, looked me up and down

before making an obscene gesture and allowing himself to be pulled away. The third man gave a last leer in Cadence's direction before quickly following his friends.

Taking my hand, Cadence allowed me to lead her away from the bar, although her gaze remained fixed on her harassers as we moved through the crowd. Even when they were well out of sight, she stared back at the area where they had stood for several long moments before turning her attention to me. Frowning, she released my hand as we stopped in front of the lift to the offices above. "I was perfectly capable of handling that situation, Chance."

"I know it," I said, nodding and leaning in so she could catch my words without my having to shout. "But given Hudd's potential feelings towards animanecrons, I thought it best to avoid exposing yourself as one by beating the snot out of three men." While we waited for the lift to arrive, I added, "I hope I didn't offend you by intervening."

"No, no – your reasoning was sound, and your intention affectionate." Cadence, still frowning, shook her head. "Those men were just...very crude."

The elevator doors opened, and I gestured for her to step inside ahead of me. "I'm sorry you had to experience that, Cay."

"No one would ever conduct themselves like that back home." Walking inside the lift, Cadence rubbed at the skin of her wrist for several seconds, and then looked up at me. "Do they really think they'll get people to copulate with them by using those kinds of advances?"

"I don't think sex is really their ultimate goal." I pressed the button for the top floor. "It's more about control. Making women feel...less than."

Cadence blinked. "Con, why? Why do they do that?"

I paused, thinking over my answer with care. I watched the people in the club below us shrink as we slid up noiselessly. At last, I shrugged, rubbing my brow. "Because they need to feel bigger than somebody, I suppose."

"Hm." Cadence followed my gaze with her own, her head falling to one side. "Humans are very...fragile."

We were silent as the lift coasted to a halt on the top floor. Waiting for the doors to open, Cadence turned to me, her eyes bright. "Have you ever–?"

"Of course not," I answered, scowling. "I was raised better than that."

The elevator doors slid open, and we stepped out into a large anteroom, our feet sinking into plush, plum carpet. Eyes fixed themselves on us from every side, suspicious and assessing. A craggy, squat man stood just to the left of the lift, pushing himself off the wall as we exited, his hands loose at his sides. A low coffee table was tucked away to the right, around which four men sat playing cards, the air above their heads thick with nix smoke. Two more men reclined on a sofa, pushed flush against the left wall, one of them standing as we entered. At the far end of the square room was a large steel door. Beside it, a small but ornate looking desk, at which sat a disinterested gentleman smoking a nix, his fine leather shoes propped up on the tabletop.

I strolled to the middle of the room with as much bravado as I could muster, my hand on Cadence's lower back. "I'm here to see Mr. Hudd. I called earlier–"

A heavy, calloused hand gripped my shoulder from behind, stopping me in my tracks. The gentleman lounging behind the desk sighed as he rocked onto his feet, stubbing his nix out in the ashtray. He walked over to us, his deep brown eyes meeting my gaze coolly, and flicked his hand up down. "Spread 'em."

I opened my mouth to say something clever but seeing the handles of two pistols sitting in the shoulder holsters under his arms, I thought better of it. I swallowed, lifting my arms over my head, and widening my stance. "Alright."

The hand on my shoulder was joined by its brother in giving me a thorough, and none too gentle, patting down. I glanced at Cadence from the corner of my eye, but she and the bored gentleman were engaged in a mutual sizing up of each other that put me on edge.

When I was deemed appropriately non-threatening, the hands from behind me retreated. The bored gentleman scratched the underside of his jaw and jerked his chin at Cadence. "And the fragger."

I bit the inside of my mouth at the slur. Cadence merely tilted her head to one side before mimicking my posture. As I watched the heavyset goon paw at her, my distemper began to grow.

"She's clean, Jacks," rumbled the man, coming around to stand next to the gentleman I assumed was his boss.

Jacks nodded, the first hint of a smile twisting his plump lips since we entered the room. He pulled a loose nix out of his trouser pocket and stuck it in the corner of his mouth, using his thumb to point over his shoulder at the thick steel door beside the desk. "He's in there."

I nodded and, glancing at Cadence to reassure myself she was alright, started towards the portal. I was about to reach out and grip the lever-like handle when I saw it turn, the door jerking inwards. Stuttering to a halt, I came face to face with a petite young woman with short cropped blonde hair. The geometric tattoos that trailed down her cheeks, under her jaw, and onto her throat told me all I needed to know about where she was from, and the determined way she was wiping at the corner of her mouth with the back of her hand told me all I needed to know about what she had been doing.

Our eyes met. Hers were green, like mine, but with that preternatural brightness that had become so familiar to me. The hunted expression they carried cut me like a switchblade. I stepped back and looked past her into the office.

Hips leaned back against the front of his desk, the man I could only assume was Noll Hudd languidly finished tucking the bottom of his grey dress shirt into his trousers, before reaching down and doing up his braided leather belt.

"Excuse me," whispered the blonde.

Her voice was higher than Cadence's, but the accent was the same. The sound of it sent a shock through me, and I stepped away to let her pass.

"Feel free to help yourself to some more party favors on the way out, dearie." There was a general round of rough chuckling from the assorted men lounging about the office foyer at Hudd's quip, the woman moving nimbly to avoid a few half-hearted swipes from a couple of thugs as she scurried into the still-open elevator.

I couldn't even look at Cadence; couldn't bring myself to see her reaction to the grotesque display. Disgust and fury wrestled inside my chest to see which emotion would win out. Staring at the floor just in front of the lift, I forced myself to take deep, measured breaths through my nose. I only turned back to the open office door when I heard Noll Hudd speak my name.

"Ah, Mr. Hale." Hudd now stood leaning against the steel frame of the doorway, his arms crossing over his chest. He looked me up and down, smiling with all his teeth. "I was surprised to hear from a captain of industry such as yourself. We don't exactly run in the same social circles."

I struggled to get my temper under control, forcing my words out in a cool, even tone. "No; we don't."

He straightened and swept his arm into the office. "Won't you come into my parlor?"

Everything about Noll Hudd was as jagged and sharp as a piece of broken glass. He preceded us into the office, a hitch in his step, as if the act of walking pained him. Piercing, sky blue eyes were deep-set above high cheekbones and a petite, upturned nose. He gave another smile as he collapsed into a high-backed desk chair, but it lacked any real warmth, purely perfunctory and gone in a flash.

"Well, what can I do for the infamous Mr. Hale?" He slid down in his seat, shifting this way and that as he tried to find the most comfortable position. "Not looking to diversify into the entertainment business, are you? Because I've got a line on a new club that's looking for investors – could get you in on the ground floor."

"As tempting as that sounds," I said, sliding my hands into my pockets and stopping just in front of his desk, pointedly refusing to sit, "I'd just as soon shoot myself in the head as go into business with the likes of you, Mr. Hudd."

At that, Hudd stopped shifting. He looked up at me, his face blank. Then, he breathed out a laugh, saying: "Save me the trouble of doing it, certainly." He nodded, the ghost of a smile twisting his lips. "Too right. Two sharks like us in the same ocean? Pretty soon we'd have to see which of us had the bigger teeth." He glanced over at Cadence as if seeing her for the first time. Pursing his lips, his brows jutted up over his eyes. "That's a nice model you have there. Wouldn't be looking to sell, would you?"

Cadence stepped forward, her jaw clenched as she stressed every word. "I am not his property."

"Well," said Hudd, sniffing. "The law doesn't quite see it that way, does it?"

Cadence met his gaze, her hands closing into fists. He let out a laugh and rubbed his cheek with one hand. "Yeah, it's got spunk." He winked at her. "Love the ones with spunk."

"I didn't come here to buy or to sell, Mr. Hudd," I said, resisting the urge to step in front of Cadence and shield her from his predatory gaze.

He leaned back, throwing his hands up into the air. "Then you just came to waste my time?"

"We came–" Cadence crossed her arms over her chest, shaking her hair behind her. "–because Elea Cerf is dead."

If he had a guilty conscience, which I doubted was possible for a man like him, Hudd didn't let it show. He looked between us and shrugged. "Yeah. Heard about that. What's it got to do with me?"

I tilted my head to one side, watching him. "Your wife left you for her and took your daughter with her."

Hudd tutted, steepling his hands in front of his face. "Oh, I was happy to see her go. Both of them." He rolled his eyes. "What's a man like me going to do with a wife and kid underfoot?"

"Hm," I nodded, an exaggerated frown tugging down the corners of my lips. I shared a glance with Cadence. She gave a slight nod in response and dug the holopuck out of her pocket. I returned my attention to Hudd. "Is this you happy?"

Cadence placed the holopuck on the lip of the desk and called up the saved message with a few presses of a button. With a jittery flash, Hudd's reddened face appeared in grainy pixels, rotating slowly, snarling and cursing out his death threat on repeat.

I watched some of the color drain out of Hudd's face, his sneer flickering off like a dying lightbulb. The only sound in the room was the sound of his recorded words, and they were deafening. He swiveled away from the puck, Adam's apple bobbing as he swallowed.

"Turn it off," he muttered after a moment. When neither of us moved to do so, he began to squirm in his seat, pushing his hand through his shock of dark brown hair. Finally, he lunged forward, coming half out of his chair to swipe at the holopuck like a feral thing, growling, "I said, turn it off!"

But his reflexes were no match for Cadence's, and she swiped the puck off the desk an instant before his hand reached it, turning it off with the press of a button. Silence filled the room. Cadence flipped the holopuck into the air like a coin and caught it with her opposite hand. "How do you like my spunk now?" she queried.

"Listen." Hudd stood, pushing his chair out behind him. "That wasn't what it sounded like."

"Really?" I said. "Because that sounded like a death threat."

"That fucking fragger was dicking around in my business!" It was a joy to watch his veneer crack, even as I realized the danger in pushing the buttons of a man like this. He pointed at me, his hand shaking as he gave in to rage. "It's not enough she steals my wife and daughter out from under me; then, she goes after my livelihood? And I'm supposed to just let some computer with delusions of grandeur get away with that?"

"What exactly was she doing?" pressed Cadence.

Hudd opened his mouth to respond, but snapped it shut, a wary expression flitting across his face.

I feigned boredom, crossing my arms over my chest, and examining the beds of my nails. "You can explain it to us, Mr. Hudd, or you can explain it to the Enforcement Office – it's really your choice."

The man's eyes narrowed into slits. "I thought the EO wasn't looking into this mess. That they had no case."

"I think they'd make an exception if they knew you were involved."

Hudd took in a deep breath, walking out from behind his desk to stand next to me, his voice lowered from a shout back to a conversational tone. "Look, there's a part of my business that may not be...strictly legal by EO standards."

I granted him a glance. "I'm shocked."

"Listen," he said, pacing around us as if he were a lawyer in a courtroom. "If people want to get their hands on drogan, or old scratch, or ponder, or MTNT, they're going to do it one way or the other – I may as well be the one making money off of it in the process."

Cadence turned to follow his circuit around the room. "What does this have to do with Elea Cerf?"

"Since the frag–" He caught himself, and with exaggerated politeness, drawled "– I should say, 'you people' have started coming to Arrhidaeus, it began to make certain fiscal sense to...diversify that part of my business." He reached down to his desk, opening a drawer, and taking out a flat, red docuchip. Holding it out to Cadence, he grinned. "Want a taste, love?"

Cadence leaned away from him but reached forward and took the chip. She turned it this way and that in the dim office light. "What is it?"

"Plug it in and find out."

I heard the dare in his words, saw the glint in the man's eyes, and I blanched. I started to shake my head, my hand coming up to reach for her. "Cadence–"

With quick, sharp movements, Cadence hinged open her jaw and clicked the red chip into the drive concealed in her upper palate, her eyes never leaving Hudd's face.

A beat of silence, of stillness, and then Cadence's entire body seized, her jaw clamping shut so hard I heard the snap of tooth against tooth even from where I stood. Her eyes rolled up into her head until only the bloodshot whites could be seen. A strangled, harsh choking sound ripped its way from her throat, and she collapsed onto the floor, twitching and shaking, all before I could move to do anything.

"Cadence!" I fell to my knees beside her. I grabbed onto her shoulders and felt her body vibrating under my hands. She jerked and flailed out of my grip, grunting and growling, as a trail of white foam began to form at the corner of her mouth.

Hudd sat on the corner of his desk and crossed his feet at the ankles, shoving his hands into his trouser pockets. "Guess I should've told her to sit down."

"What the hell did you do to her?!" I shouted, trying in vain to force her jaw open, thinking vaguely of pulling the docuchip out of her.

"I wouldn't do that if I were you, Mr. Hale," said Hudd. I looked behind me to see the man shaking his head. "Best to let these programs run their course. No telling what you'd do to her processors if you yanked it out mid run."

I shot up onto my feet, hands clenched into fists, the words tearing themselves from my throat in a rough growl. "What did you do to her?"

He responded to my anger with a dismissive sneer, leaning back to free a nix from a gilded case that sat on his desk. "Oh, don't get your panties in a twist, Hale." He ripped off the end of the nix and sucked in a healthy lungful of smoke. "She'll be fine," he said, watching the woman writhe on the floor with, at most, an academic interest. "It's a pleasure program – the frag-gers have taken to calling it RATTER. She's in heaven right now, I guarantee it."

I looked down at Cadence. Tremors wracked her body, and pitiful grunts and whimpers escaped between her clenched teeth. I swallowed hard, chewing the inside of my cheek, resisting the urge to fall back onto the floor and hold her until she stopped shaking. "How long does it last?" I demanded, my eyes fixed on my friend.

Hudd's mouth pulled down into an exaggerated frown and he wiggled his head back and forth. "Depends on how good her antivirus and firewall systems are. Could be a few minutes, could be a few hours."

"Anti–?" My eyes widened and I jerked around to face him again. "Did you just feed her a virus?"

"Their systems can handle it," he said, taking another drag of the nix. "Well, most of the time."

"Hudd–" Before I knew what I was doing I had him by the collar, swinging him around and shaking him. "If you've hurt her, I swear–"

A low, breathy sigh cut through the sound of my threat. I whipped around to see that Cadence had stopped seizing, her eyes staring unseeing up at the ceiling, but at least no longer rolled over white. I released Hudd and rushed to her, kneeling beside her once more, hands ghosting over her, afraid to touch anything, lest I cause more damage than was already done.

"Cay," I said her name softly, wiping the foam away from her face with the cuff of my shirt.

Her eyes were unfocused, pupils blown wide. But after a moment, she seemed to come back to herself, her gaze locking onto my face. She lifted her hand towards me. "Chance?"

"It's alright." I don't know who I was trying to convince, myself or her, but the desperation was clear in my voice. "You're alright."

She drew her hand across her forehead, wincing. Shifting

against the floor, she slowly began to breathe again. "That... that was a bad idea."

I chewed on the inside of my mouth as I nodded. "Yeah, yeah, it was." I sighed and wrapped my hand around her forearm. "Let's get you back on your feet. Okay?"

Too heavy for me to lift by myself, I was grateful that Cadence was regaining some of her own strength with every passing second. But she was still unsteady as she became vertical, swaying on her feet and gripping my arm to keep her balance. Half-hunched over, she reached into her mouth and removed the chip from her upper palate with her fingers.

"How was your trip?" Hudd smoothed out his shirt, smirking.

Cadence stared at him for a moment before answering, still leaning heavily on me. "You're telling me people pay you for that?"

"Not people. Animanecrons. You'd be amazed what they do to get their hands on it." He flicked ash onto the carpeted floor, lifting his brow. "Not to your liking?"

She swallowed and looked away as if embarrassed. "I was completely out of control."

"Hell of a thing, isn't it? Some fraggers, they just can't get enough." He moved back to his chair behind the desk, shaking his head. "Elea, busybody that she was, thought she knew what was best for everybody. Threatened to call the law on me if I didn't stop distributing to her clients." He settled back into his seat. "That message was just my way of telling her to back off."

Cadence grimaced and fixed him with a cold look. "And if she didn't?"

"Well, I wasn't going to kill her." He looked up at the

ceiling, as if considering the veracity of this statement, and then shrugged. "Not right away, anyway."

I glared at him. "So, you didn't care that an Animanecron was bedding your wife and raising your child?"

"Ex-wife," he snapped. He rolled his shoulders back against his chair and forced out a laugh. "Look, Simone made her choices. I may not like them, I may not understand them, but they were hers to make. I'm not happy about it, but I wouldn't stick my neck out to make a stink about it." Having said his piece, he proffered a hand up towards Cadence, gesturing to the red chip of RATTER still perched in her fingertips. "Now...can I have that back?"

Cadence looked at the chip in her grasp. Slowly, she dragged her eyes up to meet Hudd's.

The docuchip shattered with a crunch. Cadence flexed her fingers open and electrical detritus fluttered to the floor.

Hudd's tongue probed the inside of his cheek. His eyes narrowed. "I think we're done here."

I put a restraining hand on Cadence's arm and nodded. "I think we are, yes."

18

Chapter 18

We extricated ourselves from Hudd's office and exited the club as quickly as possible, pausing for the briefest of moments in the hallway outside the main doors to call for a PT to meet us outside.

The sky wept, water falling in thick, ponderous globs, pounding against the public walkways, and making frenetic music against the metal of the waiting PT as we hurried towards it.

Throwing open the back passenger door with one hand, I offered Cadence my other to help her into the waiting vehicle. When we were both safe and dry inside the cab, I shook the rain off my sleeves and asked aloud, "How did you suppose a lovely woman like Simone ever ended up married to someone like that?"

Cadence wiped her face dry, head moving from side to side. "The ways of the human heart are a mystery even to me, Chance."

The PT pulled away from the street and veered sharply upward, climbing towards the upper lanes of traffic that would eventually lead back to our flat. Cadence remained silent for a while, hand cupping her chin, gaze fixed out the rain-streaked window. I watched her closely for any signs that she was still unwell from her misadventure with Hudd's virus. Part of me wanted to chastise her for acting so rashly, for putting herself in danger like that, for letting Hudd goad her into such obvious foolhardiness. But I was stopped by the memory of the blonde animanecron when I opened the office door.

Could I blame Cadence for letting the man get under her skin? He'd certainly gotten under mine.

"Do you believe him?" she asked, breaking the silence. "When he says that he didn't kill Elea?"

"Not for a second," I said with conviction. Squirming deeper into my seat, I scowled, my hand at my lips. "I wouldn't believe a word out of that man's mouth. If he told me that rain fell up and not down, I'd have to have it independently verified."

"You think he's still our best suspect then?" she pressed, turning away from the window to face me.

I glanced at her, my brows quirked upward. "Undoubtedly. Don't you?"

She looked away, staring at her hands in her lap while she considered my query. After a few seconds of thought, her head fell to one side. "He certainly doesn't lack compelling motives. And he doesn't appear to be a man who would shy away from violence." Her lips twisted into a scowl. "But there's too many things that don't fit."

"Like what?"

Her eyes flickered up to meet mine. "Elea left the party to meet her attacker. She shared a drink with them. They were...friendly."

Nodding, I pressed my lips together. "Not a word one would use to describe the relationship between her and Hudd, that's for certain." I shrugged, my hands rising and falling in my lap. "Still, who knows? Maybe he lured her into the meeting with some kind of olive branch as part of the trap."

Cadence nodded but looked less than convinced. "Then there's the problem with Elea's manner of death."

"Hudd developed and distributes a virus targeted specifically at animanecrons. Surely technology like nanobots isn't beyond his reach."

"But someone knew how to make it look like it *wasn't* poison," she said, an insistent set to her jaw. "Someone knew how to stage the body, stage the scene to make other animanecrons think..." She let out a sharp huff and tossed up her hands. "I just don't know that Hudd would go to all that trouble. Or know that he should do so. I can't explain it, but it doesn't feel right."

The PT dropped us at The Feathers' front entrance, and Cadence and I paused our discussion while we made our way through the more public areas of the apartment complex. At length, I dragged my hand over the genetic lock, and the front door to our flat popped open with a chirp. Gesturing in with a sweep of my arm, I allowed Cadence to enter in front of me, asking, "Who would you have us investigate next, then, if you don't think Hudd fits as the murderer?"

"Eamon Lech."

I froze on the threshold behind her, staring wide-eyed at her back as she walked down the entryway steps and into the living room. Hearing his name from her lips was like hearing a holy man swear. I had hoped she had forgotten about Lech. Hoped that I had convinced her of his irrelevance.

More fool me.

I watched as Cadence slid her silk overshirt off her shoulders and dropped it to the floor, her back to me as she spoke. "Ergo Sum is making a real difference in the system's perception of the Whiston Offensive; turning the tide of public opinion against the Charcornacians and their allies." She sat down on the sofa and began to unfasten her heels. "Charcornac would have good reason to want them shut down, and killing Elea is a good start."

Forcing myself to move out of the entryway, I closed the door behind me and wandered into the kitchen, suddenly feeling the need for a strong nightcap. I chose my words carefully as I walked, swallowing to wet my dry throat. "We might be out of our weight class where Lech is concerned, my dear."

There was a scoffing cough from the living room, and I looked up to see Cadence glaring incredulously at me from where she sat on the sofa, one shoe held in her hand. I rolled my eyes, turning away to grab the bottle of Petrarchan whiskey out of the top cabinet. "He's a governmental ambassador, Cadence!"

"So?"

"I'm just saying," I said, pouring a liberal few fingers of whiskey into a glass tumbler as I spoke. "We should tread carefully."

"Perhaps you're right." I listened to the soft padding of her feet against the floor as she walked across the flat towards me. She rested her hips against the kitchen counter, leaning back to stare into my face. "Do you think you could get us a meeting with him?"

I chewed the inside of my mouth and shook my head. "I doubt very much he'd want to meet with you at all, ducky. You did bloody his face the last time."

She scowled but nodded. "True." Her face cleared and she prodded my shoulder with her finger. "Why don't you go alone, then, and report back?" I began to make noncommittal noises of a less than enthused nature and she grabbed onto my free hand with both of hers, tapping against my skin. "I can tell you all the right questions to ask. Please, Chance? This could be important."

It was an impossible position; I could no more say no to Cadence than I could deny my own name. But what she was asking would only hasten what was starting to feel like the inevitable implosion of my life.

Downing my drink in one large gulp, I winced at the burn. "Let's talk about this in the morning, alright? It's been a long day."

"Oh." She released me but gave a small shaky smile all the same. "Alright. I think I'll stay up a while longer."

I returned her smile with one of my own. "How I envy your mechanical constitution." I began unbuttoning my dress shirt with one hand as I started to walk from the kitchen towards the hallway.

The feel of her warm hand brushing across my lower back was a delicious, casual act of intimacy that made me shiver. "Good night, Chance." I looked over my shoulder to watch her disappear into the living room, waving back at me. "Sleep well."

Walking into my bedroom, I shut the door behind me,

leaning back against it with a sigh. I wasn't going to be able to keep Lech at bay forever; he'd force me into action eventually if I didn't figure some way around his demands.

Stripping as I went, I idly flicked on the screen of the computer in the corner of my room, curious to see if Solomon had gleaned any information about the poison that killed Elea. It was a long shot, but perhaps if we could trace its origins, we could gain some insight into who would have used it. Pulling my undershirt up over my head, I groaned at the sight of the vast number of unread messages in my inbox, doubtless forwarded to me from work by Miss Taylor. I sat down heavily in the desk chair in front of the screen with the intent of scrolling through the messages, when one at the top of the list caught my eye.

It had arrived less than ten minutes ago, from an address I did not recognize. The message itself had no subject but was marked urgent. Brow furrowing, I ran a quick virus scan on the item. No malicious content was detected, and I selected it, curiosity growing.

It felt as if someone had reached into my chest and crushed my heart in their fist. Wide eyed, horrified, I stared at the image which had flashed onto my screen. Cadence had her face turned towards me as I helped her into the PT outside *The Nest*, a small smile playing across her lips. My face was half visible, the collar of my jacket turned up against the rain. A large, red 'x' covered Cadence's body.

Hand shaking, I swiped the image away to read the message. It was simple enough.

You're out of time.

I jerked up away from the desk and started towards my door

at a run. My hand was on the handle when I forced myself to stop. The Feathers had topnotch security. If she was in the apartment, Cadence was safe. They could follow us out there, but in here, we were safe.

Safe for now.

I had indeed run out of time.

Early the next morning, far earlier than I usually ventured out of my rooms, I shuffled out to the kitchen. I could hear the television as I walked down the hall, and I came around the corner to see Cadence sitting on the sofa, watching the morning news. She had changed out of her club clothes and into trappings more in keeping with her usual style, but she was not in pajamas like me. I thought about cinching my black silk robe closed but decided I couldn't be bothered with human modesty today – not when I could smell freshly brewed coffee wafting through the air.

Yawning, I entered the kitchen to find the coffee maker had just finished making what was doubtless a second pot of the gorgeous stuff. I picked a wide-mouthed black mug out of the cabinet and began to pour myself a generous amount of the caffeinated liquid, breathing in the steam.

"You're up early," I said, looking at Cadence over my shoulder as the rich, black coffee streamed into my mug. "Or did you never go to sleep?"

She flicked the mute button on the television remote and glanced over at me, shaking her head. "Didn't see the point. Too much to think about; too much to process."

I nodded in answer. I knew the feeling. Sleep had eluded me all night as well, and unlike my friend, the lack of rest was already taking its toll. I put down the coffee maker and rubbed my eyes until white spots began appearing in the darkness behind my eyelids. I preferred the splotches to the images that had been playing there all night: Cadence, with the back of her head torn open, still and dead. Cadence melted down to molten metal while she still retained her consciousness. Cadence, left to the tender mercies of Eamon Lech and more men just like him.

I opened my eyes, sighing. He had me. He had me and he knew it. I would burn the entire world down with me in it if it meant saving Cadence.

I took up my coffee and trudged into the living room, robe billowing behind me as I headed for the sofa where she sat, staring at the muted television.

Nestling myself in the space beside her, I draped my arm across her shoulders and pulled her to my side, placing a chaste kiss against the side of her forehead. "Bless you for making coffee."

She smiled in response, reaching out to squeeze my knee, her attention still absorbed in the moving images on the screen.

Was this going to be our last morning together? The thought occurred to me in a flash. I swallowed hard, putting my mug down on the coffee table. I wasn't guaranteed to lose her. Maybe she would understand. Maybe...

I reached up and tucked a piece of her hair behind her ear. No. She would leave. And she would leave never knowing how I really felt about her.

"Cay," I started, the words falling slowly from my lips. "You know I..." I swallowed down the sentiment, unprepared for the fear that swelled up inside me. I tried again, shifting against the firm cushions to face her more directly. "We're...we're friends, aren't we?"

Cadence nodded but remained focused on the screen in front of us. "Of course, Chance."

"We look out for each other, don't we?" I removed my arm from around her shoulders, reaching down into her lap to grasp her hand. "You trust me?"

Something in my tone must have broken through to her. She blinked, straightening. Her hand squeezed mine and she looked straight at me, brows drawing up to a point. "Like I trust myself." She shifted in her seat, bringing her leg up under her as she turned to face me. "Con, is everything alright, Chance?"

"No." The truth came out with such ease it surprised me into dropping her hand. I pulled back, taking in a deep breath as I drew my hand down my face. "No, it's not. I have–"

The loud, sharp rap of knuckles against wood echoed through the flat like a gunshot.

I twisted around to glare at the entryway. "Damn it. Who the hell could that be?"

Cadence's hand was soft against my cheek, smooth as marble and warm as a sunbeam. She drew me back to her, her inky blue eyes bright. "Ignore it." She tapped her affection against my skin and my heart ached. "What's wrong?"

I opened my mouth, ready to tell her everything: to tell her about Lech's visit to my office and his unthinkable demands, his threats if I did not comply with those demands, and my reasons for giving into them, when a second knock pierced the air, heavy and insistent.

I shut my jaws with a snap and a growl. Vaulting over the

back of the couch, I strode to the front door and yanked it open without bothering to see who waited on the other side.

The 'who' blinked at me, his fist raised in the act of knocking again, and my childhood friend gave me a sheepish, sideways grin. "Sorry about the hour." Slouching, Henry dropped his hand to his side. "Can I come in?"

"Course." I stepped back from the door to give him room to walk inside, but my brow remained furrowed in confusion. "Is everything alright?"

He breezed past me into the entryway. "Relatively," he answered, not stopping to remove his overcoat as he strode into the living room, his shoulders hunched.

I tilted my head to one side, following his progress with my eyes as he passed. Cadence and I shared a glance. Henry's steps were long and fast. His hands were in his pockets one minute and out the next, flexing. His eyes roamed around the room, but studiously avoided landing on either Cadence or me.

Something was wrong.

I cleared my throat. "Coffee?" I started to move towards the kitchen, my hand outstretched. "We have a few promising leads on the case–"

"Good to hear," he cut in, shuffling in place in the center of the living room, his nervous hands burrowing into his trouser pockets. "But not why I'm here."

I stopped on the stair that led up to the kitchen. My hand fell to my side. I watched him for a moment, his demeanor beginning to seriously concern me. "Right then. Care to enlighten us?"

Henry took in a deep breath, casting a sideways glance at

Cadence and before turning his attention to me. "First of all, you need to know that this wasn't my idea."

"Ominous," I responded, walking back to join my friends in the living room.

He pushed a hand back through his dark hair and rubbed at the back of his neck, his gaze flicking heavenward. "Representative Peyton reached out to Ergo Sum. He wants to help put on a sort of memorial rally for Elea."

A derisive snort escaped me. "How politically expedient of him."

"Simone is on board," Henry continued, still staring at the ceiling. "She doesn't love the election angle, but she thinks Peyton's involvement will get the event more media coverage. Maybe shame the EO into doing something about Elea's death."

"I suppose I can understand that." I gave a slow nod, still failing to see why any of this demanded an early morning visit to Cadence and I.

"Does she want us to attend?" Cadence glanced between Henry and I, clasping her hands together between her knees. "It could be a wonderful opportunity to glean more information."

"She..." Henry struggled over some half-formed syllables for a moment before letting out a belabored sigh, turning to face Cadence fully, his lips a serious line. "Both she and Representative Peyton have asked if you would say a few words at the rally."

We all fell silent. We could hear the rain pelting against the windows, like dozens of tiny tap dancers.

Both Cadence and I had stopped breathing. But I was forced to resume before she was, the air shallow and cold in my lungs.

"What?" I rasped.

"Oh," said Cadence, hand coming up to her collarbone. She blinked once, then again. "What...mot, what an honor."

"Henry..." I growled his name, my hands clenching into fists at my side.

"Like I said, it wasn't my idea," he answered quickly, shaking his head. "That being said...I don't necessarily think it's a bad one."

"Have you lost your mind?" I heard myself shouting and hated myself for it. "Do you have any idea the kind of danger she'd be putting herself in?"

"She's already in danger, Chance, every day!" His volume rose to match mine. He gestured towards the grey cityscape outside the living room windows. "You don't know what it's like out there right now. Fear, anger, distrust – it's all boiling over, and animanecrons are getting the brunt of it!"

"And you want to put Cadence in the middle of that?" I demanded, blood rushing to my face.

"No one is putting me in the middle of anything," said Cadence, rising gracefully to her feet between us. She held her fist to her collarbone, staring at me with a firmness that did not invite challenge. "This is my choice to make; not Henry's, and not yours, Chance."

I struggled to keep the panic out of my voice, gritting my teeth together and closing my eyes as I spoke. "I'm trying to keep you safe, Cay."

A small smile flitted across her lips. "I don't need you to."

Shaking my head, my hands wheeling wildly in front of me, I sputtered, "They'll–they'll tear you to pieces, Cadence! You can't – I can't let that happen."

I watched as a flurry of emotions paraded across her face. Looking at me, her lips twisted into an annoyed scowl, then softened into a concerned frown. Her brows furrowed in thought and confusion, and she looked away with sadness in her eyes. At last, with just a hint of hesitation, she reached forward and placed her hand onto my shoulder.

"Chance," she said, her jaw set, her voice low. "I let fear drive me from my family, from my home. I'm not letting it drive me anymore."

I turned my back to her, shrugging her hand off my shoulder. "You don't understand! I can't–"

"What is that?"

I didn't have to look at Henry to see what he was gesturing too. I was already facing the television. Still muted, I watched in numb horror as my own face floated across the screen, the ticker at the bottom of the news program proclaiming in bold white letters, "CHANCE HALE TO GIVE PRESS CONFERENCE ON ANI-PROBLEM".

Last night I had told the communications department to move as quickly as possible to alert the media. I just hadn't expected to make the morning news.

I spun around on my heel, my hands held up in front of myself. "Cay, I can explain–"

But it was too late. Cadence had crossed towards the television, waving at it to unmute, and the booming voice of daytime anchor Omar Odeh boomed through the apartment.

"...this press conference will mark the first public statement Halcyon Enterprises has made about the so-called 'Ani-Problem' and we're being told by sources close to company CEO Chance

Hale to expect the head of the multi-billion dollar corporation to have some strong words for those who hold the 'misguided' view that animanecrons deserve equal treatment in the eyes of the law." The images on the screen cut to reveal Omar standing in the middle of the Halcyon Enterprise Campus. He gave a half-hearted smile, lifting an eyebrow. "Should be some interesting soundbites for sure. Leila, back to you in the studio."

I waved at the television to mute, cutting off Leila Lloyd's follow up remarks, my gaze focused on the floor. I winced at the sound of Henry's voice, the hurt thick in his words.

"Chance, what have you done?"

"Chance?" The top of Cadence's feet came into my view. Her hand landed on my shoulder once more. "What's... what's going on? What press conference? What are they talking about?"

I locked eyes with her, my chest heaving. "Cadence, if..." My tongue flicked out to wet my lips, but I powered on, the words ripping themselves from me, the sensation not unlike ripping a bandage from a wound. "If Halcyon Enterprises doesn't come out on the side of Charcornac– if I don't make a public statement disavowing Ergo Sum and Ani-Rights as a whole, Eamon Lech will kill you."

Henry choked out a gasp, but I didn't look at him. In that moment, Cadence was my whole world. She stared into my eyes, unblinking, her hand heavy on my shoulder. Her lips parted, but no sound came from them, not even a whisper of air. She was still; silent.

I wondered for the briefest of moments if she'd heard me, if she'd understood. But then, her hand fell away from me. She stepped back. And I knew.

She'd understood every word.

"Chance–!" Henry's hushed exclamation pierced the air, but he was cut short by a slice of Cadence's hand.

She never took her eyes off me. She took in a deep breath and let it out slowly. She blinked; swallowed.

"You're going to do it." The words came out in a whisper, but not as a question.

I closed my eyes and spread my hands out in front of myself. "What choice do I have?"

Her footsteps were heavy as she stepped around me. I opened my eyes to see her walking away, heading towards the hallway. My brow furrowed. I started after her.

"Cay?"

I followed her down the hall and into her bedroom. Her name was on the tip of my tongue, but I went silent as I watched her pull a worn, white duffel bag out from underneath her bed. Placing it open on top of the mattress, she crossed to the closet and took out a shirt and a pair of trousers. She returned to the bed and shoved the clothes into the bag without a word.

"Cadence," I asked, a sense of alarm and dread growing inside my belly as I watched her. "What are you doing?"

Still, she didn't answer. She made the circuit between the closet and the bed two more times, stuffing a few more shirts and another pair of trousers into the duffel bag, not pausing to fold them. Zipping up the bag with one hand, she picked it up with the other, and slung the strap across her torso, adjusting the weight so it would rest comfortably on her hip.

"Cay, stop."

She turned back to me and headed for the doorway where I was standing, mouth a grim line, eyes hard and focused.

"Caden–" I stepped in front of her. I might as well have stepped in front of an AN-GRAV. She pushed me to one side, and I bounced off the wall, breath knocked from me. It was a moment before I regained my balance enough to follow her, and by then she was disappearing at the mouth of the hallway, heedless to my cry of: "Stop!"

By the time I caught up with her, she had climbed the stairs to reach the front door; the only sign of her inner turmoil that I could see was the frantic way she forced her feet into her trainers.

"Cadence, please," I begged, coming to a halt at the bottom of the entryway stairs. "Stop and talk to me!"

She spun on her heels, one hand gripping the doorknob so tight her knuckles blanched. "Talk to you?" Her voice was rough with rage. She stared down at me, her eyes wide. Shaking her head, she shouted, "Talk to you?!"

I had angered Cadence before. We had exchanged shouts and insults, doing our best to hurt each other with words. This was nothing like that. What had happened was written clear on her face. Anyone who didn't believe animanecrons to have feelings, needed only to see Cadence in this moment to know how wrong they were.

I had broken her heart.

She closed her eyes, threw the door open, and stepped through. "Fas, I can barely stand to look at you."

I stood there, numb, staring at the yawning portal, listening to her retreating footsteps until there was nothing but silence.

With infinitesimal slowness, I turned my face towards Henry, who was still standing in the center of the living room. His jaw clenched, his brown eyes were narrowed. I couldn't meet his gaze, lowering my eyes to the floor.

"Henry..." I managed at last. "What...what did I just do?"

"You made your bed, Chance." Buttoning his overcoat shut, Henry shook his head. With a few quick strides, he moved past me and out the door. "Now you have to lie in it."

19

Chapter 19

I could feel the sweat trickling down the side of my face. I wiped it away with my wrist band, glancing at my trainer as I did so. The thin black band featured a chunky graphic of a stick figure running, and encouragingly flashed my time up at me in green, the seconds slowly adding up. I was a few minutes away from my goal, and pushed myself around the track, the cushioned syntho-grass keeping vibrations out of my shins and knees as I ran.

The Halcyon Enterprises Campus was a block of eight buildings in the center of District 30. It was a self-contained city and had every amenity its workers could desire. In my admittedly limited time as head of the company, I had grown particularly fond of the gymnasium, a sprawling three-floor complex that had everything from weight rooms, which I had frequented just prior to my run, to tennis courts, swimming pools, and holorooms.

The track was on the topmost floor, where the ceiling was built as a retractable dome, meant to give those running the sense of truly being out in nature. The dome was closed today, but the world was still visible through the tempered glass, such as it was. As I ran, I stared up at the angry black sky, visible through the thick crisscross pattern of PT's and cargo ships, pushing myself to run faster, harder, for just a little bit longer.

I wanted to hurt.

I wanted pain and the sweet release from thought it provided.

And it was no less than I deserved.

I hadn't heard from Cadence in two days. Not a word. She had never invested in a mobile, preferring to remain unreachable, claiming that anyone who needed could find her on the vertex. I didn't even know her v-address. I'd never needed it.

She'd always been there.

Henry was likewise avoiding my calls. I couldn't blame him. Even if he had answered, I wasn't sure what I would have said.

I couldn't go back to work as if nothing had happened, as if my life hadn't spun entirely out of control. I couldn't mope around the apartment, where reminders of her lurked around every corner and the temptation to sit in her room and weep was all too real.

I was trapped.

I thought first of drinking myself into a blind stupor, but the act felt too gentle, too self-indulgent to be what I deserved; to be a punishment. When my mobile beeped to remind me of my scheduled weekly workout, I seized on the opportunity with all the desperation of a starving dog onto a discarded bone.

Running had always been my exercise of choice – I was even on the track team at university. But it'd been years since I'd engaged in a serious running regimen, and today my body felt every minute of the four hours I had spent pushing it along the track, forcing myself to complete my own self-imposed marathon with absolutely no preparation. My grey t-shirt stuck to me, heavy with sweat. My hands shook, and my legs wobbled under me, my muscles screaming in agony.

I passed the starting line for the twenty-fourth time and, at last, my left leg gave out from under me. I managed to fall onto my knee, but the shock of the impact with the ground jittered up my aching body like the bolt from a taser gun. Gritting my teeth, I cursed aloud and tried to force myself upright, when a familiar voice addressed me from the doors that separated the track from the rest of the facility.

"As far as self-flagellation goes–" The words rang out in the silence, cutting through the pounding blood in my ears and the rasping of oxygen in and out of my lungs. "–this is inventive."

I spun around to see my oldest friend perched atop a short cylindrical stool, one of several that surrounded the entryway leading up to the track. Henry's clasped hands dangled between his knees as he rested his elbows on his thighs. He watched me, frown deepening when I staggered towards him, my mouth agape.

"Henry!" I blinked the sweat out of my eyes, ignoring the sting. "How long–?"

"Long enough." He straightened up and kicked a stool towards me as he rolled up his shirt sleeves, sneering. "Sit down before you fall down, idiot."

I didn't need further encouragement. Chest heaving, I collapsed onto the stool he offered, using what self-control I had left to keep myself mostly upright.

We were silent. As I caught my breath, watching other joggers and walkers making their way around the track, I racked my brain for something to say that wasn't the one question I wanted answered more than anything. All other topics seemed laughably trivial, however, so instead I said nothing.

Beside me, I felt him lean in. I stiffened, forcing myself to stare straight ahead and not look at him, worried what my expression might reveal.

"She's alright. She's staying with Simone."

Relaxing into a half-hunched puddle, I sighed in pure relief. "Thank y–"

"How could you be so stupid?" he demanded.

I leaned forward, my elbows on my knees, my head hanging low. "I was thinking of Cadence."

"You were thinking of yourself," he insisted, head bobbing up and down. Straightening, he flung his arms out wide, his tone turning mocking. "Thinking that you'd get to play the big strapping hero and stand between your lady love and the cruel, cruel world." Hands falling to his side, he looked down at my hunched frame with derision. "Idiot."

Shame and anger bubbled in the pit of my stomach. I wanted to answer his disdain with denial, with defense, but I resisted the urge. Instead, I sat with his words ringing in my ears a moment longer than was comfortable.

He was right.

I had acted selfishly. I'd told myself it was for Cadence, but that was a comforting lie. It had always been for me.

With a tired sigh, Henry rose to his feet. He walked to the nearby public water cooler and dispensed a cup's worth of cool liquid into a small biodegradable container. Returning to my side, he held the drink out to me, his next words no less firm, although they had lost their biting edge. "She doesn't need a knight in shining armor, Chance."

I managed a weak glare in his direction but took the water from him. "I am painfully aware of that, thank you."

"Are you? Then why didn't you just talk to her about this thing with Lech?"

Because I was scared she would leave.

I screwed my eyes shut, as if the truth I knew deep in my own heart could blind me.

I had been scared that if I told her what was happening with Lech, she would leave. And I hadn't wanted to give her that opportunity. I already didn't know why she stayed with me. With her life in danger, surely she would have left me behind and been happy to be rid of me, wouldn't she?

I let out a shallow, shaky breath. My god. Did I really think so little of her? That she would abandon me at the first sign of trouble? How could I be so stupid?

Henry sat down beside me once more. He mimicked my posture, putting his face level with mine. "Cadence doesn't need a vassal. She needs a partner." His hand came up to stroke his chin and he shook his head, sighing. "You were so busy trying to stand in front of her, you didn't realize that all she needed was for you to stand beside her."

I opened my eyes, staring at nothing. Why hadn't I trusted her? When had she ever given me cause to doubt her?

"I treated her like a child," I said, my words a whisper, more to myself than to Henry. A groan tore itself from my throat, and I slapped my hand against my forehead. "Oh god, I am such an idiot."

Henry straightened. He clapped me on the shoulder. "Yup."

"Henry," I said, my face still in my hand. "What on Arrhidaeus am I going to do?"

"Oh, I have no idea."

I swiveled my head around and glared at him. He squeezed my shoulder and let out a laugh. "What? I can't have all the answers."

I straightened on the stool, rolling my shoulders back, a plan forming in my mind. "I need to talk to her. Apologize."

"She doesn't want to talk to you, Chance," said Henry.

"I've got to." I swallowed and shook my head. "I'll just have to change her mind."

"How?"

"I'll figure something out." Struggling to my feet, I tapped the fitness band on my wrist, bringing up the date and time. "How much time do we have before the memorial? It's today, isn't it? I thought I heard something about it on the news."

"It is. But we have enough time for you to take a shower," Henry said, wiping the hand he had touched me with on his shirt. He gave a rough laugh as he stood. "God, you reek."

Heedless to his needling, I pulled him into a tight embrace, shaking my head. "What would I do without you?"

"Die stinking and alone?" He held on to me and I felt him smile for a moment before he patted my back with both hands. "Honestly, Chance, I might pass out from the stench."

I gave a huff of a laugh and released him. "Right."

20

Chapter 20

One quick, but thorough shower later, Henry and I made our way to the Unatarian Theater in District 29. Representative Peyton, known for his flair for the dramatic, had spared no expense in renting out the auditorium of the famous theater for Elea's memorial rally. The Unatarian Theater was grotesquely modern, the building itself rising from the ground like a space-craft, bronze and gold triangular panels cascading into the dark sky, as if exploding. Inside, everything dripped with red, not a surface from the floors to the ceiling spared of scarlet.

Shaking off my raincoat, we paused for a moment in the foyer, Henry looking for some indication of where Simone and Cadence might be. I was surprised by the size of the crowd that greeted us inside; there were easily 300 plus bodies in atten-dance, not counting the clusters of camera crews and reporters from both local and interplanetary news outfits. Everywhere, there permeated a buzz of anticipation that I didn't associate with a memorial, even though almost everyone was dressed in the traditional black.

Henry began to guide me towards the stages, his hand on my shoulder, trying as best as he could to give the reporters a wide berth. But it was impossible to avoid them all, and we ended up wedged in a crowd of people a few feet away from the door we needed to access, directly beside a tight cluster of cameras, lights, and microphones. In the middle of all the equipment, I spied the tall, spry frame of Leila Lloyd, one of Römer's star television journalists. But it wasn't the sight of a near-celebrity that drew my attention, but the sound of Eamon Lech pontificating for the masses that quite neatly captured my gaze.

He stood next to Leila in a crisp, black suit, shaking his head. I smiled a little when I detected the use of heavy make-up around his nose, doubtless concealing a nice bruise that was of Cadence's making.

"...what I object to–" he was saying, "–is the media's continued coverage of these clashes in ways which cast the A.F.O., and other rightly concerned citizen activists, as being in the wrong."

Leila Lloyd furrowed her brow, crossing her arms over her chest. "But, surely, animanecrons are making reasonable–"

"Reasonable? Isn't it reasonable to seek to protect your way of life? To preserve your livelihood? To defend the very notion of what it means to be human?" Shaking his head, Lech frowned, his handsome face taking on a somber expression. "Animanecrons are machines, Miss Lloyd. What's next? Giving PTs the right to vote? Thermostats the right to equal pay? Where does it stop?" Lech's blue eyes burned with righteous fervor, one hand clenched into a fist as he brought it down through the air. "It stops here. Now."

Another question was forming on Leila's lips, when Lech looked around himself and finally spotted me standing there. His eyes widened. He broke out into a tooth-filled grin. His hand shooting out like a grappling hook, he stepped towards me and pulled me effortlessly into the ring of lights, nodding. "If you really want the final word on the Ani Issue, here's the man you should be speaking to right now."

His arm was strong and firm around my shoulders. There was nowhere to go. I stared into the camera floating in front of us and, with a sickening lurch, realized that the red light was flashing to indicate that the feed was live.

Leila Lloyd's brown eyes widened. "Mr. Hale!" She immediately pivoted towards the camera, her hand flitting up under her braids to the bud nestled in her ear as she communicated back to the hosts at the studio. "Omar, I just happen to have Chance Hale here, head of Halcyon Enterprises, the company that originally created animanecrons over two hundred years ago. Mr. Hale," she said, turning back to me with undisguised relish. "Halcyon Enterprises has been very vague when it comes to the current situation regarding the so-called Ani Issue. Why is that?"

A practiced non-answer tripped smoothly off my tongue as I blinked spots out of my eyes, the glare from the camera lights blinding. "I would say that it's because there is no one issue, per say, but a multitude of complex factors at play when it comes to animanecrons reintegrating into our societies."

She nodded, gaze intent on my face. "But you do think they should be allowed to reintegrate?"

I paused a moment and took a deep breath before focusing my attention fully on the woman across from me. "Allowed?" Shaking my head, I gestured back to the crowd gathering for Elea's memorial. "What choice have we given them? We've allowed them to be butchered on their own planet, and then we have the gall to say that they're not welcome here. We should be grateful they want anything to do with us."

Lech's fingers dug into my shoulder, his grip going from firm to strangling. "I think what Mr. Hale means—"

I shook myself free from Lech and stepped forward, staring directly into the camera. "Animanecrons are not property. They are not pieces of tech to be used and discarded when we no longer find them useful or convenient. They're people, with a culture, language, and life all their own, and they have as much of a right to exist in this universe as any of us do."

Leila Lloyd's eyes sparkled with excitement as she breathlessly pressed, "Is that the official position of Halcyon Enterprises, Mr. Hale?"

"It's my official position, Miss Lloyd." I bared my teeth at her in a not-quite smile. "And I am Halcyon Enterprises. Now, if you'll excuse me, I have a memorial to attend."

I turned my back to the camera and locked eyes with Lech. Blood had drained from his face, and his hands were fists at his sides, shaking ever so slightly. Taking a step towards him, I leaned in so only he and I could hear, and whispered: "Go to hell, Lech."

I walked over to Henry without looking back, blood pounding

in my ears. Hyper aware of camera lenses trained on me, I did my best to keep my pace slow and even. Henry had opened a path to the auditorium door, and was standing next to the open portal, the only sign that he had heard any of what had happened was a reserved smile.

When the door closed behind us, Henry, his composure breaking, slapped me hard on the back. "Good for you, Chance."

"No applause, please," I muttered, my eyes darting around the crowded auditorium, more determined than ever to find Cadence. "Do you think–?"

"Hey!"

I started at the shout. Looking up, I saw Simone clambering down off the stage, which was empty except for a simple wooden podium. Once she reached the floor, she began waving in our direction, hurrying towards us.

Panic gripped me. Cadence must have told her what had happened; what I'd done. She must be furious. She probably wanted me to leave.

As she picked her way through the crowd, I lifted my hands in front of myself and leaned back, prepared to weather a barrage of well-deserved ire. "Simone, I–"

"That was amazing!" I stumbled backwards as the slight woman swept me up into a bone crushing embrace. She withdrew after a moment, still holding onto one of my arms, and I looked down to see her grinning from ear to ear, even as her cheeks carried the tracks of recent tears. "Chance, you're incredible! Do you know how many people were watching that broadcast? How many people will see that interview?"

That was when I noticed the small holopuck in her hand,

which was still broadcasting Leila Lloyd's coverage of the memorial. I blushed crimson. Staring at my feet, I shifted where I stood, discomfited by her praise. "Should've done it a long time ago." I shoved my hands into my trouser pockets. "Too much of a coward though."

Simone rubbed my arm, her smile softening into reassurance. "We've all been scared of things changing, Chance. It's human."

I didn't deserve her kindness. I was about to say as much, when the auditorium lights dimmed above us, and the crowd started to hush, settling into their seats.

She glanced over her shoulder, jumping a little. "Oh, it's time. Henry, come on!"

"See you after," said Henry, flashing me a lazy salute as he moved past me towards the stage.

Thus abandoned, I looked around for an empty seat, only to find the auditorium filled to the absolute limit. Undeterred, I strode toward the nearest empty wall as the lights went out. Leaning against the hard red surface, my feet crossed at the ankle, I had a fair view of the podium from where I stood, as well as the right wing of the stage.

I wasn't the only person without a seat; a dozen or so of us standing or sitting along the walls and watching the proceedings. So, when I felt a man move into the space behind me, I didn't think anything of it, glancing back at him in a perfunctory way.

Brisbois stared past me at the stage, applauding politely as Representative Peyton approached the podium and began his opening remarks.

I snapped my head forward, suppressing a groan. The absolute last person I wanted to see – so naturally he would appear.

Peyton's speech consisted of much of the same stuff as he had said outside of Ergo Sum the night Elea died, and I tuned him out with ease. My attention instead turned to the number of EO officers that were now plainly stationed throughout the dark auditorium, blue suits shiny in the dim light reflected from the stage.

Despite my sincerest wishes that he would maintain at least the appearance of being unaware of me, Brisbois stepped away from the wall and forward until he was beside me, his hands falling into his trouser pockets.

"Mr. Hale," he said, voice low, not deigning to spare me a glance.

"Inspector," I answered in kind, nodding. Casting a pointed look around the perimeter of the space, I asked, "You lot expecting trouble?"

He rolled his shoulders back and sighed. "It's an Ani rally. We always expect trouble."

"It's a memorial service." I glared at him from the corner of my eyes, stressing each word.

That at last garnered a look in my direction. He lifted his brows in acknowledgment of my point before turning back to face front, his voice dropping to a low murmur only I could hear. "Any progress on Miss Cerf's case?"

"Some." I did my best to sound as nonchalant as possible. I watched as Simone walked out to join Peyton at the podium. He stepped back to allow her to say a few words, setting the stage for the memorial's speakers, of which Cadence was to be the first. "You?"

Brisbois' head fell to one side, and he rubbed at his cheek.

"I've been interviewing Ergo Sum's aid recipients. None of them seem to have borne Elea or Simone any ill will."

Smirking, I turned towards him. "You don't really think an animanecron killed Elea, do you?"

"It'd be premature to discount such an eventuality."

I rolled my eyes, and was about to make a snide response, when I spied Cadence step up into the wing, Henry just behind her. The sight of her stilled the breath in my lungs for a torturous moment, my chest tightening. She was wearing a black skirt that went down to her ankles, and a long-sleeved black shirt with a deep V-neck. Sharing a whispered conversation with Henry, she looked serious and determined, even as her fingers tapped nervously against her arm.

"...now, it is my privilege to introduce someone whom Elea and I met only recently, but who has become very dear to me in a short time," said Simone, turning to smile at Cadence. "She has a unique perspective on the relationship between humans and animanecrons and is proving to be indispensable when it comes to seeking justice not just for Elea, but for all animanecrons. Please welcome Miss Cadence Turing."

With Henry accompanying her, Cadence started across the stage, her head held high as a round of applause began. She nodded to the audience, making the customary gesture of thanks, stopping as something, or someone, at the edge of the stage caught her eye.

"How's Miss Turing holding up?" Brisbois asked with a suddenness that made me start.

My heart stuttered at the sound of her name. I cleared my throat and looked pointedly at the floor. "Fine. She's fine. Why?"

"She looks...unhappy." He looked from her to me, and I felt myself begin to redden under his examinatory gaze. "You two didn't...?"

I bit down hard on the inside of my mouth, my hands clenching. I shot him a warning stare. "Didn't what?"

What happened next was a blur of sensation. From the corner of my eye, I saw Cadence lean down to accept something from someone standing at the edge of the stage. At the same moment, an explosion drowned out the thunderous applause. Henry, standing just behind Cadence, jerked backward, grabbing for her, and spinning as he fell to the floor, pulling her down with him. A second explosion, and a hanging stage light burst in a shower of sparks and shattered glass. A burning smell, acrid and earthy, began to permeate the air. The screaming started in earnest then, the gunshots recognized by all for what they were, and the room heaved with stampeding bodies, everyone rushing for the exits in the half darkness.

Flesh and bone buffeted against me as I ran in the opposite direction of the crowd, toward the stage instead of away from it. I struggled around frenzied and frightened rally goers, watching as Peyton's security detail hurried him and Simone to safety backstage. Cadence and Henry had vanished, as if swallowed whole.

I pulled myself up onto the stage and stood, heedless to the fine target I was making of myself.

"Cadence! Henry!"

I blinked in the sudden glare of the overhead lights, wandering into the middle of the stage blindly. "Cadence! Hen–"

"Get down, you idiot!" Cadence shouted, pulling me to the floor behind the podium with one strong tug on my arm.

My knees hit the floor with a thud. Cadence's hand slid across my own, sticky and wet. I drew away from her, my fingers covered with thick, red blood.

"Cadence, are you–!" Words caught in my throat as I got a closer look at what was going on. "Oh god, Henry..."

Blood gushed from a ragged, gaping hole in his shoulder. His white dress shirt was soaked rusty red, and he screamed as Cadence returned her hands to the wound, pressing into the flesh in a desperate attempt to staunch the bleeding.

Brown eyes wide, his hand scrambled to take mine, breath coming in harsh bursts from between his gritted teeth. "I'm alright," he managed. His voice was shaky, his face as pale as a bank of freshly fallen snow. "It's alright."

He was not alright. I shared a glance with Cadence, who swallowed and shook her head.

"I don't think it hit any bones," said Cadence. She looked down at herself, at the rivulets of blood running down her wrists and onto her arms and then looked back up at me, fear palpable in her gaze. "Frig, it is bleeding a lot though."

Brisbois chose that moment to vault over the lip of the stage, landing on the boards with a thud, his taser gun at the ready. He rushed towards us and knelt behind the podium, pausing to glance around the dais for any sign of the shooter.

I tugged him back, shouting to be heard over the absolute chaos which surrounded us. "We need a medic – now!"

Brisbois took in the situation at a glance. He holstered his taser gun and stuck his hand out towards me. "Give me your jacket." I did as he ordered, and watched as he folded it into a square, leaning in towards Henry. He pushed Cadence's hands out of the way and pressed the wadded fabric against the wound. "Keep pressure on it," he said, turning to Cadence. He took her hands by the wrists and placed them with precision, one directly on the jacket, already beginning to turn red, the other on the opposite side of Henry's shoulder. "Here."

Cadence did as she was told, and Brisbois produced an EO mobile from his pocket and slid it into his ear, putting in the call for EMT teams to respond to the shooting at the Unatarian Theater as soon as possible.

I heard the wail of sirens within minutes. Red suited medics forced their way through the crowds to us, and before we had the chance to put up any resistance, they hustled us away from Henry. Watching with alarm as they swarmed him, putting him on a repulsor stretcher while strapping various devices to his arms and neck, Brisbois put a hand on my shoulder, shaking me.

"Come on. We can meet them at the hospital. They're taking him to Holtzon Medical."

"Can't I ride with him?"

"We'd be in the way," snapped Cadence, dropping my ruined jacket to the floor without looking at me. She turned to Brisbois. "Let's go."

If I hadn't been so worried about Henry, it would have been the most awkward and uncomfortable PT ride of my life. I was in the back of an Enforcement Office vehicle, never a pleasant place to be, sitting beside a woman who I adored, but who seemed determined to deny my existence. Cadence didn't speak a word to me, didn't look at me the entire trip to Holtzon

Medical Center. Frowning, her entire body tense as a rod, it was impossible to read her emotional state. She relaxed only slightly, sitting outside the recovery room where Henry was eventually moved after a long hour of surgery, when one of the doctor's told us our friend should make a full recovery. The young man had lost a lot of blood, and would need time and rest to heal, but heal he would.

I looked in through the recovery room's glass door. Henry was still under sedation. He would've looked peaceful, if not for the mass of thick white bandages plastered around his right shoulder, and the bag of blood hanging beside him, dripping back into his veins.

I took a deep breath, gaze falling to my hands. Henry's blood was dry and brown, flaking away from my skin. Cadence was a horror, caked in dried blood up to her elbows, a smear of flaking brown across her forehead.

Brisbois had left us temporarily to follow up with his men at the theater, hopeful that the shooter had been apprehended. Alone together, Cadence continued her campaign of silence, staring pointedly at the floor.

Rolling my shoulders back, I was about to suggest that she ask someone about getting cleaned up, when Solomon careened around the corner of the hallway. He spotted us and rushed towards us, frantic with fear.

"Is he alright?" demanded Solomon, face drawn and haggard.

"Yes," I said, placing what I hoped was a reassuring hand on his shoulder. "He's going to be fine."

His tense frame relaxed under my hand. He put his hand to his forehead and turned away. "Thank God for that." In turning,

Cadence came into his field of vision, and he started at the sight of her, his mouth dropping open. "Cadence! Are you–?"

"Don't worry; it's Henry's blood." Cadence's gaze flickered between his face and the floor, and she quickly added: "It's alright, he's getting more now to replace it."

"That's...good," he said after a moment. Clearing his throat, he jerked a thumb over his shoulder, indicating an alcove located a little way down the hall. "I'm going to call Minerva, give her an update. She's on her way from Zahia."

As Solomon moved back down the hallway, I spied Brisbois coming from the opposite direction, a hand to his ear as he muttered into his mobile. He hung up before reaching us, his face drawn as he pushed a bloodstained hand back through his hair.

"Any news on the shooter?" I asked as soon as he was within earshot.

"None," said Brisbois, shaking his head.

"How is that possible?" My face contorted, my emotions caught somewhere between confusion and rage. "The EO was crawling all over that place, and you're telling me no one saw anything?"

Cadence straightened in her chair, gripping the armrest as she looked up at Brisbois. "You will be putting a protective detail here at the hospital, won't you, Oliver?"

He blinked down at her, his brow furrowing. "Why?"

She mimicked his expression and tossed her head toward the room across from us. "For Henry, of course."

His brow cleared. We shared a look. He lowered himself into the seat next to Cadence. "Miss Turing–"

"Cadence," she corrected.

"Cadence." With a hint of hesitation, he put a hand on her shoulder. "You were the target."

She brushed off his hand as if it were a piece of lint. "Don't be ridiculous. I was in front of Henry the whole time. The shooter had ample opportunity to take a shot at me, but they waited until I bent down to pull the trigger." Seeing the Inspector remained unconvinced, she turned to me, nodding as she insisted, "They were aiming for Henry."

"Why would someone want to kill Henry?" I asked, brow furrowed.

"Obviously, he must know something about Elea's death."

Brisbois shook his head, gaze flickering heavenward. "Now, hold on – we don't even know that these two attacks are connected."

Cadence snapped her mouth shut, her brows falling into a firm line over her eyes. She stood up, grinding her teeth, and met my gaze for the first time since the shooting. When I could offer her no more reassurance than the inspector, she rolled her eyes and let out a sharp breath through her nose.

"Someone is out to destroy Ergo Sum." Her fists shook at her sides. "And I'm not going to let that happen."

"Cadence–"

But it was too late. She brushed past me, jaw set, and strode down the hallway towards the ward's exit. I began to follow, but was stopped by the reappearance of Solomon, who stepped out from the waiting room where he had been talking to his wife, shoving his mobile into his pocket.

"Chance," he said, lifting his hand up towards me. "Do you have a moment?"

I chewed the inside of my mouth, my eyes following Cadence's retreating form, but I forced myself to answer: "Course, Solomon: what is it?"

"I've been meaning to tell you, that compound you asked me about – the nanobot solution?"

I came sharply to attention. "Yes?"

"I ran your description of it by Nguyen, our chief robotics engineer."

Nodding, I chastised myself for not thinking of running it by Natalie Nguyen in the first place. "Did she have any thoughts on who might manufacture it or how?"

He nodded. "She did."

I waited for Solomon to continue. When he didn't, I crossed my arms over my chest and nodded in encouragement. "Well?"

He gave a huff of a laugh, weak and without any real mirth in it, and waved a hand through the air. "No, Chance – *she* did. She made it. For Halcyon Enterprises. It was a DAT project from a few years ago; one of the last your father approved."

Guilt and dread, a potent, sticky combination swirled in my chest, sucking at my heart, and making it hard to breathe. "Did it make it past the prototype stage?"

Something of my emotions must have shown in my face because Solomon sobered quickly, drawing his brows up into a point. "Well past. We put it into production – called it Solution AA-22."

It took all my self-control not to grab Solomon by the shoulders and shake him. "We sold it?"

"Only as part of our defense package." He took a step back,

watching me closely. "It ended up being released to only a handful of government contractors–"

"Which governments?" I asked, already knowing the answer.

"Yann, Paraesepe, and Charcornac."

I took off after Cadence at a run. Taking the stairs down, I arrived in the lobby, just in time to catch sight of her hurrying out the revolving front doors and into the rainy night.

Sprinting through the lobby, I pushed through the doors. The rain was a light mist, dampening my face and scalp. I spied Cadence making her way towards the PT bay at the end of the block and shouted her name.

"Cadence!"

I jogged to catch up with her, dodging past people on the walkway as I continued to call out to her. "Cay, wait! I need to talk to you."

She glanced over her shoulder at me and turned away, rolling her eyes. "It isn't always about you, Chance."

"It's about the case," I tried, but Cadence spun around and cut me off with a glare, coming to a stop so abruptly I had to freeze mid-step lest I run full tilt into her.

"*My* case." She dug her finger into my chest. "It has nothing to do with you."

"But–"

Sneering, Cadence threw up her hands, shaking her head. "You think you can just say a few nice things on TV, and everything is fine between us?" Her hand sliced the air. "It's not. I trusted you, Chance. I thought we were equals; a team."

"We are." I threaded my fingers together, squeezing my hands so tight my knuckles went white. "Cadence, I know I should've told you about Lech. You deserved to know. I was stupid and selfish and I'm sorry."

But I might as well have apologized to the wind. Cadence scowled, her entire body tense and shaking. "Do you have any idea of the damage you could have done? How many people would have gotten hurt because of what you were prepared to say?"

"I..." I struggled for the right words to say. "I didn't want to lose you."

"I am not yours to lose!" Her shout drew the eyes of passer-bys, even causing several of them to stop and stare. She stepped towards me, forcing me to scurry back. "I am not a toy you get to lock away in a drawer when you're done playing with me!"

It wasn't until that moment, looking into her eyes, that it occurred to me that what I had broken, I may not be able to fix; that maybe I didn't deserve to have her back.

Tears welled up in my eyes. I could do nothing to stop them. The sight of them seemed to cool Cadence's rage to a simmer, and she took a step back, shaking her head.

"Until you realize that, Chance–" she said, shoving her hands in her jacket pockets as she turned, walking away. "–we have nothing to talk about."

21

Chapter 21

Cadence refused to listen to me. The EO would do nothing with the information I had learned. I was convinced that I had the key to Elea Cerf's death but was lost as to what to do with what I knew. What could I do?

Lech. I could make sure he didn't get away with what he'd done.

I cast my mind back to our first meeting, and remembered he'd told me he was staying at the Helios Hotel. A gaudy, decadent resort-style locale, the Helios Hotel's lobby was decorated with dark coffee colored marble and gilded golden statues, the temple style ceilings held up by rows of large pillars.

I inquired at the front desk after Lech, asking for a call to be made to his room. When the call went unanswered, I weighed my options. Either he was safely ensconced in his suite somewhere in the hotel, or he had yet to arrive back from the rally.

Either way, I resolved to wait until he appeared in the lobby, where I could confront him with what I knew.

Standing behind one of the large chocolate marble columns, I bided my time, dwelling on Cadence's last words to me. She was not mine – she never had been. She was not a thing to be owned at all. How could I have been so arrogant, so selfish, so stupid? How was I any different than Lech and his ilk?

By the time Lech and his loyal lapdog, Trafford, strode through the front doors of the Helios, I had worked myself up into a rage that desperately needed to be expressed. I hated myself but was more than willing to focus that ire on an external subject. As Lech approached, I felt my face redden, my teeth grinding.

As they walked past the column behind which I was concealed, I heard the tail end of their conversation, watching as Lech dismissed Trafford with a wave, calling after him, "...want tickets on the next ship off this miserable sphere back to Charcornac. And make sure they're first class this time, I don't want to end up packed in like cured meat!"

Trafford, fingers flying across the datapad in his hand, nodded as he peeled off from his employer, heading for the business suite behind the concierge desk. Lech continued to the elevator, scowling as he waited for the car to arrive at the bottom floor, his hands in his pockets.

Carefully timing my approach, I waited until Trafford was out of sight, and the elevator indicated its arrival was imminent, before crossing towards Lech. The lift doors opened, Lech walked inside, and I moved into the elevator after him, my hands loose at my sides. He turned to press the button for his floor, but stopped when he caught sight of me, his mouth dropping open with a growl.

"Leaving Arrhidaeus so soon?" I asked, the lift doors sliding shut.

My fist connected with his nose with a satisfying crack, the shock of the impact radiating up my arm and into my tight jaw. Lech stumbled toward the left side of the elevator, hands coming up to grip his face, but I didn't give him time to tend to his fresh wound. Pressing my advantage, I shoved him fully into the wall, the back of his head slamming against the steel as I pushed my forearm into his collar bone, pinning him beneath me.

"I know what you did, Lech." The words came out in a hiss through my clenched teeth. I leaned all my weight onto the arm I had pressed against his chest, my other fist digging into the wall next to his head. "And I don't care what the EO says, I'm going to make you suffer for it."

Lech struggled against me, blood already beginning to pour from his nose. "You're insane; get off me!"

I pulled away just enough to land another punch into his side. He began to crumple, but I forced him upright, gripping him by the collar and shaking him. "I know about the AA-22, you bastard!"

The flicker of recognition in his widening eyes was impossible for him to hide. He ceased wriggling in my grip. "What?"

"I don't know how you convinced Elea to meet with you, but it doesn't matter. What did you do; did you threaten her? Threaten Simone? Or Ayla? Think twice before you lie to me."

As I shook him, the glint of something metallic in his clothes caught my eye. I glanced down towards his hip, and my brow furrowed as I tried to understand what I was looking at. The handle of the gun was gleaming silver steel, with a smear of black on the base where the clip of bullets slotted into it.

"Is that...?" I looked from the gun to his terrified eyes and back again, my mind whirring.

Guns were illegal for private citizens on Arrhidaeus. That's not to say there weren't ways to get your hands on such weapons if you had the right contacts, and the right kind of money. But it was rare to see handguns in the hands of anyone other than criminals or the military. What were the chances that someone else at Elea's memorial had had a gun with them? Who else but the shooter would have brought one? And here I was, staring at a man that I knew was in the room, who had ample reason to shoot at my friends, looking at his gun.

I yanked the gun from its holster. Burying the mouth of the gun into Lech's jugular, I cocked back the hammer, seeing red for the first time in my life. "You fucking monster!"

"Wait! Hale!" His voice cracking, Lech tried in vain to pull away from the barrel, eyes flickering between it and my face with open desperation. "I swear on my life I don't know what you're talking about!" His hands tightened around my wrist. "AA-22 is a nanobot solution. It's designed to–"

I jerked him to me and heard him choke as the gun dug into his throat. "I know what it's designed to do, you cretin; I saw what it did to Elea!"

"That's not– what?" His brow furrowed. He shook his head. He stopped tugging at my wrist. "No, it's not– I thought– What the fuck are you talking about?"

Staring into his eyes, I saw the truth in a flash. A shiver went through me.

I uncocked the hammer and lowered the gun to my side. "You didn't know?" I shook my head with vehemence. "Of course, you knew; where else did the AA-22 come from? And what about this?" I waved the gun in front of his face, grimacing.

Sensing his opportunity at last, Lech pushed my arm off his shoulder, shouting, "A sidearm is standard issue for Charcornacian ambassadors and their staff! I've never used the damn thing!"

My chest heaved, my breathing hard and heavy. I swallowed, staring at him, and stepped away until my back hit the other side of the elevator. "Why should I believe you?"

"If – *if* – I had some AA-22 with me, why would I try and shoot your fragger girlfriend?" Lech glared daggers into me, wiping his bleeding nose along the edge of his sleeve. "You know what happens when you shoot a fragger? They don't die. They get real pissed off."

He was right. It pained me to even think it, but it didn't make sense. If the person who killed Elea had tried to kill Cadence, they wouldn't have tried to shoot her. Did that mean she was right? That Henry was the shooter's intended target after all?

With a high-pitched ping, the lift's doors opened. Since I had never given Lech an opportunity to press a button for his floor, we had never left the lobby. Trafford stood in front of the opening doors, his datapad tucked under his arm, a tired furrow to his brow.

At the sight of us, Trafford surged forward, eyes wide. "Sir!"

I stepped out of the lift as Trafford rushed in, throwing the gun onto the floor behind me. Turning on my heel, I held up my shaking finger at the men in the lift, sweat cooling on my skin. "We're not done, Lech." I sneered at him in disgust. "You run, and I'll find you. I promise you that."

"I'll get you for this, you crazy, stupid son of a–!"

Lech's shout was cut off by the closing elevator doors. Hiding my bruising knuckles in the pocket of my coat, I strode out of the hotel, more disturbed and confused than I had been upon arriving.

Now convinced that my friend may indeed be in danger, I hailed the first PT I could find, and returned to the hospital. I was perturbed to find that Brisbois had not taken Cadence's advice. The hallway outside Henry's room was empty of any kind of Enforcement Office presence, and when I inquired about security at the ward's reception desk, they informed me that they had received no special instructions. It seemed that job would fall to me as well. Without telling them why I was determined to spend the night there, I relieved Solomon and Minerva from their son's bedside, promising to keep him company and give them a call as soon as he woke. Curling up in a lumpy hospital chair beside his bed, I settled in for a long and lonely night.

At some point in the early hours of the morning, I drifted to sleep, exhaustion catching up with me. When I woke, it was to find Henry watching me with half-lidded eyes from his hospital bed, an expression of contentment on his face.

Grimacing, I unfolded myself from the chair, body creaking and cracking. "Good morning," I said, stifling a yawn.

Henry gave me a weak smile. "Afternoon, actually."

I blinked sleep out of my eyes and shook the thin gold band

on my wrist. "Afternoon?" My watch confirmed my best friend's words, the time flashing as just after three. "I didn't realize I'd been asleep for so long."

The dark-haired man squirmed against the pillows, struggling up into a sitting position. "I would've woken you, but you looked almost as knackered as me."

I pushed a hand through my hair and stood, looking down at him and grinning. "You look gorgeous. How do you feel?"

He let a long breath out through his nose, blinking up at me. "Considering that I've been shot? Remarkably well. That'd be the drugs." Clearing his throat, he straightened, shaking his head to clear the cobwebs. "Did you talk with Cadence? How'd it go?"

I tried not to wince at the sound of her name but judging by the furrow that started to form on his brow, I failed. "It didn't," I admitted, my hands falling into my trouser pockets.

"Maybe you just–"

"Henry, can I ask you something?"

He watched me for a moment, eyes narrowed in suspicion before he relaxed back into the pillows and smiled. "I'm immobile and pliant," he said. "Now would be an opportune time to interrogate me."

"No interrogation intended." I perched myself on the side of his bed. "I'm just curious; what exactly is it that you do for Ergo Sum?"

"Not as much as I'd like," he answered. "Mostly I've been acting as a kind of de facto reporter for them, writing up refugees' stories and trying to get them published around the system."

"Has the work garnered much interest?"

He wobbled his head from side to side. "Some." Grimacing,

he rubbed at his wounded shoulder. "Not to be crude, but atrocity and tragedy make for good copy. But anything that helps bring more attention to what the Charcornacians and their ilk are really doing to the animanecrons is important." He coughed, words rough in his dry throat. "People have to be forced into action."

"How do you do it?" He lifted a brow at me in response. I shook my head, reaching for a cup of water and extending it to him. "I can't imagine it's easy for you, hearing what these people have been through."

"I have the easy job; I just have to listen." He took the cup from me with his good hand, gaze falling behind me. "They're the ones who have to live with what happened to them every day – try to move on, rebuild their lives, reconnect." Swishing the water around his mouth, he swallowed, shaking his head. "I wish I could do more, but Elea said we all had to use what talents we had."

"You worked closely with her?"

Henry nodded. "Course. She reviewed all my work, arranged for me to meet with the refugees – all of it."

I did my best to put myself in Cadence's shoes. What would she ask if she were talking to Henry right now? I shifted against the thin mattress, crossing my legs. "Was anything bothering her lately? Did she ever mention the names Noll Hudd or Eamon Lech?"

Henry lifted his brows. "I know who they are, but no, Elea never made special mention of them." He glanced sharply down at the bed in which he lay. "Wait – that's not true. She asked me to get a picture of Lech last week."

"A picture?"

Nodding, his forehead furrowed as he struggled through the narcotics to remember. "Yes, she needed help searching the vertex – she wanted a photo of the entire Charcornac Ambassadorial Staff, but specifically one taken after Lech had been appointed."

"Did she say why?"

"No." He shrugged. "But I assumed it had something to do with her meeting with Ethan."

I ran down my mental list of persons involved with the case and came up empty. "Who is Ethan?"

"One of the refugees Ergo Sum was housing. He came into Ergo Sum last week when I happened to be stopping in to discuss something with Simone. He was very insistent on meeting with Elea. They were in her office for about fifteen minutes, and then Elea came out and asked for help searching the vertex." Henry's hand came up and he began pulling at his lower lip, voice falling to a murmur. "At first I thought he was unhappy with the story I published from our interviews, but I don't think that's what it was."

I shifted up onto my feet and reached towards the chair I was sleeping in to retrieve my crumpled raincoat. "Well, I think I should talk to Ethan."

Henry's eyes jerked up to meet mine. "Why?"

Shaking out the coat and slipping it on, I answered: "Cadence thinks you were the target of the shooter – not her. That you know something that Elea's killer doesn't want to get out." I frowned. "I'm starting to think she's right."

My friend gave a sarcastic snort. "Know something? I don't know anything."

"We both know that's not true." I patted my pockets to make sure I had everything before turning my attention back to Henry. "Where does Ethan live?"

"The Mawson Docks." Henry shook his head. "But he isn't overly fond of humans, Chance."

I forced a smile onto my face. "I'll just have to be extra charming, then."

After extracting Ethan's address from a reluctant Henry, I took my leave, slipping his attending nurse a hundred-credit chip to keep an extra watchful eye on him. The address led me to a dilapidated warehouse of a building that claimed to be a short-term hotel for single men, with rooms that could be rented for the month, week, day, or hour. The building was wedged between an AN-GRAV track that led straight to the Mawson Docks and a tall convenience super center, whose flashing signs and end-lessly looping ads must have made for wonderful neighbors.

I trudged up the stairs to the seventh floor, not trusting the elevator in a place like this, rainwater dripping off me as I went. I exited the stairwell and followed the crooked signs to Room 2187 but stopped short when I saw that someone else had beaten me to the door.

Cadence must have walked at least part of the way – she was drenched through, her clothes sticking to her, hair plastered to her head. She hadn't worn a coat, because of course she hadn't. She never did if I didn't remind her to. I watched as she knocked on the door once and then again, working out how it was she came to be here. She must have talked to Simone or read Henry's

work and come to the same conclusion that I had. Ethan, who-
ever he was, was well worth investigating.

When no one answered the door, Cadence looked around
herself with a scowl.

"Maybe he's not home," I said, stepping out into the hallway
behind her.

Cadence was too self-composed to jump at my sudden appearance, but she did stiffen visibly. Turning away from the door
to face me, she pushed wet tendrils of hair off her forehead,
scowling. "What are you doing here?"

Being sure to keep a respectful distance, I shrugged, gesturing
to the closed portal in front of us. "Same thing as you, I expect.
Trying to talk with Mr. Ethan."

"It's just Ethan," broke in a smooth, deep voice from behind
us. "Don't see why I should have to take on a last name."

We turned to take in the sight of a short, stout young man.
His skin was deeply tanned, the same color as his mahogany
brown eyes, which roamed around the hallway in an unfocused,
vigilant sort of way that put me on edge. Water dripped from his
bare arm, his white wife-beater soaked through and stuck to his
torso, and tools of various shapes and sizes stuck out from the
many different pockets that lined his sagging cargo pants.

I tried not to stare, but I had never seen a man with only
one arm before. Whatever had happened had severed the limb
cleanly at the shoulder. Or at least that's how it appeared at first
glance. Closer inspection revealed a halo of frayed wire ends,
plastic tubing melted shut, and dulled, tarnished metal where
his shoulder socket should be.

Ethan shifted his weight from foot to foot, his single hand holding a disintegrating paper bag to his chest.

"Ethan," I said, extending my hand towards him without thinking. "My name is –"

"Know who you are." He stared at my hand with distaste, and I withdrew it sheepishly. Tightening his grip on his brown paper bag, he continued shifting from foot to foot. "Saw you on the TV." He turned to Cadence without looking her in the face, nodding. "You too. They tried to shoot you."

My former flat mate shook her head. "They didn't, actually."

Ethan considered this for a moment. "Well." He stepped between us and, wedging the paper bag between the door jamb and his body, he punched in the code for his front door lock, still not making eye contact with either of us as he spoke. "Anyone who pisses off Eamon Lech on live TV can't be all bad. Even if they are flesh."

My brow furrowed. "Flesh?" I muttered.

"Human," shot back Cadence as she crossed the threshold after our host, hands deep in her pockets.

I blinked and shook my head. It never occurred to me that animanecrons had names for us the way we had names for them. Judging by the tone of casual condescension with which the word was laced, I took it that it was not meant as a term of endearment.

I was roused from my thoughts by Ethan's smooth voice calling out to me from inside the flat. "Hey." He jerked his head towards the interior of his rooms. "Come in, if you're coming."

I entered the apartment, and Ethan nudged the door shut behind me. It took my eyes a few moments to adjust to the dim light, and when they did, I wished they hadn't. One crammed room held a single-sized mattress that sagged in the middle, an ancient and pitifully small television screen, a wobbly table with two chairs, a food encrusted stove, and a fridge so filthy on the outside it was streaked with black. Hanging from the ceiling alongside the single uncovered bulb was a collection of strange mechanical devices, all gears, wires, and joints, some the size of my hand, some stretching from ceiling to floor.

Cadence and I picked our way through the hanging garden of machinery to follow our host, who stood by the table, emptying out the sodden paper bag. We watched as he muttered and examined a series of computer parts and metal pieces, each stranger than the last.

"You were a form fabricator, weren't you?" asked Cadence, breaking the silence.

Ethan gave a disdainful snort, his hand trailing over the items he had laid out over the table. "Were? Still am." He gestured to the empty space where his left arm should have been. "They took my arm, not what's in my head." Picking up a complex mess of rusted gears, he shook his head, scowling. "Can't get decent parts here, though. All shit." He punctuated the thought by throwing the gears into the empty rubbish bin beside the table.

Ethan sighed and turned to face us, rubbing his hand over his shaved head. "Welder at the shipyards now. They pay me half what the flesh gets. But it's enough for this..." A smile devoid of joy twisted the corners of his lips. He threw out his hand to encompass the broken windowpane, the leaking kitchen faucet, and the cracked, mold-covered wall. "...this palace."

His eyes met Cadence's for the first time. His smile

disappeared. He jutted his chin out towards her. "Where are you from?"

Cadence shifted where she stood, gaze falling to the top of her feet. "Bunker 1202."

He shoved his hand into the gaping pocket of his baggy cargo pants. "What camp did they take you to?"

"Surface Containment Camp Koma." Swallowing, Cadence rolled her shoulders back, shaking her head at the same time. "Most of us." She looked up, meeting Ethan's interrogative stare. "Tris, I'm not sure where the rest went."

He nodded. He tapped his chest with his fingertips. "Bunker 003." His gaze flitted to the window. "Containment Camp Vailir."

Cadence's eyes widened. "Charcornac."

The hushed horror in that word seemed to annoy him. Ethan threw himself down into one of the rickety wooden chairs at the table, scowling. "What do you want?"

Cadence and I shared a look. I gestured forward, content to let her take the lead. She gave a small nod of acknowledgment and returned her attention to the man in front of us. "Elea Cerf."

He shrugged. "He killed her."

Cadence's mouth snapped shut in surprise.

"Who?" I demanded.

"The traitor." He closed his eyes and rubbed at his forehead, voice quieting. "He'll come for me. He came for her."

Cadence perched herself on the edge of the table in front of Ethan. "Who? Who is the traitor?"

Ethan took in a deep breath and released it slowly. "Don't know his name. None of us at Vailir did. But without him..." His eyes stared forward into nothing, but his hand wandered back to the machine parts on the table beside him. As he spoke, he toyed with each one in turn, as if the feel of them in his grip soothed an ache deep inside him. "He told them how to keep me awake while they took my arm. Helped them do it. Smiled at me. The whole time." His hand closed around a circuit board and squeezed it tight. His eyes flickered up to meet mine, but he looked away just as quickly, his shoulders sagging. "If there was pain to be dealt, he'd help them make it worse. He enjoyed it; any twisted thing that pleased the flesh to do to us, he'd do."

In the dim light, I could see Cadence's clenched jaw, her closed fist shaking in her lap as she stared at the place where Ethan's arm should be. "Fytaq jaqit taltot."

"No." Ethan released the circuit board in his hand. "Don't... don't curse him." With a stutter of hesitation, he reached out and tapped a rhythm against the back of Cadence's closed fist. "Pity him."

"Pity?" she drew her hand back, spitting the word out in disbelief.

"All the things he did to us – the horrors – I can only imagine what they did to break him so much he came to hate his own kind," said Ethan, his head moving slowly from side to side.

Brows drawn up to a point, I stared without seeing at the space behind him. "The traitor...was an animanecron?"

"We lived in hell." Ethan stared at the floor. "Some of us became devils."

Cadence stared up at me, eyes wide. My mind reeled. How could such a thing be possible? Could an intelligent being become so lost in pain and torment that they yearned to unleash that pain on others like them? It was a hideous thought.

Tip of her tongue wetting her lips, Cadence shook her head, managing at last: "What makes you think this animanecron killed Elea?"

"Because I saw him. Here. In Römer."

Cadence and I let out exclamations of surprise. Ethan frowned and gestured towards his tiny screen. "On TV, like I saw you two." His frown deepened as he sat back in his chair. "Told Elea. She said she knew who he was. Said she'd handle it. Now she's dead."

"Did you tell a man named Henry Davers about this animanecron?" I pressed, stepping towards him.

"Davers?" Ethan's brow furrowed, but he nodded. "The human from Ergo Sum. Took my words down. Yeah, I told him about the traitor. That was before I saw the traitor in Römer." His eyes widened. "He dead too?"

"Not yet." Cadence stood. "We won't let Lech hurt anyone else."

"Lech?" Ethan sneered, coming to his feet as well. "That bekalk? He's not the traitor."

Cadence blinked in confusion. She shook her head. "But...the picture? Simone said Elea showed you a picture of the Charcornacian Ambassadorial Staff, and then–"

Ethan cut her off with a wave. "He works for Lech. Follows him around like a pet."

"Trafford." In a flash, the pale, thin man snapped into my mind, green eyes peering from under his mop of yellow hair. "Leo Trafford?"

Ethan shrugged. "If you say so." He turned away, his attention focused on his mechanical trinkets. "He'll always be the traitor to me."

22

Chapter 22

Cadence and I stood in front of the elevator at the end of the hall outside of Ethan's apartment, neither of us looking at each other, lost in our private thoughts. I pressed the call button and the cables inside the shaft began to creak and whine. I wanted to say something to her, but there was nothing to say, no words I could offer that would dull the horror of what we had just uncovered.

"Do you think Lech knows?" Cadence asked, in a voice barely above a whisper.

My eyes flicked towards her. She stared at the bottom of the elevator door, unseeing. I drew in a deep breath.

"No." I pinched the bridge of my nose and leaned my head back, closing my eyes. "Damn it, he was telling the truth."

At this, she turned to me, her eyes wide.

"Elea, she was killed with–" I hesitated over the words but

remembered what withholding unpleasant information from Cadence had done for me in the past. Squaring my shoulders, I looked her in the eyes. "Halcyon Enterprises made the compound that killed Elea. We sold it to Charcornac."

I was ready for anger, for shock, for disgust, even. But the disappointment in Cadence's face as she turned away from me cut deeper than anything else could have, and I swallowed down the pain like bile.

I shook my head. "But when I confronted Lech about it, he didn't know what I was talking about." I dug my nix case out of my trouser pocket, sighing. "No, he doesn't know about Trafford." A thought struck me, and my hand froze with a nix halfway to my lips. "Or at least...he didn't." I glanced at Cadence. She stared back at me, confusion written clear on her face. I tossed away the nix with a jerk, moving down the hallway towards the window where I hoped my mobile would get better reception. "Shit."

"What, what is it?" demanded Cadence, following me with quick, long strides.

"I told Lech that Elea was killed with AA-22. That means someone connected with the Charcornacian government killed her. If it wasn't him, it must be Trafford, and Lech is smart enough to figure that out." Fitting the mobile in my ear, I told it to dial the Helios and waited, tapping my foot, as it rang. A receptionist answered, and I cut them off before they could finish their greeting. "Yes, Eamon Lech's room, please – it's urgent."

The phone rang for what felt like an eternity before I heard the click of the line being answered.

"Hello?"

The voice which answered was familiar, but not the one I had expected. I looked over at Cadence, and then back out the window, ice water pooling at the base of my spine. "Hello, who is this?"

"This is Inspector Oliver Brisbois of the Arrhidaean Enforcement Office."

I screwed my eyes shut. Guilt washed over me like a wave off the sea, horror and fear spiking at my heart.

Brisbois' voice echoed down the line, insistent, with an edge of exasperation that cut through my dread and forced my eyes back open. "Hello?"

"Is he dead?" I managed after a moment, breath tight in my chest.

There was a pause, the sound of shuffling feet and the closing of a door. "Mr. Hale?"

I turned to face Cadence fully, my hand at my ear. "Is Eamon Lech dead?"

"I – yes. Yes, he's dead. What's going on, what do you know?" demanded Brisbois, his voice strident.

I pulled the bud from my ear, cupping it in my hand so that only Cadence could hear what I said. "The docks. Lech had Trafford buy two tickets for the next transport back to Charcornac. He's going to try and get off planet."

Cadence pointed to the phone in my hand, and then started running for the stairs. "We need the EO to meet us there!"

I slid the mobile back into my ear, barking: "Brisbois, it's Trafford. He's an animanecron. He's trying to escape on the next transport to Charcornac, out of the Mawson Docks; you need to get there, now!"

I hung up before he could respond, feet pounding against the threadbare carpet of the hotel hallway as I chased after Cadence. We burst out onto the street, startling a few pedestrians.

"What's the fastest way to get to the Mawson Dock Terminal?" demanded Cadence, casting about herself wildly.

I grabbed her hand and pulled her toward the tracks. "ANGRAV; come on!"

We were lucky the next train to the Mawson Dock Terminal was about to leave when we raced onto the platform. Once aboard, it was a quick ten-minute ride to the hub of off-world travel in Römer. A bustling complex, it represented the largest free-standing structure in the city, and Cadence openly despaired at the sight of it.

"We'll never find him in all that," she groaned.

"Flights to and from Charcornac have been restricted for months," I said. "There should only be a few scheduled every day – all we need to do is find which terminal he's headed for and beat him there."

When we entered the main terminal, we split up, scanning the departure and arrival boards for any sign of our quarry. I found the flight to Charcornac first – leaving in one hour from Terminal AB. I called to Cadence as I ran by her and together we headed for the AB security checkpoint, thinking that we would have to wait for Brisbois and the EO to arrive to back us up, when fate intervened.

Trafford was dressed in the same baggy suit he always wore. He stood in the security line looking, for all intents and purposes, bored. Cadence and I spotted him at the same time, just as he was about to hand his ticket to the person at the check-point booth.

I'll never know what made him glance in our direction, but his eyes flickered up and found us in the crowd. His pupils widened; his hand convulsed around the handle of his bag.

Cadence cupped her hands around her lips and shouted as loud as she could, caring nothing for the fact that we were still a good hundred yards away from him.

"Trafford! Stop!"

But it was too late. Trafford was already running, knocking travelers and terminal workers out of his way as he careened across the crowded lobby, throwing his bag away in the process. Cadence and I took off after him, people darting out of our way, lest they end up trampled.

The shouting and screaming of the public alerted terminal security to the fact that something was amiss and soon scowling people were rushing towards us, their hands on their tasers. Not wanting to take time to explain that we were not in fact the threat, but were in hot pursuit of a murderer, Cadence and I did our best to dodge and weave around these well-meaning public servants, though one did manage to grab a hold of my coat with both hands. Luckily, I didn't have to fastened shut and was able to slip out of it without stopping, leaving the woman holding nothing but soggy fabric.

Two guards managed to get ahead of Trafford and attempted to tackle him around the waist and legs. They might as well have thrown themselves at an AN-GRAV for all the effect they had on him. The young man who went for Trafford's legs was knocked to one side immediately, flung off into a nearby pillar which he hit with a sickening crack. The older guard managed to hold on to Trafford's waist for a foot or two before the animanecron reached down and wrenched the man's arms free of him, bending the arms back in a way human appendages were not meant to be bent. The guard screamed, his scream taking on an extra edge of terror as Trafford flung him into the air behind him, using him to attempt to shake off any more pursuers following behind.

Knocking aside a man at a ticketing kiosk, Trafford eventually forced his way behind an employee-only door. We followed, moments behind him, but when we entered the murky room, it was to a cavalcade of sound.

The baggage sorting room was a raucous din of activity, conveyor belts and claw machines moving parcels from one place to the next. We froze by the front door, peering into the crowded mess of a room, looking for any sign of our quarry, but it was impossible to tell one shape from the other in the dimly lit space.

"Come on. He can't have gotten far." Cadence took off into the room at a slow jog, and I had no choice but to follow her.

"It doesn't have to be like this..." Trafford's words bounced off the machinery and baggage piled around us, making it sound as if he were speaking from everywhere at once.

"No, it doesn't." Cadence paused, waiting for an answer, head cocked to one side. When none came, she continued, slowly moving forward through the detritus of the room. "If you give up now, I can talk with the EO – try and see if I can convince them to go easy on you."

I followed Cadence, reluctance slowing my step. The room was large, noisy, and crowded – a perfect place to trap someone or surprise them. Going further inside, when there was a known killer lurking within, seemed like the definition of foolhardiness.

There was a flicker of movement to my right. I twisted towards it, but it was too late. Trafford advanced from behind a sorting machine, gun drawn.

"Easy on me?" Trafford cocked the hammer back with his thumb, grinning with all his perfect teeth. "When do humans ever go easy on us?"

"I don't know what they did to you," Cadence's voice remained calm, but she took a small step in front of me. "But it's over now."

A sliver of light broke through the gloom behind Trafford, and I saw, for a fraction of a second, Brisbois and a handful of officers slip into the room via a side door. My heart jumped into my throat, but I did my best not to let the surprise show in my face, forcing my gaze back to Trafford, who shook his head.

"You don't get it, do you?" Trafford's shoulders fell, the barrel of the gun bobbing as he spoke. "Men like Lech – they're right. We're a disease. We're an aberration. A mistake. We were never supposed to exist." He blinked several times, shaking his head. "It must be made right. I have to make it right. We have to be corrected. Expunged." His smile shrank. He leveled the gun at Cadence's head and moved his finger to the trigger. "There's no place for us in this universe."

Cadence's attention remained fixed on Trafford's face. Her lips firmed into a thin line. "You know that won't kill me."

Trafford's jaw clenched. "It will slow you down." His hand jerked and the gun was pointed at me. "And him–" He smiled at me, his gaze dreamy. "–him it will definitely kill."

"Trafford." I did my best to keep my attention focused on him, wary of giving away Brisbois' position in the darkness. I thought of Ethan in his dingy apartment and tried again, keeping my voice low. "Leo. We want to help you."

Trafford barked out a laugh. "Like Elea?" He sneered, looking from me to Cadence and back again. "I don't need your help. I'm doing what I was put here to do. And no one is going to get in my way."

"Then why kill Lech?" I asked. I had lost track of where Brisbois and his men were in the room, but I prayed they were close to being in position.

At the name of his deceased employer, Trafford snapped to attention, his body straightening, even as his jaw went slack. "Mr. Lech..." He shut his jaw with a snap, grinding his teeth together. "He – he was going to shut me down. He thought I was like her." He gestured to Cadence with his free hand, waving dismissively. "No, he couldn't see my potential. None of them can see! I'm the solution! The savior!"

The man was insane. There would be no saving this one, no matter how badly Elea, Cadence, or I may have wanted to.

I gritted my teeth, nodding to the shadows behind him. "Do it."

Eyes widening, Trafford began to spin around, both hands wrapping around the butt of his gun, but it was too late. It only took Brisbois the length of a heartbeat to step out from the darkness, press his taser gun against the back of Trafford's neck, and pull the trigger.

After it was all over, Brisbois explained to me that he had intentionally overridden the safety voltage of his taser to maximize the charge delivered to Trafford, hoping to overload his systems. He wasn't sure it would work, given how little was known about animanecron design, but it was the only thing he could think of to do.

In the moment, however, as I watched Trafford convulse and fall to the floor, the gun clattering out of his hand, I felt only an overwhelming sense of shame. None of this should have ever happened. If people like Eamon Lech, if humans like me, had just left the animanecrons in peace, had accepted them as friends rather than treated them as enemies; as people rather than as things – how much less ugliness would there be in this universe right now? How much more beauty? Why did we corrupt everything we touched?

Ten minutes later, Brisbois, Cadence, and I, stood near the outer edge of a deserted docking bay, watching as Trafford was loaded into the back of an EO PT, his hands double manacled in front of him. The taser had taken much of the fight out of him. He sat hunched and unmoving, staring out the window at the milling EO officers, a grim expression on his pale face.

With a suddenness that startled us both, Cadence turned to Brisbois, her face somber. "I want to go with him."

Brisbois' brow furrowed. "That's really not necessary–"

"I want to go with him." Her tone made it clear that 'no' was not an acceptable answer, her hands clenched into fists at her sides.

I placed a steadying hand on her shoulder, directing her attention away from Brisbois, and to me instead. "Why?" I asked.

Looking over her shoulder at the EO PT, she began to wring her hands. "Now that I see him...really see him..." she said, "I understand what Ethan meant." She turned to me, her eyes wide with pain. "Tris, I do pity him."

I nodded, my hand sliding from her shoulder. "Go."

She swallowed hard. "Sinc, thank you, Chance." With a slight nod to Brisbois, she walked away, heading for the EO PT. I watched as she spoke to the officer who was about to climb into the driver's seat, gesturing to the passenger cab. The officer glanced back at Brisbois, who waved an assent. Shrugging, the officer opened the passenger door, and allowed Cadence to slide in beside Trafford.

I pulled my gaze away, unable to watch her go. My heartbeat felt slow and sluggish in my chest, and the oppressive black clouds looming overhead matched my current mood.

"She's a remarkable woman," said Brisbois.

I looked over at him, watching as he dug into his jacket pocket, his gaze focused on the EO PT as it pulled away from the docking platform. He pulled out a crumpled box of nixes, thin, brown sticks, shorter than my elegant, black-wrapped brand choice. But I still took the one he offered to me.

I rolled the nix between my fingers, my attention returning to the society beneath my feet. Beside me Brisbois inhaled deeply, a cloud of smoke floating by a moment later.

Without thinking, I twisted the end off the stubby nix, setting it sparking, and drew on it sharply. My body convulsed, and I released a mouthful of smoke in desperate choking gasps, curling in on myself slightly.

"Oh god," I managed through my hacking cough. "That – that's hideous." I took another pull of the nix. My eyes watered and I grimaced, examining the stubby, thin roll held between my fingers. "Augh, it's like licking a sooty fireplace! How do you smoke these?"

Brisbois chuckled, speaking around his own nix with ease. "They're an acquired taste, I'll admit."

I smacked my lips together and shook my head. "These can't be local." I gave the nix another puff, hissing as I let out the acrid smoke. "Imported?"

He nodded and flicked ash over the lip of the dock. "Being an Enforcement Officer has its advantages."

We stood there in silence for several long minutes, smoking our nixes and staring out over Römer. It hadn't occurred to me that the man's presence could be anything other than an irritant, but in this instance, I was surprised to find his company reassuring. Though I'd be damned if I'd ever admit that to anyone, least of all him.

"You're in love with her, aren't you?"

I looked up at him sharply. He wasn't turned towards me, his olive eyes fixed somewhere out on the horizon. I let out a long breath through my nose, a rueful smile twisting my lips. "Yes."

Swallowing down the lump in my throat, I examined Brisbois' placid facade with care, considering for the first time the ways in which we were similar. "You're rather taken with her yourself, aren't you?"

His eyes narrowed and he gave a derisive snort, bringing his nix back up to his lips. "Of course, I am."

"And it doesn't bother you? What she is?"

"Why should it?" Brisbois turned to me at last, one brow raised. "She can't help what she is; a lot of people can't. You, for example, can't help being an entitled, smarmy ass; it's just the way you were born and brought up."

I smirked. "Thanks."

Brisbois smiled back at me, before resuming his examination of the city skyline. "Cadence can't help being an animanecron." He shrugged, sharp shoulders rising and falling quickly. "I like who she is, regardless of what she is. She's a smart, funny, lively woman." He sighed, his head falling to one side. "Damn gorgeous too."

"You noticed."

He heard the goading in my words and glared at me. "I'm a policeman, Hale; it's my job to notice things." Sighing, he dropped his nix and ground it out with his heel. "You're very lucky to have found each other."

Pulling in a large lungful of coarse smoke, I nodded. Cadence and I had known each other for less than a year, and yet I realized now that her friendship was a gift, not a right, and I had wasted it.

I flicked the still burning nix out into the ether. "I just hope I haven't lost her," I said. Turning to face him, I looked him in the eye and offered him my hand. "Am I dismissed, Inspector?"

Brisbois took my hand with a nod and gave it a firm shake. "Dismissed, Mr. Hale."

23

Chapter 23

A month later, and the monsoon season was coming to its dreary end. Cadence had yet to resurface in my life. The "Mad Ani Killings" had already begun to fade in the public consciousness, despite the initial zeal with which the Arrhidaean media had covered the story. Used to stoke up more fear and hate toward the animanecron community, the whole affair had nearly cost Representative Peyton his highly coveted chancellorship. But, in the end, his support of animanecrons was not enough to defeat him, though many in the pro-ani community were left to wonder if the man could now be trusted to follow through on his promises.

From what I could glean from Brisbois, Trafford was being held in isolation in the Anteries Penal District, a victim of legal limbo. He'd committed murder, but how to prosecute a 'non-person' in the eyes of the law was proving problematic. Given his status, however, the Enforcement Office was able to hold him indefinitely, and that was what they intended to do.

"Is he allowed visitors?" I asked, tipping a puddle of whisky back into my mouth.

"Certainly," answered Brisbois, his brow furrowing. "But who – ah, I see what you're thinking." Leaning back in the booth, he threw his arm over the plush seat top as he shook his head, smiling ruefully. "No. No, she hasn't been to see him. I'd know it if she had."

No one was more shocked than I, but this post-work drink with Brisbois had become a not unpleasant habit over the last month. We shared a booth in one of the nicer EO bars, a pub called *The Anga's Head*, a few nights every week. We spent as much time in silence as we did in conversation, which suited my current disposition quite well. When we did talk, the conversation somehow always seemed to circle back to one topic, despite our best efforts.

"It was a thought," I grumbled, withdrawing farther into my corner of the booth.

Brisbois sipped at his dark, dense beer. "Still nothing?"

"Not a word." Sighing, I spun my empty glass in my fingertips. "Simone's put the word out to her people at Ergo Sum, but no one matching Cadence's description has shown up at any of their events. Henry hasn't heard from her either. Even he's starting to get worried now."

"How is Mr. Davers? Recovered?"

"Never better." I pushed my hand back through my hair, considering if I should stop at two double whiskies or go for three. "Are you sure there's nothing–?"

"She has to be a person in order for me to file a missing person's report; I told you." Brisbois rubbed at the back of his neck, wincing. "Besides, I don't think I could find her if she doesn't want to be found."

"It's not like her," I said for the hundredth time. "She knows people would worry about her. She wouldn't just disappear."

"She's going through a lot right now." Shifting forward, Brisbois shook his head. "Give her time."

"How much more time do you suggest?" I shot back, glowering.

Brisbois' only response was to stare at me from over the rim of his pint glass. Squirming, I threw my hands into the air. "What if something's happened to her?"

He lifted his brow, lowering his glass. "Like what?"

I opened my mouth to respond, but stuttered to a halt, mind scrambling through scenarios, each one more unlikely than the next. It was hard to imagine a situation in which Cadence would be at a disadvantage, either physically or mentally. Leaning my forearms against the table, I waved my hand through the air, my head hung low. "I'm just saying, she could be in trouble."

"If she is, she knows she has people she can reach out to." Brisbois craned his head around towards the bar, signaling to the barkeep for the check. "You said it before; you need to give her space. This is part of that. She'll come back when she's ready. If she's ready."

"And if she doesn't come back?"

Brisbois turned to me, a wry smile twisting his lips. "My evenings remain free for the most part."

Rolling my eyes, I heaved a sigh. "Oh, goody."

It was close to fifteen o'clock when we parted ways, and my eyes were bleary with drink and sleep. *The Anga's Head* was close enough to *The Feathers* that I felt comfortable walking from one to the other, trudging through a haze of rain. The lobby and elevators were deserted as I entered, and I felt as if I were the last man on the sphere as I dragged my hand over the corrugated handle of my front door, waiting for it to pop open.

Entering the flat, cool wind picked at the bottom of my long overcoat, sending the fabric fluttering. The rain sounded loud and insistent, and I couldn't tell why, until my weak eyes picked out the open living room window in the darkness. I was about to call out for the lights, when the sound of fabric shifting against fabric drew my attention to the sofa beneath the window.

Cadence crossed her legs, one arm thrown over the back of the couch. She looked away from the open window to me, her eyes glowing unnaturally bright in the unlit room. "You didn't change the lock."

My throat tightened. I forced myself to look away from her, not fully convinced that what I was seeing was real. I undid the buttons of my coat one at a time, trying in vain to calm myself. I cleared my throat and glanced back at her. She was still watching me, unmoving, unbreathing. I struggled to paste a smile onto my face.

"Of course not." I shrugged off my coat and hung it on the peg next to the door. "You paid rent through the end of the month, after all."

I had hoped for a smile, but Cadence gave me nothing more than a low hum of acknowledgement before she twisted back to the window.

I wanted to be angry with her. But all I could find in my heart was relief; relief that she was alright, and relief that whatever path she now found herself on had brought her back to me.

The sound of rain permeated everything, covering the sound of my soft, slow footfalls as I stepped down from the entryway and crossed the living room. Still as a frozen image on a screen, Cadence seemed content to watch the rain fall. I wondered how long she had been there, waiting for me. The thought sent tremors through me. I stopped a few feet in front of her, cautious of making any move, or saying anything that would encourage her to leave.

"Things are never going to go back to the way they were." Cadence crossed her arms over her chest, leaning into the cool wind blowing in through the open window. She turned to me, sighing. "They're not, are they?"

I shook my head. "Not unless you have secretly designed some way of traveling back in time."

The edge of Cadence's lips twitched up into a lightning strike smile. She returned her gaze out the window, her stoic expression reclaiming her face. Far off in the distance, thunder rumbled and roared. The air once again smelled like rain.

I shifted uncomfortably in front of her, shoving my hands in my pockets. I cleared my throat, my brow furrowing. "That's not all bad, though. Right?"

"How so?"

"Cadence..." I licked my lips. Feeling awkward, I collapsed onto the sofa beside her. "I was wrong. I couldn't see how what I was doing was hurting you." My hands clenched. "It was the last thing I wanted to do, and I did it anyway. I've never–" I swallowed down the next few words that were ready to come tripping off my tongue and shook my head instead. "No. No, I'm not going to make excuses for myself. I was scared and selfish and I tried to keep you in a box without thinking about what you wanted, or even needed." I looked away from her, out into the darkened living room we used to share. "I should have been supporting you. Instead, I was smothering you."

I felt Cadence's hand land just above my knee. Her fingers began tapping out her familiar, arrhythmic beat. "I...didn't always mind being smothered."

"I understand if you don't–" Shaking my head, I put my hand over hers, stilling it. "You don't have to come back. Here, to the apartment. If you need your own space, I get it. But I hope we can still be friends."

Her hand was warm against my cheek as she pulled my face around to look into my eyes. Her summer smile was soft and soothing, like a sprinkling of rain. "We'll always be friends, Chance."

My chest ached. I wanted so badly for that to be true. I looked into her deep blue eyes, with words of love on the tip of my tongue, when it occurred to me that she deserved so much more than words. I lifted my hand to my jacket's breast pocket and slid out the tissue-wrapped parcel I carried around for the past week. I glanced between her face and the item in my hand, fingers stuttering nervously over the thin paper.

"Here." I sat the package onto the table in front of us. "For your new place, wherever it happens to be."

She stared at the package. She lowered her head towards the table, catching her chin in her hand. "What is it?"

"It's...a present."

She reached down and poked it. "What kind of present?"

I rolled my eyes, pulling the knot of my tie loose. "The kind you have to open before you ask me another question."

Cadence made no further move towards my offering, her eyes narrowing.

"Oh, come now," I chided, picking it up and shoving it at her directly. "It's not going to bite."

She took it in one hand, leaning back in her seat and sighing. "You didn't need to get me a present, Chance. Not after–"

"Shut up and open it; I'm begging you."

My pleading got through to her at last, and Cadence began unwrapping the package with a huff.

Her movements stuttered to a halt once she uncovered the edge of the optric. Like a true idiot, I had wrapped the damn thing upside down; so, all she could see of it was the shiny silver backing. Still, too clever by half, I think she suspected right away what I had done.

Cadence sat up slowly, her eyes widening. She turned to look at me, one brow crooking upwards in a question. I refused to answer with anything but a wavering smile, half hidden behind my hand as I stroked my chin.

She swallowed. Her fingertips gripped the edges of the optric gently, as if she were handling a dry, cracking leaf. She flipped the optric right side up, and laid it on her knees, all the while locking eyes with me.

Then, as if afraid, Cadence glanced at it from the corner of her eyes. They flickered shut. She swallowed again.

"Impossible."

Her head hung low between her shoulders; she opened her eyes once more. Her frame began to shake. "But...I..." She drew her fingers down the edges of the picture. "Wea, I smashed it." She lifted her optric off her knees, bringing it mere inches away from her face. "Didn't I?"

"You most certainly did," I said, giving a dry chuckle despite the gravitas of the moment. "The techs I had working on it counted all the original fragments. You broke this into exactly two hundred and sixty-seven pieces."

"Two hundred and sixty-seven..." Cadence was transfixed with the item in her hands. Trembling, her fingers traced the faces of her family. "...that's quite a lot."

"They couldn't save everything of course," I babbled on, wringing my hands until they were banded with red. "They had to replace a lot of the basic components – even my engineers aren't that good – but they kept what they could and recovered most of the picture off the memory chip. They used this stupidly complicated program to repair the image, pixel by pixel, where data had been lost and – and..." I leaned over towards her, eyes roaming desperately over the optric. "Is it alright? Does it look like it should?"

"Alright?" Cadence put the optric down on the table in front of us. She leaned back, her hands in her lap. She shook her head.

My heart stuttered to a halt. It was wrong; I had done it all wrong!

Cadence's hands flew up to her face. Her palms began rubbing her cheeks in slow circles. She shook her head again. "Alright? Chance..." She began shaking her head in time with my name, repeating it over and over again like a personal mantra. "Chance, Chance, Chance, Chance, Chance–"

I slid towards her, my head fuzzy with alarm and fear. "What, Cay, what's wrong with it? I'm sure I can fix it, I can–"

"Tris gav gav tris, Chance!" She turned and launched herself at me, seemingly unaware that I had closed the distance between us until it was too late. She knocked into me with such force that I ended up splayed across the sofa with her lying on top of me, her arms wrapped tight around my chest, her face buried in my shirt. "It couldn't be more alright; more perfect! Wea gav, it's the nicest, kindest, sweetest thing anyone's ever done for me!" I could feel her trembling all over, like an overworked PT. "Sinc, thank you, thank you, thank you!"

It was impossible to get my breath back with her squeezing me. But I managed to suck in enough air to wheeze out, "You're very welcome..."

Cadence eased up on me, perhaps detecting the thinness of my voice, and realizing that she was affectionately suffocating me. She lifted her head off my chest and gazed up at me, wide blue eyes shining like pieces of the sky. "Urio, why did you do this for me?"

I smiled. Reaching down to brush her wavy bangs off her forehead, my other hand began caressing her arm. She was heavy and warm, like a familiar, beloved winter blanket. I felt safe and protected under her; and more shocking than anything else, not the least bit embarrassed or afraid of the words tripping off my tongue.

"You're my friend, Cay. And I love you."

She sat up from me with a start. "What?"

My smile widened. "I love you. Quite madly, too."

She sat back on her haunches. Her face was blank. She huffed hair away from her mouth. Eyes fixed on the far wall, she began tapping on her thighs so quickly that I could barely distinguish one beat from another.

"Oh." It was like the coo of a dove. The tapping stopped for a moment. She cleared her throat and cast me a quick glance before looking away once more. "I suppose that is...an adequate explanation."

I propped myself up on my elbows. "Is that really your only response?"

Her brow furrowed and she scowled, holding up a hand. "Well, give me a moment to process it!"

I flung my arms around her hips, threading my fingers together against her back. I rested all my weight on her, delighted at the way she didn't even sway at the additional burden. "It can't really be that much of a surprise; I've been after you since the moment we met."

"Sex is different than love, Chance." Cadence looked down at me, her hand falling to caress my back. "And I've never been in love with a human before."

I rested my head against her shoulder and neck, focusing on the sound of my own pounding heart. "Do you think you could be?"

"I am...open to the possibilities." With a final pat on my back, Cadence looked up and away from me, and gave a single firm nod. "Yes. We will see what happens. I will allow you to court me."

"Allow me to...?" I pulled back from her, mouth agape. "Well, what the hell have I been doing all this time?"

About the Author

Robin Jeffrey was born in Cheyenne, Wyoming to a psychologist and a librarian, giving her a love of literature and a consuming interest in the inner workings of people's minds, which have served her well as she pursues a career in creative writing. She holds a BA in English from the University of Washington and a MS in Library Science from the University of Kentucky. She has been published in various journals across the country as well as on websites like The Mary Sue and Introvert, Dear. She currently resides in Bremerton, Washington. More of her work can be found on her website, RobinJeffreyAuthor.com.

Robin would like to take this opportunity to extend her sincerest thanks to everyone who made this book possible. The covers for both this and the first book in the Cadence Turing Mystery Series were created by the incomparable Julianne Stone (https://www.juliariaart.com/). This book in particular would not have reached completion without the wonderful booksellers at the Kitsap Barnes & Noble in Silverdale, WA, where the author spent many, many weekends working. Finally, to the supportive voices of her editor, Megan Jeffrey, her husband, Philip Allen, and all the wonderful readers who gave Cadence Turing and Chance Hale a spot on their shelves: thank you.